EMBER IN TIME SERIES

PROTECTORS

OF TIME

BOOK THREE

EMBER IN TIME SERIES

PROTECTORS OF TIME

BOOK THREE

KIM MALAJ

Protectors of Time

ISBN: 9781958502013 (Paperback)
       9781958502037 (Hardcover)

Kim Malaj
Haxhaj Nd. 19
Ivanaj, Albania 4306
www.kimmalaj.com

Second Edition: August 1, 2022

To my protectors...

I know this middle child was wild and stubborn in many ways.

I love that I have earth to stay when I travel back from far away.

Cheers to you and the parents who raised a wanderer soul to write the old untold.

N
NW
NE
W
E
SW
SE
S
MONTENEGRO

FORT KELMEND
ALBANIAN ALPS
ASTLE OF TESKOM
BAJZE
LAKE SHKODER

1

Itra tears off his gloves and slides the pruning shears into his back pocket. He pulls out his phone and swipes to accept the incoming call, but it's still vibrating. He rubs a finger across his jacket sleeve and swipes the screen again.

The call connects and he shoulders the phone to his ear.

"Itra!" Anton shouts.

Itra winces and pulls the phone away from his ear. He bristles as a cold shiver runs the length of his tall frame.

"Anton?" Itra asks warily, placing the phone on speaker. "Why are you shouting?" He jogs from the vines and into the house.

"Sorry," Anton apologizes, his voice hoarse and shaking. He swallows and sucks in a breath. "Is Elis with you?"

Itra finds Danae bent forward, gripping the edge of the kitchen counter. She is rocking side to side, a little breathless.

"No, why?" Itra turns up the call volume before running the water. He quickly washes his hands and turns to Danae. She tosses him the hand towel from the counter. He catches it with ease.

Following a long sniffle. Anton says with a weak voice, "He didn't make it home from Nada's apartment."

Danae rubs her tight, round abdomen and rests her hips against the counter.

"When was this?" Itra asks.

"An hour ago."

Itra tosses the hand towel onto the counter near the sink. He takes and squeezes Danae's hand.

She squeezes back. Her frown and worry lines mirror the creases next to his brown eyes.

"Elis left her apartment on his bike." Anton continues. "Nada watched him from the balcony until he turned the corner." Anton sighs and mumbles a curse. "It's less than two blocks!"

"I know, I know." Itra shakes his head. He nudges Danae and holds the phone closer to her.

"Anton, it's Danae." She takes a breath. "Does Elis have friends in your building, or a favorite spot between his cousins and you?"

"Iana would know, but she isn't here to ask!"

Danae stiffens.

Itra grips her hand harder.

She places her free hand around her belly.

"Ok, what would my sister have done to find Elis?" Itra asks.

Anton is silent.

Itra taps the phone to make sure the call didn't drop.

"Anton?" Danae asks.

"I went outside to wait for him when Nada called. I never saw him turn the corner like she saw him do. It's like he vanished." He clears his throat twice before continuing. "We've only done this once before and we had a visual on him the whole time."

Danae feels a vibration against her chest. She palms her ember amulet. *It's hot!* She looks down and it's pulsing a faint orange glow.

"Does the corner store have cameras?" Danae asks. She shifts her weight from side to side.

On the other end of the phone, a door slams and there is an echo of pounding footsteps.

"Anton?" Itra asks.

"I'll call you back!"

Itra's phone lights up as the call disconnects. He looks from the phone to the floor as liquid splashes at their feet.

"Oh, no!" Danae whispers. She arches her back and lets out a long moan.

"Is that your water breaking?" Itra asks, eyes wide.

Danae nods, breathing through another contraction.

"Stay here! I'll get the bag and the truck."

Danae nods again.

Itra kisses her forehead and sprints out of the kitchen.

Danae breathes in and out slowly, looking past her swollen belly to the mess on the floor. Her contraction subsides. She grabs a few towels from a drawer. She attempts to bend over, but only makes it halfway, finding it hard to breathe. She straightens.

"Just breathe," she whispers to herself. "We have plenty of time."

Itra rushes back in and takes the towels from her. He cleans up the floor and takes her hands. She waddles towards the washroom.

"Can you," Danae says, but stops to breathe, "get the blue maxi dress and fleece jacket from the top of the dresser?"

"Sure, anything else?" Itra asks before leaving her at the washroom sink.

"Take a few towels to the truck," Danae says.

Itra's face goes from tan to pale white in an instant.

"It's just a precaution." She half smiles.

He nods and races to the bedroom.

She peels off her wet clothes and tosses them in the washing machine. Itra returns with her dress and fleece. He squats with a warm washcloth and wipes down her legs as another contraction kicks in. She bends forward and leans against him. She rocks from foot to foot.

Itra's phone vibrates. He fumbles his phone before answering.

"He vanished!" Anton yells.

"Danae's water broke!" Itra yells back, throwing the washcloth in the washer.

"What?"

"She's in labor," Itra says. "I'm sorry. We can't be there for you at the moment. But I'll make some calls on the way to the birthing center."

Danae straightens and extends her hand towards the phone.

Itra hands her the phone while she waddles to the front door.

"Anton," Danae says, "what do you mean he vanished?"

Itra kneels and directs Danae's feet into slip-on shoes.

"Danae, dear God," Anton says, "you're about to…"

"Anton, explain," Danae says, stepping out of the house. She grasps the porch rail with one hand while Itra locks the front door. "What do you mean he vanished?"

Itra helps her down the front steps.

"The store had a camera facing the street. They rolled it back, and you can see Elis riding down the sidewalk. And then he wasn't."

Itra helps her into the truck after lining the seat with a few towels.

"What do you mean he wasn't?" Danae asks, turning to her side and reclining the seat back. She spots the two car seats and their packed bag in the back seat before relaxing for just a second as another contraction begins.

"As he turns towards my building," Anton says, "the bike falls, and he's gone, just gone!"

Itra gets into the car, turning towards Danae as he pulls down the drive. Tears are streaming down his cheeks. She reaches to touch his face. He shakes his head and hops out to open the gate. When he gets back in, he punches the gas, peeling out of the drive onto the gravel road. He hops out again to close the gate.

"So, the bike is still there?" Danae asks, placing the phone on the charger on the center console. It connects to the truck speakers.

Itra hops back in and throws the truck in gear. His acceleration makes Danae wince. He reaches out his hand to her and slows a bit. She squeezes his hand.

"A young woman walked the bike into the store less than a minute after he vanished." Anton's voice fills the cab. "That is why I didn't see the bike when I initially walked down." The jangle of the store door chimes through the call. "Nada is on her way. I can see her jogging towards me. She had to wait for her husband to return home before leaving the kids."

"Call the police," Itra says, turning onto the main road to the highway. "I'll call Ermal and see if we can get his police department to encourage the city cops to take it seriously. We will find Elis."

"God, I hope so!" Anton mumbles. "A squad car just arrived. Nada must have called them. Drive safe, and Danae, just breathe!"

The call disconnects.

Itra pounds on the steering wheel.

"Easy," Danae says, reaching over to touch Itra.

He meets her eyes with a crease furrowed deep between his eyebrows.

"Why would someone take Elis?" Itra asks.

The ember amulet under Danae's dress lifts, pushing out the fabric.

"Itra! Watch out!"

Danae braces against the door and center console.

Itra jerks the wheel to the left, missing a large cow by a hair. He straightens the wheel and takes his foot off the accelerator. Taking in a deep breath. He looks over at Danae.

She opens one eye. "Cow?"

"Alive."

"Ha, ha."

Itra turns his focus back on the highway. The overcast clouds and early winter dusk add a layer of foggy mist across the pavement. He turns on his high beams. "Why did your amulet move?"

"Truck versus cow in the road?"

Itra chokes back a laugh.

Danae shifts in the seat as another contraction starts. She pulls out the amulet. "It's still warm."

"Warm?"

"It was hot just before my water broke," Danae explains, breathing slowly in and back out.

"So, it was a warning?" Itra asks.

She lets out a long breath and shifts again. "I guess." She looks down at the amulet and back up to Itra as a contraction ends. "So far, the amulet has been useful, especially for keeping our memories of the time in the castle intact, for the family, Ermal, and us. Speaking of Ermal, you said you would call him and let him know Elis is missing."

"Right," Itra says, glancing over at his phone. "Can you dial? I want to keep my eyes on the road."

"Yep," Danae says, swiping through his contacts and selecting Ermal's name. It goes straight to voicemail. She disconnects before leaving a message. "I'll text Ermal the details after I text the on-call number for the birthing center that we're on our way."

Twenty minutes later, they pull into the emergency entrance at the birthing center. Itra hurries around the truck to help Danae out.

A nurse immediately comes out with a wheelchair and helps Danae into the chair.

"Park the truck just over there," the nurse explains, pointing to a few open spaces near the entrance. "Take the elevator up to the third floor. She'll be in room 317."

Itra kisses her firmly. The nurse blushes and looks away.

"Grab the bag on your way up," Danae whispers when the kiss ends.

Itra nods with a grin and runs back to the driver's side.

The nurse pushes Danae through the doors and toward an awaiting elevator. "How far apart are the contractions?"

"Less than two minutes." Danae shifts as another starts.

"And you're having twins?"

"Yes, a boy and a girl," Danae answers between breaths.

The ride up to the third floor is short. The elevator doors slide open to a nursing station. The cool blues and warm yellows of the unit are inviting. A few nurses dressed in lavender scrubs look up and smile.

The nurse pushing Danae shouts a command to the smiling faces. "Less than two, twins, and prep the room for immediate delivery!"

A rush of activity follows them into the assigned room. Danae is shifted from her chair to the bed with ease.

When Itra arrives, he has to pick his way around the lavender crowd to Danae's bedside.

6

"What's happening?" Itra asks, finally reaching Danae.

"I think we are about to become parents," Danae says sarcastically.

Itra's face goes very pale.

"Chair!" Danae shouts. "He needs a chair!" She watches Itra teeter from side to side.

A nurse pulls up a stool and slowly lowers Itra down.

"There, there," the nurse says, patting his shoulder. "We've got this. Just sit down and hold her hand."

Danae snorts out a laugh. This brings Itra back to reality. He looks up at her and down at his seated position. He frowns.

"Sorry," he whispers. "Too much, too fast."

Danae nods and breathes through another contraction.

The nurse slides out and unfolds the stirrups and shimmies Danae down to the end of the bed.

After a quick examination, the nurse looks up at Danae. "The doctor is right next door with another delivery. You're clear to push with your next contraction. The first baby is in position."

Ring, ring

The people in the room pause and check their phones.

Ring, ring

The nurse standing behind Itra taps him on the shoulder. "I believe it's your phone." She points down to Itra's jean pocket.

He stands up quickly, digging in his pocket. His vision goes spotty. The nurse catches his elbow and holds him up. He fumbles the phone and swipes the screen, gently sitting back down.

"It was Teuta!" Anton says as Itra connects the call.

"What?" Itra asks.

"The young woman who walked the bike into the corner store was Teuta," Anton says.

"But why, how, I don't understand?" Itra looks up. Danae is glaring at him. "Sorry, she is about to push. I'll call you back in a few." Itra hangs up and tosses the phone on the bed-side table. He takes Danae's hand and kisses her sweaty brow. "Right then, we are pushing?"

Danae frowns. "Did he say Teuta?"

Itra nods. "But let's focus. Baby time!"

She squeezes his hand so hard he winces.

"Ready when you are," the mid-wife says, watching the next contraction start on the monitor.

2

Kaly hands back the graded exams to her final class of the week. She overhears a quiet, whispered exchange between two students towards the front. She waves her hand and the students quiet down.

"As many of you are new to this subject, I am impressed at your theories for the Kelmend tribes." Kaly nods to the two students who were whispering in the front. "For example, your research supports some of these theories, especially the reference in an ancient Greek logbook and another cited entry from an ancient war diary from the Ottoman archives here on campus. The Kelmend people seem to be fierce warriors with the agility to climb and fight on rugged mountainsides to defend their small villages."

The two students respond with smiles and nods. She nods in return and then turns to address the entire class. "My final for this class will not be a traditional exam." A murmur of conversation starts from the back. "Now hold on, before you freak out. At the beginning of this semester, I assigned each student to a tribe noted in Illyrian history. All of your assignments have been strategic."

Kaly pauses, acknowledging a few head nods before she continues. "Your final will be a ten-minute oral presentation about an individual from your assigned tribe. You must present in first person, like you are sharing their story as your own."

A few hands shoot up.

Kaly continues without addressing the eager students. "Now the details of this story can be factual or fictional, but they must apply to that person's timeline, struggles, lifestyle, and family dynamics."

A few hands fall, but two remain up. Kaly nods to a young man sitting towards the center.

"Are you talking about cosplay?" the young man asks, pointing his pen as he talks. "Like, do we need to dress like these people or what?"

Kaly smiles. "That is totally up to the presenter. The breakdown of the grading scale will be equal parts length and relevance. If you can talk for a full ten minutes, you're halfway to a full grade."

One hand from a young lady remains up in the back.

Kaly nods.

The woman stands.

"And if the professor is a no show," the woman says with a hint of an accent. "Is that an automatic pass?" She swirls her dress from side to side.

Kaly steps closer to get a good look at who is speaking and coughs to cover a curse word.

"Alright, class dismissed," Kaly says, almost yelling. She levels her tone before addressing the students again. "Have a good weekend and don't mind the little messenger. She is an old— friend."

The class gathers their belongings. They try not to stare at the smiling woman dancing down the steps of the lecture hall towards their professor. After the last student files out, Kaly closes the door before turning to address the intruder.

"Teuta, what in the hell are you doing here and so far away from the Castle of Teskom?" Kaly asks.

"Nice to see you too," Teuta greets her with a curtsy. Her wide green eyes stare up at her.

"Seriously, what's going on?" Kaly asks, gathering her lecture notes, laptop, and markers, and stuffing them in her bag.

"Where to begin?" Teuta sings.

"Start with why you are here in the flesh." Kaly glares at her and shoulders her bag.

"Danae is delivering time, and the compass was taken."

Kaly's mouth falls open.

Teuta hands her a square piece of parchment that clearly states Time to Serve in purple cursive ink.

Kaly takes the card and opens her mouth to speak, but Teuta waves her hand.

"You've been served," Teuta sings and disappears.

"Seriously!" Kaly yells as the lecture hall doors open. The students for the next class walk in. She turns in a slow circle, looking for Teuta, but she's gone. She sighs before exiting the hall and attempts to find her phone buried inside her bag. It is already ringing when she grasps it. Her husband's face fills the screen.

"Hey," Kaly answers.

"My sister is in labor," Leon says, his pitch low and rushed.

"I know."

"How? Anton just called me a minute ago."

"Your favorite fairy messenger just served me my orders with the news."

"In person?" Leon asks.

"Yep!"

"She was actually there?"

"She even caused a scene at the end of my class. Her flair for dramatics is ever present."

Leon mumbles something that sounds like a string of curses.

"Teuta mentioned something about a compass being taken," Kaly says, walking faster across campus.

"Elis is the compass," Leon says.

Kaly secures her bag across her body and breaks into a full run towards her car, her phone pressed to her ear.

Leon continues. "Elis vanished right before Danae went into labor. Anton claims Teuta is on surveillance footage from the corner store where he was last seen. I've packed a bag for both of us."

Kaly yanks open her car door and tosses her bag into the backseat. "In my car." She takes a big breath in. "Be ready in thirty minutes."

"See you soon, drive safe."

Kaly tosses her phone down and screams loud and long enough to make her throat hurt. Tears prick the corners of her eyes as she pulls out of the parking lot and merges into midday traffic.

Leon is outside waiting for Kaly when she turns down the winding drive to their farmhouse, bathed in the afternoon sunlight. The sight of home and Leon tampers her rising anxiety.

"Need anything from inside?" Leon asks, as he pulls her from the car into a hug.

Kaly holds on to him until he releases her. It's something she started doing after returning from her stone statue days. She never breaks an embrace from him or any loved one first.

Kaly shakes her head and grabs her lecture bag from the car. She turns back to Leon.

"Why are you grinning from ear to ear?" she asks.

He holds up his phone. A squishy newborn face with a light blue cap fills the screen. "I'm officially an uncle!"

Kaly zooms the picture in and out to exam each detail of the tiny human. Her eyes water as she hands the phone back to Leon. "It's a boy, right?"

Leon nods. "Baby girl is on the way." He pockets his phone. He spins the gold ring on his left thumb. "Anton's apartment?"

Kaly nods and clinks her gold ring against his.

"Ready?" Leon asks.

Kaly sucks in a breath and nods.

"Protect time," they say in unison. "Unite to fight. Ember of mine."

A portal door opens to the interior of Anton's apartment. They join hands and walk through.

Anton comes out of the kitchen disheveled, his tie hanging loose, his dark wavy hair standing on end and the top three buttons of his dress shirt undone. Startled, he throws a water bottle at Kaly and Leon, standing in his living room.

Leon catches the bottle mid assault.

"Jesus!" Anton yells. "How did you? When did you?"

"Do you really want us to answer that question?" Leon asks, raising an eyebrow at Anton's pale face.

"Probably not." Anton pulls out a chair and sits down hard.

"Any news about Elis?" Kaly says, walking to sit beside Anton.

"Nothing new," Anton says, raking a hand through his hair.

"Can you walk us through what you know?" Leon asks, placing the water bottle down in front of Anton.

"From my cousin Nada's apartment, you can see the sidewalk up to the corner. We've let Elis ride his bike to that corner and back since he turned seven, but only ever with supervision and once to come home from Nada's apartment to here." He pauses and shakes his head. "I waited at street level while Nada watched from her balcony, but he never made it around the corner." Anton sighs and takes a sip from the water bottle. "When I called Nada and ask if she could still see him, she said no. She went back inside when he turned the corner." Anton shakes his head. "I jogged down to the corner but saw nothing. I called his name and jogged back and forth for several minutes. Still nothing. I jogged back to my apartment and checked every room. I called Itra after nearly an hour in full-blown panic mode. They suggested going to the corner store and asking about security footage. The store owner showed me the footage of Elis riding down the sidewalk on his bike. The bike falls when he vanishes. A minute later, a young woman walks the bike into the store. That young woman is a dead ringer for Teuta."

Kaly relays her visit from Teuta in the lecture hall.

Anton's phone chimes as she finishes. He taps the notification, and a rosy-cheeked baby girl fills the screen. Anton turns his phone towards Leon and Kaly.

Leon tears up. "Danae did it. She had twins."

3

Itra sets his phone back on the bedside table. He gently pats Danae's face with a cool, damp cloth.

"They're perfect," she whispers.

He leans over, touching his nose to hers.

"More than perfect," he says, kissing her softly.

Two nurses bring over the babies. Itra helps Danae into a comfortable position as they hand over Emit, their son, and Ora, their daughter.

Danae whispers, "They're here. It's not a dream."

The room activity falls silent, giving Danae and Itra a moment to soak up the joy. A gentle suckling sound is coming from Emit.

"Like father like son, you're already hungry." Danae teases Emit, snuggling his cheek with hers.

Itra laughs, startling Ora. She winces in response. He covers his mouth and continues to laugh softly.

The room empties of delivery staff, leaving them alone for the first time. They each take turns with skin-to-skin time with the babies.

"If we could only freeze this moment for eternity," Danae says and then immediately looks up at Itra.

"Time," they say in unison.

Teuta appears between Danae and Itra in an instant.

Itra and Danae instinctively cover their babies and turn away from Teuta.

"What in the hell!" Danae shouts.

"Leave it to you to ruin the first private moment with our children, you heartless wench!" Itra glares at her.

Teuta simply smiles.

"What could you possibly want from us at this moment?" Danae asks, pulling her ember amulet out from under her hospital gown.

Teuta hums and then sings. "Illyria of mine, the heirs of time, arise in your place. We must haste. The compass and only guide has been taken inside. Illyria of time."

The babies cry in unison and vanish with Teuta.

Itra and Danae scream and reach for them.

The nurses come in running.

"She took them!" Danae cries. "She took them! She took them!"

Beep, beep, beep

"Can you describe the woman?" a security officer asks hovering at Danae's bedside.

Danae shakes her head and covers her ears.

The beeping alarm is ringing her every nerve.

Itra opens his mouth several times, but no words come out.

"Get out!" Danae cries after several minutes. "Leave us! Everyone, get out!"

The nurses hesitantly step out to the hall with the security officers.

Itra closes and locks the door.

Danae reaches for Itra's hand when he returns to her side. He taps her thumb, the one with the gold ring. She nods and closes her eyes, picturing the twins.

"Protect time," Danae whispers, "unite the fight. Ember of mine."

A portal door opens.

Itra picks up Danae and walks through.

Anton's phone lights up with a missing child alert notification, which blasts three quick warning sounds. The first is Elis, the next two are newborn infants from a birthing center up north.

Anton immediately dials Itra's phone. It only rings once before a woman's voice answers.

"Hello?"

"Danae?"

"No, I'm a nurse at a birthing center. Do you know Danae or her husband?"

"Yes, why are you answering Itra's phone?" Anton puts his phone on speaker for Kaly and Leon.

"Their babies…" the nurse says, speaking over the shouting from the hall. "And then they, um, vanished. Our staff is freaking out over here."

A loud beep screeches over the shouts.

Leon reaches over and ends the call before Anton can respond.

"If I find out," Leon says, "Teuta had anything to do with this, I'll put her back in stone and leave her there for eternity!" He stands and motions for Kaly to follow.

Anton holds up a hand. "Where are you going?"

"The Castle of Teskom," Leon says. "My best guess is the archive suite. It has a nursery."

Kaly stands, looking from Leon to Anton.

"Do you want to split up?" Kaly asks.

Leon laughs and shakes his head. "Never! Not after the last stoned fiasco."

Kaly shivers at the thought. She frowns at Leon.

"Wait, I can't leave," Anton protests. "What if Elis returns and I'm gone?"

"Call Nada," Leon suggests. "You can have her keep watch here until you return."

Anton stands and leaves the dining room without a word. The bedroom door shuts.

Leon paces, overhearing a bit of Anton's phone conversation.

Anton says, "Just trust me." A second later, he exits the bedroom and slams the hall washroom door. The sound of retching immediately follows.

Kaly and Leon exchange a worried glance.

"Shit," Leon mumbles.

Kaly searches the fridge for a ginger ale but settles on a pack of gum from the counter.

Anton walks back in, sweaty and slightly green.

Kaly hands him the pack of gum.

Anton nods.

She takes Anton's hand and Leon stands beside them.

"To Danae and Itra," Leon says, looking at Anton. "Focus on that thought only for the moment, ok?"

"Ok," Anton whispers.

"Protect time," Leon and Kaly say in unison. "Unite to fight. Ember of mine."

A portal door opens.

Anton steps back, but Kaly tightens her grip on his hand. They all walk through together.

The room is dark, and Anton panics.

"We are definitely in the castle," Leon says.

"Leon, a light?" Kaly asks.

Leon calls his ember staff, taps it once, and fills the space with a warm ember glow.

Anton points from the ember glow to Leon.

"Ember's idea of a gift," Leon says, showing him the tattoo of the staff on his forearm. "I think this is the future cavern." Leon pauses, scratching his chin. "What was the phrase to activate it?"

"We are here, we are open, we are present," Kaly says.

Leon turns and winks at her.

A flicker of light appears in the center and expands until the room is nearly white.

They blink and shade their eyes until their pupils adjust.

A figure appears tall and ominous in the middle of the room, draped in a dark hooded cloak hiding their face.

Kaly and Anton take three steps back.

Leon starts a slow circle around the figure.

"Hear this now!" The figure's low, gravely tone echoes in the space. "See her bow. I am Father Time. The compass near for a year. Ember of mine."

Anton lunges forward as the room falls to darkness minus the warm ember glow once again. He curses under his breath but goes silent as a flurry of images appears in quick succession: the twins sleeping in a crib, three women chasing two figures through the woods, and a circle of red dots just before the image fades to the ember glow of Leon's staff.

"The woods image is what the pot ladies described during their visit to the future cavern," Kaly says.

Anton raises an eyebrow at her. "Pot ladies?"

Kaly shrugs. "The 'Protectors of Time' descendants. It is too long. I like acronyms."

A door hisses open to a stairwell.

Leon nods, walking towards the open doorway and talks over his shoulder. "The other two images are what Itra and Danae described during their last visit in here."

"And Father Time?" Anton asks, following Leon.

Kaly joins them at the base of the winding stone stairs.

"That's new as far as I know," Kaly says.

Leon nods and starts climbing the steps.

Anton and Kaly follow in silence.

Leon looks back to check their progress.

Anton's pale face and Kaly's fierce glare stare back at Leon. He flares his nose and increases his speed up the steps. He halts on the last step, taking in the castle's main foyer.

The cool night breeze chills his face from the open door. The entry to the conservatory directly across from him is vacant of people just the shadows of the plants lining the path.

A faint whisper floats in from the open door.

Leon rubs the standing hairs on his arms. He turns back to Anton and Kaly, holding a finger to his mouth.

They nod.

18

He creeps along the wall and peeks out of the main entrance. Two figures are standing in the shadows at the bottom of the large stone steps. Leon double taps his staff, transforming the warm ember glow to a long glowing scythe.

Anton squashes a grunt of surprise.

Kaly shakes her head at him.

Leon smiles and steps out, filling the doorway to the Castle of Teskom.

Itra steadies Danae as her legs give way at the first sight of the twins wrapped in soft white blankets asleep in a crib.

"Is this the archive suite?" Itra asks in a whisper.

Danae nods, wiping the tears from her cheeks with trembling hands.

Itra wraps an arm around her and feels her shaking.

"Bed?" Itra suggests. "Not sure you should be standing at the moment."

"Only if you agree to bring them to me at once," Danae says without taking her eyes off the babies.

"Of course." Itra takes her by the hand to the adjoining room. He helps her to the bed and positions a few pillows around her.

"Enough!" Danae pushes him away with a grin. "Bring me our babies."

Itra smiles and returns to the nursery. He hovers over the crib, taking in the view for a moment. He wipes his cheek, surprised at the fallen tear. His sister tried to warn him that having children is like wearing your heart on the outside. He feels a pang of longing for Iana.

Ora coos and scrunches her nose. He smiles and swallows his emotions. He picks up Emit and adjusts him in the nook of his arm, holding him close before leaning back over to pick up Ora. He walks with care through the nursery back to Danae. She opens her arms, taking Ora. Itra circles the bed and climbs in with Emit.

Danae unwraps Ora and nods to Itra. He unwraps Emit. She scrutinizes Ora for any injuries or harm. She only finds a small birthmark on Ora's right shoulder blade, twelve red dots in a perfect circle, with one slightly darker at six o'clock.

"Itra look!" Danae carefully turns her back to Itra to show him the mark.

Itra counts the red dots. "There are twelve of them?"

Danae nods.

Itra carefully turns Emit around and on his left shoulder blade is nearly the same mark—twelve red dots in a perfect circle, but the dot at twelve o'clock is slightly darker.

Itra moves him closer to Danae.

"The future cavern," Danae whispers. "Two pulsing dots at twelve and six." She shakes her head. "Were these on them at the birthing center?"

Itra shakes his head. "I don't honestly know. I kept their backs covered when we were doing chest to chest and during the clean up I didn't see any marks on their backs."

Ora and Emit sigh and cry in unison.

Itra laughs. Danae raises a finger to her lips.

"What? It was cute," Itra says with a shrug.

Danae sticks out her tongue and crosses her eyes.

Itra laughs again, startling the babies to silence.

Danae barks out a laugh, and they cry again. She covers her mouth and shakes her head.

Itra points at Danae, silently laughing, but then yawns.

Danae yawns behind her hand. "We should get them wrapped back up." She nudges Itra. "Can you check the nursery for bottles and formula?" A tray lands with a soft thud on the bedside table. Two full bottles and white burp cloths appear on the tray. "Ok, scratch that off the things we need until my milk comes in."

"Thought provoked food includes baby formula, cool," Itra says, wrapping Emit back up in the white blanket. "Does it include diaper duty?"

"Yes," Teuta answers, appearing in the adjoining doorway.

"You monster!" Danae whisper screams at Teuta. She attempts to move from the bed, but Itra pats her leg and hands her Emit. "How could you take them? Why!"

"They are time," Teuta says.

"They are our children!" Itra says, bounding over the foot of the bed and landing inches in front of Teuta. "They should've left you stuck in stone!"

"I was only doing what I could to protect them until the Protectors of Time arrived."

"We can protect our children!" Danae hisses.

"Not from him," Teuta says peeking around Itra's shoulder to meet Danae's glare.

"Really?" Danae says, shifting the babies in her arms. "You're claiming Itra is a threat?"

"No! Goodness no. Chronos is the threat. He has Elis."

Itra's knees go soft, and he leans a hand against the wall.

"Explain. Every. Single. Detail. Now." Itra says.

"Ember asked me to check on Elis," Teuta says, side-stepping Itra and inching into the room. "I have been checking in on Elis every week since he left, from a distance. But when I arrived today, all I found was his bike and this." Teuta holds up a tiny rock shaped like an hourglass. "I walked his bike into the corner store, hoping Anton would find it with the camera footage, but I couldn't stay. I had to alert Ember and the Protectors of Time. Elis may not be time, but he is as much a part of their legacy. He is their guide."

"So, you just left Anton there to figure it out?" Itra asks, moving closer to the bed to stand between Teuta and Danae.

"Yes," Teuta states and blinks twice. "May I continue?"

Itra glares at her in response.

"When I arrived back here, I received the messages to serve to the Protectors of Time. The grey sisters sent Enyo. Kaly is here with Leon and Anton. And Avi has just arrived."

"Hold up, my brother is here?" Danae asks.

Teuta nods. "And he is in a mood." Teuta shifts from side to side. "After I returned from delivering the messages, Ember had one last task. She believes the stone left with Elis's bike confirms that the threat of Chronos is real and sent me to retrieve time—I mean, the babies. I wanted to warn you, but my orders were precise: sing the message and time would follow.”

“They were barely out of my body before you snatched them away! Do you even comprehend the trauma you have caused?”

Teuta frowns. “I’m afraid I had no choice. Remember, I’m just the messenger.”

“So, you’re saying we should take this up with the goddess Ember?” Itra asks. Teuta’s eyes go wide. “Fine! Ember, I call to you. Make yourself present or I’ll end your messenger.”

Teuta steps back towards the adjoining door, out of Itra’s reach. The room fills with a warm ember glow.

Danae’s ember amulet moves towards the center of the light.

“I hear your call.” The soothing tone of Ember’s voice fills the room. “I understand it all. Time to protect and serve upon your request.”

“Enough with the riddles!” Itra shouts into the light.

The babies let out a single cry in unison.

Itra continues. “You ripped our children from our arms. They’re not even hours old. Hell, Danae shouldn’t be up and moving.”

“I hear your call. I understand it all. The compass erased increases the pace.”

Itra starts toward the light with a raised fist. “What do you mean erased?” His voice cracks on the last word.

“Misplaced,” Ember whispers.

“Which one is it?” Danae asks.

No response as the light fades.

Danae shifts the babies to one arm and reaches for Itra.

He whirls at her touch. His expression softens, but then Teuta knocks on the doorframe. He turns and advances on her in three steps. She disappears and reappears across the room on the opposite side of the bed.

“I know, I know,” Teuta says, holding up her hands. “We are prepared to take care of you and the babies, and we will find Elis. I promise.”

Danae reaches for Itra's hand. "We can take care of them. You and the others have only one job. Get our nephew back unharmed. Nothing, I mean, nothing else matters right now!"

Itra takes her hand. He attempts to calm the rage pulsing in his ears.

Teuta nods. "One last question," she asks, dancing from side to side.

"Make it count," Itra states.

"The family would like to visit," Teuta says quietly. "Are you ready for visitors?"

Itra waves to Danae to answer. "Give them free access to the archives and the suite," says Danae. "At their will, not yours. Just ask them to knock on our door before entering."

Teuta holds up a hand to protest.

Itra waves his hand. "You'll do what she says, no objections."

Teuta twirls and disappears without another word.

"We have to find Elis," Itra whispers, kneeling on the floor next to the bed.

The babies coo in unison.

Itra reaches for them.

Danae shifts the babies closer, and he pulls them in. She reaches up to hold the amulet and touches his arm.

Itra's shoulders droop in response. "What is that?"

"Thought provoked calm."

A woman's voice calls out from the darkness. "Leon?"

Leon tightens his grip on the scythe. He squints into the darkness below and makes out two figures.

"Who is asking?" Leon says, extending his staff with the glowing scythe to illuminate the steps.

One figure moves out of the shadows. Her dark hair is pulled back in three separate braids. The hilt of a dagger glints in the moonlight, just visible over her right shoulder.

"Enyo?" Leon asks.

"Yes, and Avi."

Avi joins Enyo in the light, moving her long, dark hair away from her face. She tightens her scarf and pulls the zip up on her jacket. She stares past the fog of her breath at Leon and the two people standing behind him in the entryway.

"Who is with you?" Avi asks.

Kaly walks forward next to Leon.

Without a word, Avi and Enyo climb the four giant steps.

Kaly hugs each of the ladies before turning to Anton.

"Anton, this is Enyo," says Kaly. "Anton is Itra's brother-in-law and father to Elis, our missing compass."

Anton flinches. "I hope I never hear Elis's name and missing in the same sentence after tonight!"

"We will do everything we can to find and bring him safely home," Enyo says. She offers her hand.

He shakes her hand.

"And you remember Avi," Kaly asks Anton.

Anton nods and swallows. He recognized her from his wife's funeral.

"War room?" Leon asks, releasing his scythe.

The others nod in agreement and move through the conservatory to the dining hall door. The stars in the night sky shine through the glass above.

Leon and Enyo discuss Teuta appearing near Elis's bike moments after he disappears, her message to Kaly, and the future cavern images.

Anton follows a few paces behind.

Teuta appears next to him.

Anton jumps away from her, knocking over a plant.

Enyo turns, unsheathing her sword in one smooth assault maneuver.

Kaly and Avi step aside, giving her space to charge.

"Wait!" Teuta cries. She vanishes before appearing further away. "Give me a minute to explain."

Leon calls his staff with a double tap and joins Enyo, scowling at the tiny figure, their weapons drawn.

"Speak!" Leon shouts.

Teuta nods. "Danae and Itra are in the archive suite with both of their babies." Leon inches towards her. "Ember asked me to retrieve them after Elis was taken."

"Taken by you!" Anton says, his tone low and menacing.

"No!" Teuta protests, holding up her hands. "Ember sent me to check on him. I arrived too late."

"And what does that mean?" Enyo asks.

"Chronos took him," Teuta says, lowering her hands to fists at her sides.

"Where did Chronos take him?" Anton asks.

Teuta shifts from side to side. "We don't know yet. That is why they were summoned here."

Kaly steps forward. "I want to see Danae and Itra to confirm your story."

Kaly disappears.

Leon swings his scythe towards Teuta, missing her by an inch as she fades and reappears a foot away.

"You have full access to the archives and the suite, per Danae's request." Teuta states. "Just knock before entering." She vanishes from the conservatory and doesn't reappear.

"Head to the war room," Leon says, releasing his staff. "I'm going to check on Kaly. Anton, you can come with me."

Avi and Enyo nod.

Anton and Leon disappear.

6

Anton bends at the waist, trying to catch his breath.

Leon pats Anton on the back. "Sorry dude, traveling around the castle gets a little easier over time."

"What was that?" Anton exhales, straightening.

"A portal," Leon says, motioning him to follow.

"Where are we?" Anton says, taking in the space for the first time.

"The archives."

A maze of shelves filled with books expands across the great hall. The walls, nearly three stories high, are covered with framed paintings and other pieces of art, including shields and swords. Anton's eyes dance around the space, but fall on the glass dome in the center of the room.

"Wow."

Leon tilts his chin towards the far corner. "The suite is there. Feeling better?"

"Yes."

Leon leads Anton through the maze by memory. He calls his staff as they cross the threshold of the open suite door. Leon hears Kaly's voice before he knocks on the last door on the left.

"Come in," Itra calls.

Kaly turns to face the door with a baby cradled in her arms.

Leon audibly gulps and releases his staff.

Anton steps past Leon.

Itra meets Anton halfway and hugs him tightly.

"We will find Elis," Itra whispers.

Anton hugs him tighter.

"I promise," Itra adds.

Leon moves around the men to Kaly and Danae.

Danae smiles. "Hi bro, glad you could make it. Would you like to meet your niece?"

Leon kisses Kaly's cheek before leaning over the bed to mess with Danae's hair. "Good to see you too!"

Danae swats him away.

"This is Ora. Ora, this is your Uncle Leon," Danae says, lifting the swaddled baby girl. She places Ora in his arms. He eyes Kaly, moving his arms to copy how she is holding his nephew.

Kaly smiles at him, and a single tear falls down her cheek. She sidles up next to him and pushes the blanket down around Emit. "And this is our nephew, Emit." She holds Emit so Leon can see both of the babies side by side.

"Well done, sis," Leon says, admiring their tiny, beautiful faces.

"Thanks," Danae says, fighting a yawn.

Anton leans over the bed and hugs Danae.

"You're officially Uncle Anton," Danae whispers.

Anton stands with a smile, wiping his watery eyes.

Kaly shifts Emit towards Anton.

Anton cradles him with ease, lifting him up to his nose, inhaling him softly before he strokes Emit's cherub cheeks.

Itra sits on the edge of the bed next to Danae. He wraps an arm around her. She nuzzles into him and yawns.

Itra yawns in return. "Tired?" he whispers into her hair.

"What do you think?" Danae asks. "It's late and I delivered two humans today."

Anton and Leon exchange their bundles.

Anton marvels over Ora as the tears fall in rapid succession. "I know she is watching over you." Her eyes brighten at his soft whisper. He nuzzles her nose.

Leon blinks his tears away, taking in the sight of Emit's wide gaze.

Kaly nudges Leon's hip. "We should let Danae get some rest."

Leon nods, not taking his eyes off of Emit.

Anton looks over at Danae. "Yes, of course we should go." He gently hands off Ora to Itra. "They're perfect."

"Tiny perfection," Leon says in agreement. He moves closer and hands over Emit to Danae. "

"We think so, but of course we may all be biased," Danae says with a small laugh.

"Keep me in the loop with what you find out from your search," Itra says, walking them to the door. "After Danae and the babies are asleep, I'll pull books from the archive for any clues."

"You need rest too," Leon says. Itra attempts to interrupt. Leon shakes his head. "We'll keep you in the loop, but Danae will need your help here."

Itra looks over at Danae with Emit and then down at his daughter. He nods. "Just find Elis."

Leon and Kaly nod.

Anton hugs Itra again. "Congratulations! Iana would be so proud."

Itra nods.

Anton walks through the stacks of books. He whispers, "This place is huge."

"I know," Kaly says. "It's a wonder I can ever bring myself to leave."

Several books float above their heads.

"How is that happening?" Anton asks, pointing up.

"It's a thought provoked catalog," Kaly explains.

"Where are they going?"

"You'll see."

Kaly leads their way through the maze of bookshelves to a round open seating area just under the glass dome

A stack of books fills a table near the center.

Anton points up at the dome. "Is that a clock?"

Kaly looks up and frowns. "Leon, look up."

"At my striking…" Leon freezes.

The glass dome is a giant clock with two red pulsing dots at twelve and six.

"Your what?" Anton asks.

"There was a stained-glass panel of a man with my face yielding a scythe." Leon shakes his head. "Plus a few other people, including one that looked like Danae." He looks at Kaly. "What the hell is that?"

Two books fly towards Leon. He catches the first one and misses the second.

Kaly reaches up and catches the second book.

"The compass," Kaly reads the cover aloud.

Anton takes the book from her and flips it open. "It's freaking blank."

"Hapur," Leon and Kaly say in unison.

The pages fill with text and images.

Anton gasps. His hands tremble and the book shakes as the pages turn by themselves.

Kaly places her hands under his to help steady the book.

The pages stop turning on an image of a gold arch with a single caption.

"Seek, and you will find," Anton quietly reads aloud.

Kaly and Leon's eyes meet in an instant.

Leon holds up his left thumb. The gold ring glows.

Kaly nods and holds hers up.

Anton looks between them. "Care to fill me in now?"

"In the previous assault against the castle," Kaly explains. "The gold cubes that were used to portal were collected, forged, and transformed into two gold arches. Each bloodline from Zeus and each of the pot ladies took possession of the arches." Kaly holds up her ring. "And these are the results."

"They're thought provoked," Leon says. "They let us go where we want. Like when we arrived at your place and startled you earlier and then when we brought you here."

"You can find Elis the same way?" Anton asks, his urgent tone gaining volume as he speaks.

"Possibly," Leon says. "We should take these books back to the war room." He turns the cover of the book he's holding towards them.

Kaly covers her mouth in surprise.

A symbol of a judgment scale with the words Emit and Ora are etched in gold over each side.

When they arrive in the war room. Anton grabs a vase from a side table and hurls for several minutes before joining the others at the table.

32

A cool glass of ginger ale, water, crackers, and mints appear on the table in front of him as he sits down. He nods in thanks but doesn't make eye contact with anyone. He sips on the ginger ale and listens.

"Enyo, I hear you," Leon says. "But if this is our direction, we should all go."

"I can't leave time and their parents here alone," Enyo says.

"Anton is here," Leon says.

"With no bloodline, power, or ability to protect and serve," Avi says, nodding towards Anton. "Sorry Anton."

"No offense taken," Anton croaks.

"Well, if I'm not late to the party, who is?" a voice hollers from the door.

Enyo and Leon stand and push Avi and Kaly behind them. Hermes slides into the room and bows.

"Hermes, at your service," he says, standing back up with a wide grin.

Anton coughs, but the others remain silent.

"It's good to see you, too," Hermes says with a frown and reaches to pull out a chair.

"No!" Leon says.

Avi and Kaly giggle.

Enyo just shakes her head and gestures to Leon.

Hermes pauses, raising a single eyebrow.

"Dude!" Leon shakes his head. "You're naked minus your winged shoes!"

Kaly and Avi lose their composure, laughing in unison.

Hermes puts his fists on his hips and stands up taller. "I fly faster with less resistance. Cool, right?"

"Negative!" Leon barks and turns away. "Dude, cover it up!"

Hermes uses the thought provoked wardrobe for new threads. He checks out his new outfit matching Leon's tan, long sleeve shirt and black cargo pants. "All good!" He smiles and hooks his thumbs through the belt loops.

Anton laughs.

Leon looks at Hermes and then looks down at his own clothes.

Leon scowls at him. "Original."

Enyo smirks. "Let's get Hermes caught up." She pauses, looking around the room. "Unless we're expecting a few others?"

Teuta appears near the doorway. "Maybe a few more in the morning, but that is all for now." Enyo nods and Leon glares in Teuta's direction. She prances out the door.

Hermes listens to the incidents that called them here and raises a hand to interrupt when Leon mentions Danae and her children.

"Wait, if time is here, does that mean that time has stopped outside of this dimension?"

"Oh dear," Kaly whispers. "What was the exact verbiage used in the prophecy for time?"

A book flies into the room and lands open in front of Kaly. She runs her finger down the page. "The Legacy of Time. Once the heir crosses under the ember archway, time will freeze in every dimension." She looks at Leon. His jaw is hanging open.

"Teuta took them from the birthing center, right?" Anton asks.

Leon nods.

"Teuta!" Enyo demands.

Teuta skips in the same door she left earlier.

"Is time frozen in the other dimensions?" Kaly asks.

"No," Teuta answers. "Not yet."

Enyo pounds the table with her fist. "Explain."

"The infants only received the gift of time once they arrived here."

Leon's mouth forms a grim line.

"Bringing them here put them in more danger?" Avi asks.

"Ember sent me, so I went." Teuta rolls up to her toes and down with a bounce.

"So, if they leave and come back through the ember archways, time will stop?" Kaly asks, reaching for Leon's hand.

"It depends," Teuta says. Leon tries to speak, but she holds up a hand. "The compass is essential to guiding time. Without him we will be subjected to an infant's mind of start and stop."

Kaly glances in Anton's direction. He runs a shaking hand through his hair and frowns.

"This is on you, all of it!" Leon says, pointing a finger at Teuta. "A minute late to save Elis and you put my family in more danger by bringing them here."

34

Teuta frowns. "I am just the messenger."

Leon snatches a book from the table and hurls it in her direction, but before impact, the book vanishes along with Teuta.

Enyo stands, checks her dagger strapped to her back and sheathes her sword. "Hermes, Avi and I will—"

"No," Kaly interrupts. "We need someone Elis will know and trust. Leon should be one of the three." Leon turns to her. "I know the whole 'never out of my sight again in this place' rule, but it's Elis. He needs us to divide and conquer. Avi, Anton, and I can handle anything here. She can send an alarm to Enyo if we run into any danger."

"How would she do that?" Anton asks.

Avi taps the infinity pendant around her neck. "A gift or curse," she says to Anton. "I am soul bound to the protectors of time."

Anton looks from Kaly to Leon back to Avi. "Just bring my boy home. I don't care how you do it."

Kaly reaches over and pats Anton's arm.

Enyo nods and walks over to the corner wardrobe and pulls out three red and purple feathered cloaks. Leon and Hermes stand and join Enyo. Hermes turns and extends his arms. Enyo drapes the cloak on his back, and it disappears. Leon turns and Enyo repeats the process. When Leon lays the final cloak against Enyo, it glows purple as it disappears.

"Why does hers glow and the others disappear?" Anton whispers to Kaly. A book from the table floats up and opens. It turns and faces Anton and Kaly.

An illustration of the cloak fills the page. Three small captions are written below.

"Safe passage through time and dimensions," Kaly says, leaning forward to read the text. "Flight to soar above or below. And with a glow, refract the light from matter and space."

"Below?" Hermes asks.

Avi claps twice. She eagerly turns to Enyo. "Can you try to make yourself invisible?"

"How?" Enyo asks.

"Teuta said these are thought provoked like everything else here," Leon says.

Enyo rolls her eyes at him. She takes a deep breath in. She slowly vanishes.

"It's working!" Avi exclaims. "Can you move or walk around?"

A chair beside Avi moves.

Hermes and Leon watch, mouths open, as several items in the room hover and are gently sat back down.

"Boo!" Enyo whispers in Leon's ear after sneaking up behind him. He jumps forward and calls his staff.

The others laugh as Enyo reappears with a smug grin. "You can't see me at all?"

"Not even a shadow," Kaly explains.

Enyo nods. "Good to know. Are you two ready?"

Hermes nods.

Leon releases his staff, leans over the chair and kisses Kaly. He pats Anton on the shoulder.

"Ready," Leon states. He stands in between Hermes and Enyo and spins his ring. "I will think only of Elis, just keep a hand on my shoulder as we go through."

Hermes and Enyo nod.

"Protect time," Leon says. "Unite to fight. Ember of mine."

Leon coughs as their feet find solid ground.

Hermes tightens his grip on Leon's shoulder.

"This is wrong," Hermes whispers.

Enyo unsheathes her dagger and sword.

"Do you know where we are?" Leon asks, glancing at Hermes.

"Turn around," Hermes says.

Leon calls his staff and taps once. The warm ember glow surrounds them. He slowly turns, examining the clearing and curses when he faces the five ember archways. He whirls around and takes in the vacant land.

"Where is the Castle of Teskom?" Leon asks.

"The ember archways were created before the castle was built," Hermes says. "I think we are far in the past."

"But why would Elis be here?" Leon asks.

"Chronos," Enyo says with a shrug. "Father Time was pursuing Ember in this timeline."

"I have an idea!" Hermes pushes off and flies over to the edge of the clearing high above Lake Shkoder.

Leon and Enyo sheathe their weapons and push off, flying up to follow him.

"Why are we flying?" Enyo asks, hovering back from the edge.

Leon wobbles in the air when he looks down at the shear drop to the water.

"The present and future caverns weren't built," Hermes says. "They were already here." He looks at them with a wide grin and wiggles his brows. "Are you ready to dive?"

Leon and Enyo shake their heads in unison.

Hermes flies higher over their heads and then dives, tucking his arms down to his side, increasing in speed as he bolts straight down.

"What is he… no way!" Leon says.

Hermes' laugh drifts up in response.

Enyo inches closer to the edge. She spots Hermes, barely visible far below, hovering in place. "I think he is waving."

"Smug bastard," Leon mutters, flying over the edge and copying Hermes' technique.

Enyo chuckles.

"Too fast, too fast!" Leon panics, flailing his arms and legs, somersaulting out of control.

Hermes flies down towards Leon.

"Just relax," Hermes calmly teases. "Think up and you fly up."

"Up!" Leon shouts. His tumble through the air halts just feet above the lapping water and rigid stones. He flies back up slowly.

Enyo is standing inside a cave when Leon lands beside Hermes.

"Rough flight?" Enyo says, barely keeping a straight face.

"Zip it!" Leon says, turning towards the dark interior of the cave.

The wide opening allows the moonlight to dance over the water dripping from the large stalagmites to the smooth stone surface.

Leon takes a breath, walks a few steps further away from the edge. "Show me Elis."

The interior remains dark.

"Show us Elis," Hermes says.

Nothing happens.

"We are here," Enyo says. "We are present. Show us Elis."

A flicker of light in the center glows and then fades to darkness.

"Damn it!" Leon kicks a rock across the cave.

"We are here," Enyo repeats. "We are open. We are present."

A bright white light fills the space.

Leon squints and shades his eyes.

A single figure dressed in a black hooded cloak appears in the center of the cave.

Leon blinks, adjusting to the light.

Enyo and Hermes nod at each other and they circle the figure.

"You will find the guide to all time," a deep male voice echoes in the cave. "In a place between space and mine."

"What place?" Leon asks, calling his staff.

No response.

"He's seven!" Leon yells, double tapping his staff. The figure turns towards the glowing scythe and points.

Leon tightens his grip around the staff, feeling it pull towards the figure.

"Leon!" Enyo yells, watching him struggle to hold on to the scythe. She unsheathes her sword. "The scythe can cut a hole in time! Create a window!"

Leon raises the scythe and swings once, decapitating the cloaked figure.

The figure dissolves, but a gash of darkness remains.

"Elis!" Leon shouts, moving closer to the darkness as it flickers to life.

Elis uncurls and rolls over.

"It's him," Leon says, squashing the panic rising in his voice. He sucks in a breath. "Elis, it's me, Leon."

Elis sits up and looks around.

"I can't see you," Elis whispers.

"I know buddy," Leon says. "Can you tell me what you see around you?"

"Stone walls and a small window," Elis says. His bottom lip quivers. "I miss my dad."

"I know buddy," Leon says. "We're here to help you get home. Can you tell me what you see out of the window?"

Elis nods and stands.

The perspective through the gash shifts to Elis facing the window.

"The lake and the moon."

Hermes flies out of the cave and hovers looking for any windows carved out of the cliff face.

"Can you see a man flying below you?" Leon asks Elis.

Elis rolls up on his toes to peer further out the window. "Not below but above."

Hermes flies down, searching for any openings.

"Who is that?" Elis asks.

"Hermes," Leon says. "He is—um, a friend. Is he getting closer?"

"He just flew past my window," Elis says. "Hermy, over here!"

Leon watches Elis wave and jump up and down.

"You just passed him," Enyo shouts over the edge to Hermes.

Hermes circles and slows, moving closer towards the cliff.

"When you see Hermes again yell, stop!" Leon instructs Elis.

"Stop! Hermy, stop!" Elis shouts and waves.

"Stop!" Enyo shouts down.

Hermes looks up and shakes his head. "I can't see him."

"I'm right here!" Elis jumps up and down, continuously waving his arms around.

"He can see you!" Enyo shouts down.

Hermes nods and moves closer to the rocks inch by inch.

Enyo looks back towards the image with Elis. "It's flickering. Hurry!"

Leon taps his staff once transforming the scythe to an ember glow and sprints to the edge.

"Catch!" Leon shouts down.

Hermes pushes away from the cliff and looks up.

Leon lets go of his staff. It falls fast.

Hermes catches it, but it slides through his sweaty palm. He tightens his grip around the staff. "Whew!" he mumbles, flying closer to the face of the cliff. He methodically inspects every rock and shadow.

"I see a light!" Elis calls out.

Leon walks closer to the image of Elis. "He's trying to find you. Keep talking to me."

A warm ember glow fills the window. Elis disappears from view and the cavern goes dark.

Leon curses and runs out of the cave, flying down to Hermes, but he's gone.

"Up here!" Hermes calls down to Leon.

Leon hovers and searches the night sky. The glow of his staff appears over the edge of the cliff.

Enyo flies out of the cave, following the light.

"Where is he?" Leon yells, landing next Enyo.

"Leon!" Elis says, running from behind Hermes.

Leon falls to his knees and scoops him up. "Are you hurt?"

"Starving!" Elis groans into Leon's neck.

Leon laughs. "I bet!"

Hermes hands Leon his staff.

"Thanks, Hermy," Leon says, smiling.

"Hermy?" Hermes laughs. "No, thanks to me really." He points to the ember glow. "The second you tossed the staff down, the entire cliff face transformed. It's a full castle with courtyards, look-out towers—basically an entire village." He shakes his head. "What I can't figure out… it looked like home, my home."

Leon and Enyo exchange a glance.

Elis shivers in Leon's arms. "Let's get this little man back to Anton."

Enyo and Hermes nod and place a hand on Leon's shoulder.

"Protect time," they say in unison. "Unite to fight. Ember of mine."

9

"Heading upstairs for a second," Kaly says. "You two ok?"
Anton and Avi nod.

Kaly climbs the stairs to the Zeus family suites she stayed in during their last visit. She pauses at the landing.

A door opens a few feet down on the left. She cautiously walks down and pokes her head in the open doorway. It's a bedroom with a large bed with soft grey and blue pillows and linens. A smaller bed is set on the opposite side of the room, with colorful sheets, pillows, and a stuffed animal.

She smiles. "If Ember is prepping for Elis and Anton, this must be good news!" She retraces her steps towards the landing.

Click

Kaly pauses and turns around. "Teuta?"

She hears a whoosh of air. *Was that a door?* She strains to see in the dark. She gasps as a figure steps out into the corridor and walks towards her.

A light stone illuminates a familiar face.

"Aunt Xena!" Kaly says, hugging her tightly. "How and when did you arrive?"

"I returned home and found the Time to Serve message left on my dining table," Xena says, holding up the card. "I used the ring to return to my suite. I wasn't sure if the grounds or castle were compromised."

"Where's Pem?" Kaly asks, looking over Xena's shoulder.

Xena shakes her head. "Making up for lost time."

Kaly raises an eyebrow.

"Ten years of manipulation and torture by Poseidon and Medusa have not been too kind to my daughter," Xena says, the frown and concern etching deep in her brow. "She's still weary of strangers, even my friends, and don't get me started on her reactions to tall men in public places." Xena shakes her head.

"That's heartbreaking," Kaly whispers and frowns.

"I've asked her to stay home and on standby. I promised to summon her if needed."

"And she was ok with that?" Kaly asks.

"My summons to return wasn't a complete shock. I had a dream two nights ago I would be called here. She sends her best, by the way."

Kaly nods. She loops her arm through Xena's as they walk towards the landing.

"Is she still attending therapy?" Kaly asks.

"Twice a week," Xena says, taking the first step down. "It helps, but it's hard when you can't explain Ember and the Castle of Teskom to any outsider." Xena laughs. "Pem tried it one day out of frustration in a session. The therapist said it all came out like she spoke in another language."

Kaly stops and turns towards her. "Really?"

Xena nods. "They record their sessions, and the therapist replayed the recording. Pem just bolted without an explanation. When she got home and explained what happen we cried and then laughed at the level of Ember's control."

Kaly smiles and shakes her head.

A loud burst of conversation fills the stairwell from the war room.

Anton's cries carry over the rest.

Kaly and Xena jog down the remaining steps.

Avi turns to them, clapping and crying. She runs over and hugs Xena.

"What's happening?" Xena asks, hugging Avi.

"They found Elis!" Avi says.

Leon moves to the side and reveals Anton holding Elis.

"Oh! Thank God!" Kaly cries.

Leon turns, noticing Xena and Kaly for the first time. He walks to Kaly, kissing her on the cheek, and hugs Xena.

"Glad you could make it," Leon says.

Xena smiles and releases him, reaching up to squeeze his cheek. "I'm glad it looks like all good news here."

Leon smiles. "It's good, but we definitely have a lot of questions."

Elis pushes back from Anton. "I'm starving! Can we have pancakes for dinner?"

"Absolutely," Kaly says, walking over to tousle Elis's brown curls. Hermes pulls out a chair for Elis. Elis giggles at the size of the pancakes he uncovers.

Kaly turns to Anton. "We have a room for you and Elis ready upstairs."

Anton frowns. "We can't stay here."

"It's the middle of the night," Leon whispers. "We need to make sure he is safe."

Anton flinches.

Leon presses a hand to Anton's shoulder. "That you both are."

Elis squeals as a giant mug full of marshmallows appears next to his plate.

"Look dad!" Elis says, holding up a handful of marshmallows.

Anton smiles and nods at Elis. Then cuts a look towards Leon. "We leave tomorrow."

Leon nods and pulls out a chair for Kaly to sit. She shakes her head. "I'll let Itra and Danae know Elis is back and safe."

Leon nods and takes the seat himself.

At Itra's name, Elis turns. "Is Uncle Itra here?" He looks around the room.

"Yes," says Anton. "Danae had the babies earlier. They are resting tonight but you can see them in the morning."

"Whoop!" Elis says, raising a fork in the air. "I have baby cousins!"

Leon laughs. "You sure do, kid."

Kaly lands in the archive suite. The portal from one space to another leaves her breathless, but it is getting easier. She takes two steps down the hallway towards the nursery but pauses when Itra steps out, gently closing a door.

Itra turns and jumps in surprise. He immediately throws one hand over his mouth to squash a curse and one hand goes to his chest.

"Sorry," Kaly whispers.

Itra shakes his head, meeting her halfway. "No worries. I just wasn't expecting to see anyone."

"How are the babies and Danae?" Kaly asks, walking with Itra to the archives.

"Resting." Itra smiles and fights a yawn.

"Well, maybe you can sleep soon, too." Kaly smiles and yawns in return. "I bring good news!"

"Elis?"

"He's currently eating a plate full of pancakes and a mug full of marshmallows."

Itra hugs Kaly, letting out a soft cry of joy and relief. When he pulls back, he has tears falling down both cheeks.

"Is he ok?" Itra asks.

"I think so," Kaly says. "Anton is relieved, but doesn't want to stay here. Leon mentioned that we have a few more questions to figure out."

"Details?" Itra asks.

"I overheard Enyo and Hermes discussing an old village, but we can question all of them in the morning."

Itra frowns.

Kaly shrugs an apology. "I stayed with Anton and Avi."

"Who found Elis?"

"Hermes, Enyo and Leon," Kaly says, a blur in her peripheral makes her turn.

A book flies towards her face. She catches it before the cover collides with her nose.

Itra whistles. "Great catch!"

Kaly turns the dark blue book over. No writing appears on either side or the spine, but it's heavy and thick. She opens the cover. Like most books in the archive, it's blank.

"Hapur," Kaly whispers. The pages turn quickly, filling with lines of text and illustrations.

"What were you thinking to prompt this book?" Itra asks, watching the magic happen.

"I was thinking about the old village," Kaly says.

The book flips back to the opening page. Kaly reads the text, scrawled in a flowing blue ink, several times before looking up at Itra.

Kaly shifts to show Itra. "It says the City of Time is beneath what's mine."

They look down simultaneously at the floor and softly chuckle.

"On that weird note," Itra says with a yawn. "I'm too tired for Ember's riddles. Tell Anton and Elis to come down in the morning."

"And Xena?" Kaly asks.

"Your aunt and cousin are here?" Itra asks.

"Just Xena, Pem's on standby."

"Danae would love to see her," Itra says, fighting another yawn. "Thanks again for the good news and good luck with that." He points to the heavy book.

Kaly smiles. "Good night!" She vanishes from the archives.

"Good night to you too." Itra laughs at the empty spot where Kaly was standing.

Kaly appears near the table in the war room.

Leon is sitting alone.

"Where did everyone go?" Kaly asks.

"Bed," Leon says. "Elis made it halfway through his pancakes before his eyes drooped." Leon smirks and wipes syrup from the corner of his mouth. "All good?"

Kaly sets the book down. It thuds in the quiet space.

He stands to pull her in for a hug.

46

She leans against his chest and sighs. "Yes, all good."

"What's this?" Leon asks, pointing to the thick book.

"Something that nearly hit me in the face when I was giving Itra the updates about Elis."

Leon inspects her face.

"I caught it in time," Kaly says with a soft laugh. "Can you tell me more about the rescue?" She yawns. "Preferably from bed."

Leon nods and picks up the book. He takes her hand and leads her up the stairs to the Zeus family suites.

Leon spends the next half hour pacing their suite, explaining their trip to the past. The clearing without the Castle of Teskom but with the five ember archways, the cave, images played out inside, and what Hermes described as an entire castle with a village below the cave.

"Was it the same dark figure we saw in the future cavern when we arrived?" Kaly asks.

"Yes, I think so," Leon answers before sitting on the side of the bed.

Kaly taps her forehead, and a pen with paper appears in her lap. She writes something down and reads it to Leon.

"The first message from the hooded figure was: Hear this now, see her bow. I am Father Time. The compass near for a year. Ember of mine."

Leon nods.

"And the second?" Kaly says.

Leon recites. "You will find the guide to all time. In a place between space and mine."

Kaly writes the rhyme down.

Leon leans back on the bed. "We can double check the rhyme with Enyo in the morning."

"What does Hermes call home?" Kaly asks, tapping the pen on the paper.

"All good questions," Leon says, rolling to his side.

The book flips open, near the center. A detailed illustration of a castle and courtyards fills both pages. The caption is in the same flowing text as the opening: *City of Time*.

Kaly hovers a finger over the illustration. She points out the fine details of the cobblestone paths, the small narrow windows on the second and third floors, and a sundial in the middle of a courtyard.

"This is under the castle?" Kaly asks, looking up at Leon.

"According to Hermes," Leon says. "I didn't see it." He leans closer and snuggles her shoulder. "Can we hit pause till morning?" He pulls out a pouty lip and bats his eyes.

She kisses his nose.

He bats his lashes again.

"Maybe," she says, placing the book and paper on the bedside table. "But I will need to be thoroughly distracted."

Leon rolls on top of her. "Distraction is my specialty."

10

Teuta appears in the war room. She attempts to blink away the darkness and tosses up her light stone.

It remains dark.

She rubs the hair standing on end at the base of her ponytail.

"Who's there?" Teuta asks, slowly turning around.

"Ah, so perceptive," a male says, coming out of the shadows from the dining hall entrance.

"Leon?" Teuta guesses by the looming height of the man whose face is still covered in darkness.

"I see you don't recognize your younger brother." the man teases.

She takes a step back, bumping into a chair.

"Half-brother!" she corrects.

"A new version of him." He laughs.

"How did you get in here?" Teuta asks, transforming from her fairy stature to her queen height.

He clicks his tongue. "We have our secrets and so do you."

He lunges and clasps a hand on Teuta's forearm before she can vanish.

"Get off of me!" She attempts to loosen his grip by transforming back to her fairy form, but he only tightens his hold. She pulls harder.

She freezes. A cool, metal object clamps around her forearm near her wrist.

Her light stone flares to life, brightening the room in an instant. Pax laughs.

Teuta's face falls pale as she inspects her arm, and she blinks several times.

"Ah, you know what it is then?" Pax asks.

"It's not possible." She stares down at the tattoo of a gold cuff inked on her olive skin. She rotates her wrist, seeing where the ink came together, encircling her tiny forearm.

"A new gift from me and an old friend," he says, leaning over to her small height.

She looks up for the first time and spits in the smooth, contoured, familiar face of Pax.

He slaps her hard across the face.

She doesn't wince or even blink.

Then he wipes his cheek with the sleeve of his blue tunic.

She points her chin up and flares her nostrils. "Chronos, you'll regret the day you took Pax as your host. He is nothing but a conniving, self-absorbed creature that will eat you alive from the inside."

He throws back his head with a full body laugh.

She stomps on his foot.

He levels his gaze to her glare. "Pax has zero consciousness left. I own his physical form. Like you said, he's just the host."

A warm white glow starts in the center of the room.

"Time to go," he says, yanking Teuta's arm and dragging her towards the light.

She throws all her tiny weight against his pull, but free falls into the light, landing a few seconds later on a sandy surface. She quickly stands and tries to portal. Nothing happens. Her eyes adjust to the dark space after a few deep breaths.

She rolls to her toes and peeks out the only opening in the small stone wall.

The moon is high, reflecting on the water below. The cool night air seeps in and through her thin dress.

She folds into a ball, covering her exposed legs with what little fabric she has.

11

Anton rolls over and feels cool air on his wet cheeks. He opens one eye. *Still dark.* He flips the tear-soaked pillow and feels the bed shift.

"Elis," Anton whispers.

"Is it morning?" Elis asks, excitedly.

"No, son," Anton answers, and sits up. He wipes his cheeks with his sleeve. "Not quite."

Elis stands and then kneels on the bed next to Anton.

"But dad!" Elis whines. "I want to see Uncle Itra and the babies." He folds his hands together in a pleading prayer. "Please?"

"Soon," Anton says, pulling him closer and wrapping his arms around him. "I promise, but Danae will need all the rest she can get with two babies to care for."

"Is she going to die like momma?" Elis whispers into Anton's chest.

Anton stiffens and pulls Elis away to look at his face. His bottom lip is pushed out.

"Danae is perfectly well," Anton says, stroking his cheek. "She is just tired. It's hard work giving birth to one and she gave birth to two!"

"Promise?" Elis asks, squirming a bit.

"I promise," Anton says. "Not anytime soon."

Elis jumps off the bed, taking three strides into the washroom.

Anton sighs. He lays back on the bed.

The door cracks open a second after the toilet flushes.

"Wash your hands, young man!" Anton says in the high-pitched mocking tone of Elis's new after-school nanny.

Elis laughs and returns to the sink.

"You sound just like her!" Elis says over the running water.

"One day you will remember to do it without a reminder!" Anton says, in his regular voice.

Elis returns to the bed but doesn't climb up. "Can I eat while we wait for morning?"

A door opens on the opposite side of the room.

Anton taps the light stone on the nightstand and tosses it up, a lesson he remembered from his first visit to the Castle of Teskom. The glow expands, lighting the bedroom and the adjoining room.

He throws back the blanket. "Can you order on your own?"

"I think so!" Elis squeals. He jumps up and down in place.

"Great," Anton says, patting Elis on the head. "Give me three minutes and wait for me in here."

Elis nods before Anton closes the washroom door.

Anton turns on the faucet and splashes his face. He contemplates a shower but hears Elis pacing just outside the door. He wets his hair and pats it down. He turns off the water and attempts to smooth the wrinkles from his disheveled button-up shirt and trousers.

He opens the door and Elis bolts across the room to the adjacent open door.

The large living room has two additional doors. An iron and glass door opens to a balcony and a large wood door to the corridor.

Anton laughs and follows him to the room. He tilts his head up to admire the high ceilings and the round glass dome centered over a large round table as he passes a sofa and chair set near a fireplace.

Elis sits at the table and closes his eyes. Seven trays of food appear on the table all at once.

"Whoa!" Anton says.

Elis opens his eyes and throws back his head with laughter.

"Really, son," Anton scolds him, "magic castle or not, it's not polite to waste food."

Elis ignores him, lifting the purple dome plate covers off each tray.

"Yum! Oh yea! Bacon!" Elis wiggles side to side in his chair as he uncovers a plate of chocolate chip pancakes, scrambled eggs, and an entire plate of just bacon. He pops a slice of bacon in his mouth and uncovers a bowl of cereal with brightly colored marshmallows. "Cool!"

Elis winks at Anton. The next three trays reveal Anton's breakfast. A pot of coffee and creamer, the next oatmeal with honey and blueberries, and the last has a plate with two eggs over easy with hash browns and toast.

"Did I get it right?" Elis asks, examining the items.

Anton smiles and pulls out a chair. "You thought of all of this just for me?"

"More like what mom would make you," Elis says over a mouth full of marshmallows.

"How about you save the sugary treats for last?" Anton says, laughing and pointing to the scrambled eggs.

Elis frowns but stabs a fork full of eggs. He swallows the eggs, and a large mug of hot chocolate arrives on the table.

Anton blinks twice and shakes his head.

"I was thirsty," Elis says before taking a long sip. He smiles.

Anton reaches over and wipes the chocolate-stained mustache from his upper lip.

Elis swats his hand away. "Dad!"

Anton pulls his hand back and returns to eating.

"Do you think Danae will let me hold them?" Elis asks a few minutes later, finishing the eggs and moving on to the pancakes.

"Of course," Anton says after sipping his coffee. "They are pretty small. If you sit down, you could probably hold both of them at the same time."

"Cool!" Elis takes another few bites. "Was I pretty small?"

Anton laughs. "No son, you came into this world large and in charge." Elis frowns. "There is an average size for a newborn, and you were above average in both weight and length."

Elis smiles and nods. "Above average, cool." He finishes the plate of pancakes and fists his chest. "Brah!" He giggles when his burp echoes in the room.

Anton looks up. "Do you see what I am dealing with down here?"

"Are you talking to mom again?" Elis asks.

"Every day, all day," Anton says, raising his mug to Elis's hot chocolate. Elis clinks his mug to his.

"Me too," Elis says after sipping.

Anton smiles and wipes his left eye before a tear spills over.

Elis alternates between the bacon and the cereal.

"Do you want to talk about yesterday?" Anton asks, pushing his tray of food away.

Elis doesn't look up from the cereal. "Father Time said he needed my help."

"Who is Father Time?" Anton asks, waiting for Elis to look up.

Elis doesn't respond. At first, Anton thinks he's absorbed in his food. But then he can see that Elis is avoiding the question.

He scoots his chair over until he is next to Elis and puts a hand on his shoulder. "What is it?"

Elis blinks back tears. "He told me—I could see her again."

"See who again?" Anton furrows his brows. "Mom?"

Elis nods.

"Can you tell me what he looks like?"

Elis shakes his head. "I never saw him. I was riding my bike when he spoke to me. He told me, come and see your mom. I didn't mean to say yes, but I nodded my head and then I was in the dark, stone wall room."

Anton pulls Elis into a hug. "I'm sorry you experienced that."

Elis sighs into his chest.

"Were you scared?"

Elis nods.

Anton squeezes him a little harder. "Did the man say anything else?"

"Just to wait for time," Elis whispers.

Anton brushes the brown curls away from Elis's forehead and kisses his temple. "You're safe now."

"Ember will always protect me and time."

54

Anton pulls away and touches his nose to Elis. "I will always protect you."

"Father Time is bigger than you, dad."

Anton frowns. "You said you didn't see him."

Elis shakes his head. "I didn't see him—yesterday."

"Ok, when did you see him?"

"In my dreams every night since we buried mom."

Knock, knock

Anton's mouth is still hanging open when Elis hops off his chair to run to the door.

"Who is it?" Elis asks, dancing side to side.

"Leon."

Elis swings open the door. "Is it time?"

Leon smiles at Elis. "Time for what?"

"To go see the babies," Elis says.

"It's barely morning," Leon says, patting his belly. "I need breakfast."

"We already ate," Elis says, patting his full belly. "Please, can we go?"

Leon looks past Elis to Anton. "Hey buddy, go brush your teeth and clean up your face." He touches Elis's cheek. "You're sticky!"

Elis sighs and marches back through the living area to the bedroom.

When the washroom door shuts, Anton curses.

"What's up?" Leon asks, gripping the back of the chair across from Anton.

"Father freaking time!" Anton says, standing to pace the room.

"Explain," Leon says, "I haven't had coffee yet." A steaming mug appears on the table in front of Leon.

Anton gestures with a nod to the bedroom door. "It was Father fucking Time who took Elis. And the man has been invading his dreams since we buried Iana."

Leon chokes on the coffee. "He saw him?"

"Not yesterday," Anton says, shaking his head. "Elis only heard him promise he could see Iana again."

"Son of a—" Leon cuts off the curse, hearing the door to the washroom open.

"Cleaned and brushed!" Elis says, skipping back into the room.

Anton walks past Elis towards the washroom. "I need to—clean up."

Leon watches Anton retreat. He walks with his coffee to the sofa. "Let's give your dad a chance to shower." He sits and pats the cushion next to him.

Elis groans. He stomps his way over to the sofa and sits. After readjusting several times, he settles and sighs.

"Did Father Time keep his promise?" Leon asks between sips.

Elis tilts his head to the side.

"He promised you could see your mom, right?" Leon asks.

"That's what he said," Elis says, shaking his head. "But no, I didn't see her."

Leon sets his mug down on a side table and leans forward to Elis's eye level. "What do you dream about?"

Elis curls his legs in, wrapping his arms around his shins and resting his chin on his knees. "Father Time."

"What does he look like?"

Elis scrunches his little nose. "An old man with a long white beard." He tucks in his chin and waves his hand from his lips to his waist.

"That long?" Leon asks.

Elis nods.

"And what does he say in your dreams?"

A smile crosses Elis's lips. He stands and puffs out his chest, placing his fists on his hips. "Hear this now, see her bow. I am Father Time." He giggles and collapses back into the sofa.

"That's it?" Leon says, picking up his mug. He finishes the last of the coffee and the mug vanishes.

"Sometimes he shows me things," Elis says. "I try to draw them when I wake up but those drawings are at home."

A pile of papers plops on the cushion between Leon and Elis.

"Cool!" Elis exclaims, picking up a drawing and showing Leon. It's a clock with the hands pointing at twelve and six.

"How did you get these here?" Leon asks, picking up a drawing.

"I pictured my desk at home and then boom!" Elis dances from side to side.

Anton pokes his head through the doorway. "Can I borrow a set of clean clothes?" He feels a tingle from his toes to his shoulders. The towel wrapped around his waist has been replaced by a blue spandex suit with an orange capital A on his chest and a red cape.

Leon barks out a laugh and doubles over.

Elis runs over to Anton. "Do you like it?"

Anton gives Elis a slow twirl, fighting his own laugh. He smiles, facing Elis again. "I don't think I need a superhero costume today."

"Ok," Elis says, letting his smile and shoulders fall.

Anton feels the tingle and examines his new threads: a long sleeve blue shirt and jeans with running shoes.

"Cool!" Anton's mimic of Elis is nearly spot on.

Leon laughs again. He stands and takes the drawings from the sofa. "Let's take these to show your uncle."

"Yes!" Elis says, running for the suite door to the corridor.

"Hold up!" Leon calls. Elis pauses mid stride. "We have to portal there."

Elis turns to Leon with his mouth hanging open. "You know how to do that?"

"Sure do! Come, take my hand and your dads."

Elis runs over and grasps Leon's hand. Anton joins them, holding Elis's other hand.

"Hold on," Leon says as they vanish from the suite.

12

Danae sits up and blinks away the sleep. She hears approaching footsteps in the hall. She nudges Itra.

He groans.

"I think we have visitors," she whispers.

He moans and rolls out of bed, adjusting his pajama pants and pulling on a shirt on his way to the door.

"What's your problem?" Danae teases. "We had a good two full hours of sleep!"

He looks back at her with a single eyebrow raised.

She smiles and shrugs, pulling out her ember amulet from under her top.

Itra pulls open the door and meets Leon's surprised face with his fist raised to knock.

Elis pushes past Leon and into Itra.

Itra rocks back a bit to counter his weight.

"Hey buddy," Itra says, ruffling his hair. "Good morning to you too!"

Elis looks up, grinning ear to ear. "Are they sleeping?" he loudly whispers.

Danae laughs.

Elis releases Itra and bounds across the room to Danae.

"Easy, Elis," Anton says, patting Itra on the shoulder after Leon enters.

"You're a mom!" Elis says, climbing into the bed to sit next to Danae.

"And you're a cousin!" Danae says, tickling his side. He giggles. "Would you like to hold them?"

"Yes!" He claps twice.

Anton and Leon lean against the bedposts at the end of the bed.

Itra goes to the bassinet and picks up Ora, passing her to Danae.

Danae places a pillow on Elis's lap and gently rests Ora in the middle.

"Elis meet Ora," she whispers, taking Emit from Itra.

Elis strokes her tiny fingers. She purses her lips in response. He bends and rubs his nose to her. He hears a sniffle and looks up, meeting Anton's teary eyes.

"Why are you sad?" Elis asks.

Anton smiles and wipes his cheeks. "Only happy tears, I promise."

Elis looks back down. "She will be a queen one day."

"A queen of what, silly?" Danae asks.

"Time."

Danae looks over at Itra. He shakes his head.

"What do you mean?" Leon asks, placing Elis's drawings on the bed.

Itra leans over and immediately picks up the drawing of the clock with the hands pointing to twelve and six.

Elis looks up and shrugs. "Father Time showed me her as the queen and I was a guide to him." Elis points to Emit.

Emit squirms a little. Danae leans over and adjusts Ora to one side and places Emit on the other side.

Elis repeats the nose gesture to Emit.

Itra sits on the other side of Elis. "Can you tell me what this means?" He holds the drawing of the clock up for Elis. Elis glances at the drawing before returning his gaze to the babies.

"Father Time shows me a clock like this right before the dream stops."

Itra and Danae exchange a look with a shrug, but Leon holds up another drawing. They stare at the small girl with a crown atop her brown hair, hand in hand with a white bearded man.

"Elis," Danae whispers. "Can you tell us about this one?" She takes the drawing from Leon to study it closer.

"It's Ora with Father Time," Elis says, looking up at the drawing. "She will live in a place between space and mine with Father Time."

There is a chorus of gasps from the adults in the room.

Elis scans each face, which frown back at him. His brow furrows. "Is that bad?"

"Elis, son," Anton says, raising a hand to his racing heart. "We were terrified when you were taken. Why would this be good?"

"But Emit and Ora are time." Elis states. "They can't stay together."

Danae wraps an arm around Elis. "They can't stay apart. They will need us."

Elis looks up through his long, curled lashes. "She won't be alone. She will be with Father Time."

Danae frowns and feels the ember amulet lift away from her chest. "Why her? Why would he take her?"

"She is the queen," Elis says, smiling.

Itra pats Danae's arm as the color drains from her face and she wraps a hand around the ember amulet.

Itra stands and clears his throat. "It's their breakfast time." He bends and takes Ora.

Danae brushes away a single tear and takes Emit from Elis's lap. "Did you eat?"

Elis grins and nods, patting his belly. "I ordered it all by myself."

"Is that right?" Itra says, looking at Anton.

Anton nods. "He even ordered for me, along with my clean clothes." He tugs on his shirt.

A steaming mug appears in Itra's hand. He sighs with a smile and raises his mug to his wife. He recites a passage from the Zeus book that has replayed in his mind since their first trip to the castle. "Danae, your heir will bind our blood in time. The infinity loop combines. Oh, Ember of mine, our Ember in time."

The babies cry in unison.

The room chills in an instant and the air swirls at the floor and rises quickly, blowing the covers up and stirring the drawings around. The bedroom door slams shut.

Leon calls his staff.

Anton reaches for Elis.

Danae looks down at her hand. "Oh, God!"

Leon and Itra look down at the ember amulet Danae is holding. It is broken into two pieces.

Danae looks up at Itra's bent, empty arm. He looks down and drops his mug. It disappears before spilling and hitting the floor.

Elis jumps from the bed and circles Itra. "Where did you hide her?"

"She's gone!" Danae cries.

Elis stops circling Itra. He inches away towards Anton.

"She was here," Itra panics. "She has to be here." He looks from the bed to Leon to the floor. He scans the entire room… anywhere but Danae's face, dripping with tears.

"Find her, now!" Danae cries, holding Emit closer.

Leon charges out the bedroom door and runs into Kaly. He holds her steady before she falls.

"Problem, big problem!" she whispers, catching her breath.

"We know!" Leon says, looking over her shoulder at the grim faces of Xena and Enyo.

"You do?" Enyo says, marching forward. "How did you know Avi was taken? Is she down here?"

"Her too?" Itra asks at the door.

Kaly bolts past Itra into the room. "The babies?"

Danae shakes her head.

"Ora disappeared," Anton says, kneeling with Elis hugging his neck.

"How?" Xena asks, moving into the room to stand next to Kaly.

"A whirl of air and then the door—slammed," Itra says, his voice cracking on the last word. "When I looked down Danae's amulet was split in two and Ora—"

"What was the phrase you said right before this happened?" Leon asks, pointing a finger in Itra's face.

"I, um," Itra chokes out a whisper. "It's a quote from the Zeus book about the merger with Mui."

"Where is this book?" Kaly asks, stepping between Leon and Itra.

"The study, Ivan's study," Itra says. "It just says Zeus on the cover." A book appears and hovers in the air between Kaly and Itra. "That's it!"

Kaly takes the book. "Show me what you said."

The book opens at her request.

Itra scans the translated page in his Uncle Vincent's handwriting and finds the line. He points it out to Kaly.

Kaly reads the line silently. She coughs and then reads one part aloud. "Bind our blood in time, the infinity loop combines."

Enyo whirls on Itra with her dagger raised. "What—did—you do?"

Itra takes a step back. "Why are you pointing that thing at me? My daughter was just taken."

"You gave him time and Avi!" Enyo hisses.

"I don't understand!" Itra takes another step back.

Kaly reaches over and attempts to lower Enyo's arm. Enyo stiffens and keeps the blade pointed at Itra.

Xena steps between Itra and Enyo. "Weapons down and egos aside. We have two missing people. We need to come together, not tear each other apart."

"Can you explain what happened to Avi?" Leon asks.

Kaly nods. "We had just sat down in the war room to eat breakfast. A whirl of air blasted through the room like it did when I recited the castle reset passage on our last visit. When the doors slammed shut, Avi was gone."

"And Teuta?" Leon asks.

"We haven't seen her since last night." Kaly shakes her head. "And she didn't answer when we called for her."

"Teuta!" Danae and Leon yell in unison.

Emit cries in response.

Hermes appears next to Kaly.

Leon lunges towards him but stops in recognition.

Hermes holds up both hands and shakes his head after assessing the mix of shock and horror on each face before speaking.

"I flew the grounds and there is no sign of Avi. And I went through the ember archways." He tilts his head and continues. "There is no movement anywhere."

"The stone of judgement," Xena whispers.

"What did you say?" Danae asks, sitting up straighter and adjusting Emit.

"The urtar stone," Xena says. "The fable of the ember stones on one side and the glowing red rocks on the other side of the scale until the cry of an infant."

Enyo frowns. "That thing we saw in the hand of that statue after we left Pax in the helix?"

Xena nods.

"The scale has tipped?" Hermes asks, rolling up on his toes.

"I'm open to another interpretation," Xena says, looking from face to face.

"We had a book with an illustration of a scale with Emit and Ora's name on the cover," Leon says. "But we never read it." He turns to Kaly.

"It was the book you launched at Teuta," Kaly says with a frown. The same book appears next her. "Bless the book fairies at least." She flips open the book and studies the text. "I can't read this. Enyo?" Kaly turns the book.

Enyo reads the text. "A balance of true, attest for two. The lines of time and divine are truly aligned." She looks up from the text.

Elis turns away from Anton. "Father Time."

Itra kneels to his level. "Tell us everything you know about Father Time."

Elis walks over to the drawings on the bed. He lays them out on the floor across the room. He moves a few around and then stands at one end. He points down to a drawing of a blue sky split with a vertical gap of black crayon scratches in the middle.

Danae moves with Emit to the foot of the bed.

"The place between space and time," Elis says.

"What does—" Enyo asks.

"Give him a second to explain the drawings!" Itra interrupts. She glares at him.

Elis moves to the second drawing with twelve red dots in a perfect circle, like the other drawing of the clock, but the dots at twelve and six are larger. "Father Time shows me this time in each dream."

Elis moves to the third drawing. "This one is Ora with Father Time. He takes us on a tour of his castle."

Kaly squats, tracing the outline of the crown on the little girl's head.

"She is a queen!" Elis says. He smiles and dances to the next drawing of a bridge across mountain peaks.

"Father Time stands here and shouts," Elis says, pointing to the bridge. He puffs out his chest and holds out his arms. "Hear this now, see her bow. I am Father Time. Illyria of mine."

Kaly looks up at Leon. He nods.

"We heard a cloaked figure say something similar in the future cavern," Leon says, kneeling in front of the next drawing. A woman with dark hair and a yellow dress stands on the same bridge without Father Time. "And her?"

Elis nods. "The goddess Ember." He points to the bottom of the drawing. A man with a white beard is at the bottom of the mountain. "She pushes him off the bridge in my dreams. It was scary the first time."

Anton moves next to Elis.

"And the last one is you?" Kaly asks, moving to look at the drawing of a little boy holding hands with another little boy. They are pointing at the sky.

"Me and Emit," Elis says, skipping to Danae. "He is time, and I am the compass."

Danae loosens the blanket and pulls down the corner of Emit's sleeper, showing Elis his left shoulder blade.

Elis points and giggles.

"See! He is time!" Elis says, motioning for the others to see. One by one, they step closer and count the dots.

"Twelve red dots in a perfect circle," Kaly whispers.

"Ora has the same mark on the opposite shoulder but the darkest spot at the sixth mark," Danae says. "We only noticed the marks when we got here."

"Are they tattoos?" Leon says, holding up his forearm with the ink of the staff.

"Maybe," Enyo says. "Last night, Teuta said they weren't time until they came here."

Itra mumbles a curse.

Elis turns and points a finger at him.

"I heard that," Elis says.

"Sorry buddy," Itra apologizes.

13

A cry from below stirs Teuta from her hollow void of self-pity. She creeps towards the high window. The cool breeze from the lake bathes her face. She squints at the morning dawn.

"Ember!" Teuta shouts.

"Not Ember," a woman calls up. "Who are you?"

Teuta sucks in a breath. "Avi, is that you?"

"Oh dear," Avi answers. "Teuta?"

"Yes," Teuta whispers and then repeats louder. "Yes!"

"What the hell happened?" Avi asks.

"I was taken last night by Chronos, you?"

"I just sat down to eat breakfast with the ladies and then poof. I'm here with Ora."

"You have one of Danae's babies?"

"Yes, at least I think this is Danae's daughter. We were going to meet them after breakfast."

"No, no, no!" Teuta shouts, pacing the small space.

"Where are we?" Avi asks.

Teuta pauses and takes a breath. "Tell me what you see."

"The lake and the mountains, like you can see from the clearing near the ember archways, but below is an entire village with a castle and small buildings."

Teuta finds a few stones to stand on. She grips the window ledge, pulling with all her might to lift herself up and looks out.

"It's the City of Time," Teuta calls to Avi.

"When are we?" Avi asks, her voice shaking.

"Before or near 1 or 2 BC, maybe?"

"Hermes described a village like this where Elis was found." Avi adjusts Ora in her arm. "Maybe they can find this place again."

"True, true," Teuta says, "but what if that is his plan to trap us all here?"

"Why?" Avi asks.

"To make Ember bow."

"Can you portal us out of this mess?"

"I wish," Teuta laughs. "He has full control of me."

"Excuse me, what?" Avi asks shrilly.

"He marked me before taking me from the castle," Teuta explains. "It's a keeper's cuff. It enslaves the marked to the will of their keeper."

"We are so screwed!" Avi cries. "Why would Ember allow him in, or let him take you?"

"Something I would love to know myself," Teuta answers. "Is Ora ok?"

"For now," Avi says, looking around the small stone space and gritty floor. "But I have nothing here to feed or care for her."

"Can you call the grey sisters?" Teuta asks.

Avi palms her infinity charm. "I've been trying, but it doesn't seem to work here."

"Try calling for an original grey sister, Deino or Pemphredo."

Avi closes her eyes, squashing her anxiety. "Here me call, one or all."

Tap

She opens her eyes and the ring on her left thumb taps against the charm. "I'm an idiot!"

"What's happening?" Teuta asks.

Avi clears her throat. "Protect time, unite to fight. Ember of mine."

A door opens.

"Wait, no!" Teuta shouts.

"We'll come back for you!" Avi calls out before walking through the door.

Ora cries out once and then quiets.

Avi pulls her close, trying to make out her new surroundings. A whip of cold air makes her skin prickle.

The rising sun filters in sparse rays through a thick forest.

"Not the castle," she mumbles.

She turns in a slow circle and spots a narrow path. She carefully high steps through thick, damp bramble.

Ora squirms.

Avi tightly wraps her cardigan around herself and the baby.

A small bird flutters above, drawing her attention. She follows its flight towards a small gap in the forest ahead.

"Thank you!" she whispers to the bird.

Avi continues towards the break. She stumbles over the last thicket and on to a stony ledge. A few rocks scatter across the ledge dropping over the side. Avi sucks in a breath. It's nearly five full second until a tinkle of noise floats back up through the thin air. She tip toes forward and immediately steps back at the sight of the valley below.

"It's a cliff!" She looks down at Ora. "We are on top of a bloody mountain." She creeps back closer to the edge. The rugged sides of the mountains are too steep to even think of navigating a climb down alone—and a hard no with Ora. She shades her eyes and squints as she looks towards the rising sun. *A bridge?*

She looks in the opposite direction only to find more forest.

"Bridge or forest?" Avi asks Ora. She smiles at her absurd question to a newborn, but another bird flies overhead towards the bridge. "Are you speaking to the birds, Miss Ora?"

Ora purses her lips and suckles.

Avi's moment of hilarity passes into urgency. She will need some way to feed Ora soon. She maneuvers her way up and over a few small boulders. She adjusts Ora and inspects a worn path along the edge.

The air whips and howls.

A shiver of cool air runs straight through her layers. She bends and rests Ora on a boulder, removing her cardigan and carefully

68

wraps Ora snuggly into the fabric. She rubs her hands together before picking her back up. She hesitantly follows the path. She peeks around a blind corner and her eyes land on a small rickety footbridge over the valley far below.

"No, no, that is not happening." She looks up for the bird. "New path please!" She palms the infinity charm again. "Enyo!"

"Avi?" Enyo calls back.

Avi turns her eyes back towards the tree line. "Are you here?"

"I can hear you!" Enyo shouts back.

"We are on a mountaintop near a footbridge," Avi says. "I need a way back."

"We?" Enyo asks.

"Ora and I. It's cold! Hurry!"

"Keep the connection," Enyo commands. "I'm coming!"

14

Enyo exhales and looks around the room at each worried face. "I found Avi and Ora. She needs a cloak." She vanishes from the room.

Leon curses and vanishes.

Kaly and Xena exchange a glance and vanish without a word.

Hermes looks from Danae to Itra and shrugs before vanishing.

Anton blinks at the near empty room. He turns to Itra. "Where are they going?"

"Your guess is as good as mine!" Itra states with a frown. He moves to Danae's side and scoops up Elis, putting him on his lap. "Do you know where they are, buddy?"

Elis shrugs and reaches over to pat Danae's arm. "Don't be sad."

Danae sniffles and kisses his head.

Leon lands in the war room in front of the wardrobe. He calls his staff and points it at Enyo. He scowls at her. "You can't just drop a bomb like that and leave!"

"No time, grab a cloak!" Enyo gestures, holding up one cloak.

Xena and Kaly appear next to Enyo.

Leon shakes his head and releases his staff. He tosses them each a cloak and they shrug them on.

"Focus on Avi!" Enyo states, taking Xena's and Kaly's hand. "Protect time, unite to fight. Ember of mine."

A door opens and they walk through together. Before Leon can enter, the door shuts in his face.

"Son of a—" Leon shouts just as Hermes appears in the war room.

"They're gone?" Hermes whispers.

Leon clenches his jaw and nods once.

Hermes raises both hands and slowly backs toward the dining hall door. "I'll go check the clearing."

Hermes jogs to the conservatory. He pauses at the wide-open front entrance. A long shadow fills the foyer, covering the mural on the floor.

He pushes up and hovers, waiting for a person to enter. A man enters a few seconds later. Hermes claps and flies to the giant.

"Junior!" Hermes says and bows.

Junior tilts his head to the side and barks out a laugh.

"Did you open the door?" Hermes asks, straightening.

"It was open when I arrived," Junior says. "Where is that awful fairy?"

"Missing, along with two others."

Junior walks through the conservatory into the dining hall. He frowns upon entry. The wall color, once a pale yellow when his bloodline failed to protect and serve, is now the vibrant purple of Zeus's line. He mutters, "I'm still not a fan of this color." He turns to Hermes. "So Teuta is missing? Who are the two others?"

"Avi and Ora," Hermes says, attempting to keep up with Junior's giant stride.

Junior raises an eyebrow.

"Avi is the one with the infinity charm, a descendant of the grey sisters," Hermes explains. "And Ora is Itra and Danae's newborn daughter."

"Time is missing?" Junior bellows. His voice echoes around the giant hall.

Hermes winces. "Half of time."

"Where are Itra and Danae?" Junior asks, walking towards a door across the dining hall from the conservatory.

The once locked door swings open with ease.

"They are in the archive suite," Hermes says.

Junior climbs up a small iron spiral staircase to a loft.

Hermes sprints and catches up to Junior.

He finds him in an open area with a large circular dark wood table in the middle surrounded by gold and blue ceramic pieces on various shelves lining the bottom half of the walls. The walls above are covered with maps. "What is this room?"

"My war room," Junior says, sifting through a pile of books in the corner. He looks up and shrugs. "Well, the descendants of Mui's war room, to be more specific."

Hermes nods and inspects a few maps. "What are you looking for?"

"Ana said this day would come and documented her vision," Junior says, flipping through a few journals.

Hermes nods. "Who is Ana?"

"Ana is a descendant of Mui. She is a doppelganger for Itra's sister, Iana. Ember gave her the gift of vision. She can see events in the future, present, and past." He finds the journal he is looking for and opens it, reading a single line. "A bridge of time and mine to discover all realms of thine."

"Bridge?" Hermes asks, jogging to his side. "Elis drew two bridges."

"The compass?" Junior asks in alarm. "He's here?"

"We recovered him from Father Time last night."

Junior heads for the door and then stops to face Hermes. "If Teuta is gone, how do we get to the archives?"

Hermes reaches out and touches Junior's arm.

Junior yanks his arm away as they land in the archives.

"I'll warn you next time," Hermes says in apology.

Junior frowns and nods.

"Hermes?" Leon calls from the stacks.

"And Junior," Hermes answers.

"Junior?" Leon says, coming into view. "When did you arrive?"

"Ten minutes ago, give or take," Hermes says.

Leon frowns at Hermes.

"Did you open the front entrance?" Hermes asks.

"No," Leon says. "Why?"

"It was open when Junior arrived, and it was closed and secured before I joined the family in the archives." Hermes rocks up on his toes and back down on his heels. "And we know the ladies didn't open it on their way out."

"Who else is here?" Junior asks.

Leon runs a hand over his head and glances up.

The dome with the clock has transformed back to Zeus and Mui's descendants. They are etched into the stained glass.

"Leon?" Hermes asks, following his fixed gaze. "What's wrong?"

"Last night this was a clock and now this," Leon whispers.

"Why are you concerned with the dome?" Junior asks. "They change constantly. It's Ember's way of expressing current events."

Hermes and Leon fix their gaze on Junior.

He shrugs.

"Really?" Hermes says.

"As an original, you're surprised?" Junior asks.

Leon shakes his head. "It doesn't matter. What does matter is we have two missing descendants and an intruder. Who summoned you?"

"I received my card." Junior holds a piece of parchment with '*Do you remember?*' scrawled in blue cursive writing. "It was late last night. I came as quickly as I could, but there was an issue at the ember archway. It didn't work until midmorning."

Hermes nods. "Avi and Ora were taken near dawn, time appeared frozen beyond the archways."

"And if I was summoned, others from my line are probably here or nearby," Junior states. "But if they were stuck like I was, it may have delayed their climb up." He holds up the journal. "Ana wrote about this day after a vision."

"Show me," Leon says.

"I'd also like to show Itra," Junior says, nodding towards the suite door. "I want his insight on what Ana wrote."

"Fine," Leon says and points to Hermes. "Round up whoever has made their way into the castle and wait for us in the dining hall."

Hermes nods and vanishes.

Leon taps on the closed door to the bedroom.

"Come in," Danae calls from the bed.

"Junior is here," Leon says, hesitant to open the door.

"He can come in," Itra says.

Leon swings open the door and enters. Junior ducks to enter and nods to Itra and Danae, who are sitting on the bed with Elis and Anton is rocking Emit in the corner.

"Junior," Itra says with a nod in return.

"Leon explained your daughter is missing," Junior says. "We will do everything we can to bring her back." He holds up the journal. "Ana described this day from a vision."

Danae extends her hand.

Junior opens it to the marked page and hands her the journal.

"When the sun rises two will disappear from the castle between space and mine." Danae pauses and sucks in a shaking breath. "A bridge of time and mine to discover all realms of thine."

Elis stands on the bed. "The bridge!" He jumps off the bed and picks up the two drawings. "Like this one?" He holds it up for Junior.

"You drew this?" Junior asks. Elis nods. "Did you see this bridge?"

"In my dreams with Father Time," Elis answers.

Junior slowly turns from Elis to face Itra.

Itra just nods and frowns.

"How long have you been dreaming about Father Time?" Junior asks.

"Almost six months," Anton answers for Elis.

Junior turns to face Anton.

"Since we buried my wife."

Junior opens his mouth to speak but closes it again. He shakes his head. "We are truly sorry about Iana."

Anton stops rocking and stands. "And my niece?"

Junior holds up his hands. "Like I said, we will do everything we can to get her back."

"My son will not be part of this," Anton says, narrowing his eyes. "So, before you ask, the answer is no!"

Junior nods and turns to Leon. He gestures for him to follow him out into the corridor.

Leon shuts the door behind them.

"Can you tell me what happened last night?" Junior asks.

16

"Avi!" Enyo shouts.

She scans the thick forest and follows the tree line up. Her eyes land on the top of a tall evergreen tree. Two heads emerge between the thick green pines and dive towards her.

"Run!"

Kaly and Xena sprint after Enyo, dodging trees and thick bramble.

Kaly chances a look behind her and spots wings expanding— she stumbles. "Shit!"

Xena pulls Kaly up.

They catch up with Enyo as she burst out of the woods on to a stone ledge. She teeters over, but Xena yanks her back.

Kaly pulls them both down as the monster breaks free of the forest, squawking just overhead.

"What the actual f is that!" Kaly breathlessly whispers. The creature soars over them. It's not just a bird, but an eagle with two heads. Except it's the size of a cargo plane.

"An usmu," Enyo says, searching the sky and tree line.

"That thing could carry tanks!" Xena says.

A shriek of caws echoes from the valley, followed by a woman's scream.

"Avi!" they yell in unison, and they scramble up.

Enyo takes the lead, climbing over a small boulder. She races down the path and around a bend, spotting the footbridge.

Avi is crouching in the middle of the bridge with Ora. The usmu circles just over Avi's head.

"Help!" Avi screams. The bridge sways. "Hurry!"

Ora's cry echoes back.

The usmu squawks again and circles closer to Avi.

Xena waves her hands and whistles.

The usmu turns towards Xena.

She nods to Enyo and Kaly. "I can distract the damn thing! Go get the girls!"

Kaly hesitates to leave Xena.

"Go! Fly!" Xena shouts.

Enyo takes Kaly's hand and they vanish over the edge.

Xena pushes off and flies straight for the usmu. It flaps hard, letting out a long call, extending long, sharp talons toward Xena. She banks left just out of reach, and it follows. She dives forward into the valley, keeping her arms pinned to her side until she hears the piercing high pitched *ah dah, ah dah.*

She tucks and rolls, facing the talons extending down towards her and banks to the right. She catches sight of Avi and the others safely landing near the cover of the trees. She makes a wide circle, passing directly over their heads, and holds up her thumb with the gold ring.

"Use the ring!" Xena yells.

Kaly shakes her head, but Enyo doesn't hesitate.

Xena watches the portal door open.

Enyo pushes Kaly and Avi with Ora through.

The usmu silently reaches and digs its talons into the skin of Xena's back and shoulder.

"Ah!" Xena screams and tries to pull away.

The usmu flaps harder to counter her weight.

"Protect time," Xena says through gritted teeth. "Unite to fight. Ember of mine."

A portal opens mid air. She swings her legs through. She feels hands grasp her ankles. "Pull!" she shouts.

The usmu squawks in protest and bends to peck Xena's head, but she falls hard through the portal to the floor in the war room.

"She's bleeding!" Kaly shouts. "Xena, are you ok?"

Xena moans and tries to stand.

"Not a chance!" Kaly scolds, holding her down.

"I'm sure it looks worse than it is," Xena says, patting Kaly's cheek.

"You were attacked by a giant two-headed eagle," Kaly says and then laughs. "What the hell has our world turned into?"

Enyo cuts the back of Xena's top free with her dagger and inspects the damage. "You will need stitches and a salve."

Leon skids into the war room. Junior and two women come in directly behind him.

"What happened?" Leon kneels next to Kaly.

"Is Ora ok?" Xena asks.

Leon nods. "Ora is feeding now." He looks at her back. "You're bleeding. Tell me what happened."

"My aunt distracted an usmu," Kaly says. He stares at her blankly. "A giant double-headed eagle."

A woman steps around Junior.

Kaly gasps. "Iana?"

"I'm Ana." She gestures to the second woman. "And this is Dita. She is our healer. Do you mind if she…?"

"Please!" Kaly says, moving to the side.

Xena nods.

Leon and Enyo stand, giving Dita and Xena space.

Dita places her hands over the punctures on Xena's back and shoulder. A warm ember glow shines from her palms over the wounds.

Xena takes in a deep breath and sighs.

Dita holds up a piece of the black curved talon.

"Jesus!" Leon stammers. "That's only a piece of it?" He shakes his head. "The talon would be as big as my forearm."

Xena turns to Dita. "Thank you!" She frowns at the talon and turns back to Kaly. "Is Avi ok?"

"Here!" Avi says, appearing next to Xena. "Are you?"

"Yes," Xena says, replacing her shirt with a thought. She grasps Kaly's hand and stands with her and Avi's help.

"I'm so sorry!" Avi apologizes. "I used the ring to escape the stone room but when I ended up in that forest, I was terrified to use it again."

"What stone room?" Leon asks.

"I transported to a small stone room with a window that looks out over the lake," Avi explains. "Ora appeared a second later."

"In the castle?" Junior asks.

"No," Avi answers. "Teuta called it the City of Time."

"She was with you?" Kaly asks as they move to sit at the table.

"Not with me, but I could hear her above me from the open window," Avi says, taking a sip from the hot tea she conjures. "She was taken last night by Chronos."

"He was here?" Junior asks, pacing the room.

Avi shrugs. "But he has some sort of control over her now. He's using a keeper's cuff."

Enyo curses.

Avi raises an eyebrow. "You know what that is?"

Enyo nods with a frown. "The keeper's cuff is like the infinity charm you wear. Not soul bound but will bound. The marked carry the burden of acting out the owner's will."

Leon mumbles a curse. "Is there an undo button?"

Enyo shakes her head. "Not that I know of."

"Do we just leave her there?" Avi asks.

Junior and Leon make eye contact and shrug.

Leon shakes his head. "I'll put free Teuta on the to-do list."

Kaly rolls her eyes and turns to face Ana. "Ana, when did you arrive?"

"About an hour ago," Ana says. "Dita was climbing the steps when I was crossing the clearing."

Dita nods. "I had to try the ember archway several times before it worked."

"Have Elis or Anton seen you?" Kaly asks.

"No," Ana says. "I have no desire to upset either of them with my presence."

Leon shifts in his chair. "I had just finished telling Junior about last night and this morning when Avi and Ora appeared in the archives. Junior thinks the bridge is a space between time."

Junior smirks. "A fairy legend I heard as a kid."

Xena nods. "The bridge to nowhere."

Junior laughs. "Yes! You've heard of it."

Xena smiles. "It's a common tale." She removes a tea bag and takes a sip from the steaming cup.

"Go on," Kaly says, encouraging Xena.

"The legend I've heard," Xena says, "starts with the fairies in the Accursed Mountains. They would lure trespassers to this bridge. It appears narrow but short. The eager trespasser is promised wealth if they successfully cross to the other side. They can see the end but never reach it." She smiles at the frown on Leon's face. "The trespasser would eventually turn around and try to backtrack, but the same fate awaits—an end they cannot reach. A cruel act to the greedy trespasser but endless entertainment for the fairies."

"Wow," Leon says, shaking his head. "Do they eventually starve to death or jump?"

Junior chuckles. "The version I've heard is like Xena's tale, but the ending is infinite." He nods to Xena.

Xena nods. "The echoes of cries sing in the night wind of those fallen prey to the fairies' fool bargain."

Kaly shivers from her neck to her toes.

"In a place between space and mine," Leon whispers.

Ana leans across the table. "What did you say?"

"A phrase we keep hearing applies to this," Leon says. "In a place between space and mine."

"I've heard that before," Ana says, "but from where?"

A book appears and opens in front of her. The page falls open on the village illustration Kaly discovered the night before.

Kaly looks at the book's dark blue cover. "I was nearly assaulted by this book last night." She looks up as Hermes strolls in.

Hermes looks over Ana's shoulder. "This is the village where Elis was held, but the caption says City of Time. I swear, this is

Illyria." He turns the book towards Enyo. "Do you recognize the rise of the castle here?"

"The third-floor addition, Zeus added late last year?" Enyo asks.

"Yes!" Hermes says. "I thought so too."

"I will head to the archives and see what we can find out about this city," Kaly says, pointing to the open book. "And the keeper's cuff."

"Xena," Avi says. "Danae has asked to see you once you're rested."

"I'm good," Xena says, vanishing.

"All of you can portal with a thought?" Ana asks, blinking at the empty chair.

Leon laughs. "Danae made Teuta give the family access to the archives after she stole the twins' moments after their birth."

Ana and Dita exchange a surprised sly smile.

"And she actually listened to Danae's request?" Ana asks.

Leon nods and raises his mug.

Dita laughs and shakes her head. "There's a first time for everything. Junior, can you look through Ivan's study for anything that may be helpful?"

Hermes raises a hand. "Who is Ivan?"

"Mui's descendants designated host," Junior answers. "Did Zeus's line have a designated host?"

Hermes frowns. "Zeus, I guess."

"I'm going to get cleaned up and meet you down in the archives," Avi says to Kaly. She stands and the rest of the table disperses except for Leon, Enyo, and Hermes.

"You left without me!" Leon hisses at Enyo, pointing his finger a little too close to her nose.

Enyo scoffs. "It's not my fault you're slow."

Hermes steps between them. "Before you two throw punches— I think we should come up with a plan for Teuta."

"Avi's description suggests she is in the same location as Elis," Enyo says, her nose still flaring at Leon. "But we can't go in without a resolution to the keeper's cuff."

"He can keep her," Leon says, heading for the dining hall door. "She only makes things worse."

"Wait!" Hermes yells.

Leon slows and turns.

"She is Ember's messenger."

Leon rolls his eyes.

Hermes continues. "We are here to protect and serve Ember and the Castle of Teskom."

"Ember can assign a new messenger," Leon says, folding his arms across his chest. "I've done it in her stony absence."

Hermes shakes his head. "Ember wants her found." He holds a piece of parchment. A burnt edge cuts off part of the writing. He hands it to Enyo.

"Find her in ti…," Enyo reads. "Her could regard Avi and Ora." She hands it to Leon.

"Agreed," Leon says, handing it back to Hermes.

"I found this burning on a dish in the other war room."

"What other war room?" Leon asks.

Hermes motions them to follow. He walks back to the dining hall and down two doors. He climbs the iron spiral stairs. They enter the space and stare.

"Is this Junior's war room?" Enyo asks, looking around the open space and the maps hanging on the walls.

"Mui's descendants are welcome here," Junior says from behind them.

Enyo whirls in surprise. He towers over her, standing on the top step.

Hermes holds up the burnt parchment. "I smelled something burning when I was crossing the dining hall. Care to explain?"

"It's nothing," Junior says with a shrug.

"What did the full message say?" Leon asks from the corner near a pile of books.

Junior crosses the room in four long strides. "None of your business or your bloodline's business." He stands between the books and Leon.

"We are allies," Leon says in a level tone. "All of this is the Castle of Teskom. Ours to protect and serve. There are no lines in the sand or areas off limits."

Junior looks down his long straight nose at Leon, meeting his eyes. "We are allies but I'm in charge and what I say goes."

Hermes laughs. "Wrong!"

Leon and Junior face Hermes.

"If you want a person in charge, look no further than Enyo," says Hermes. She frowns at him. "She is the oldest grey sister and it's her descendants ordered to protect time. I am the only original Zeus descendant here so technically," he points to himself and Enyo, "we're the most senior members of this alliance."

Leon smiles and turns back to Junior, calling his staff with a quick double tap to the scythe. "What was on the parchment?"

17

Teuta sits on the sandy floor in the light from the high window, tracing the outline of the gold cuff on her forearm. She feels the ground shake and stands.

The floor cracks open, and sand slides towards the opening. Another rumble and the crack widens. She jumps up and grasps the edge of the window. The floor falls away. She adjusts her grip, looking for any foot holds on the stone wall but slips and free falls into a dark abyss.

"Welcome to the City of Time."

Teuta winces at the cool stone under her face. She attempts to roll to her side, but groans. Her head throbs with the effort.

"Some welcome," Teuta says, coughing and groans again.

A light flickers in the corner. A face framed with long, brown waves appears.

Teuta struggles to sit up but finally manages. "Ember?" She blinks away the darkness.

"Really?" the woman says and walks closer to Teuta. She squats to her level and tilts her head. "Recognize me now?"

The small round face of a teen—small button nose and big brown eyes—meets Teuta's glare.

Teuta shakes her head. "It's not possible you're a—no, it can't be."

"I'm a what?" The girl stands. Her white gown swishes the floor as she walks away. "A child? An infant?"

"Ora," Teuta whispers.

"Ding, ding, ding!" Ora says, slowly spinning to face Teuta again.

"But Avi—this morning," Teuta says, shaking her head. "How long have I been down here?"

"How long?" Ora says, tapping her lips and looking up.

Teuta follows her gaze.

A large gold circle divided into twelve sections appears inside the dark dome overhead. It shifts clockwise.

Teuta lowers her gaze to Ora, but the space transforms to four stone walls with a single window and a sandy floor.

"Ora," Teuta whispers. She stands and grunts with the effort. "Ora!"

Knock, knock

Itra opens the door to Xena. He immediately hugs her. "Thank you for coming!"

Xena pats his back. She catches Danae's teary face and feels Itra tremble. "Where's Elis?"

Itra releases her and steps back. "Anton and Elis are resting in the room across the hall." He looks down the corridor before closing and locking the door.

Xena walks to the small bassinet beside the bed. She admires the two babies for a few seconds before looking up at Danae. "My dear, why are you crying?"

Danae swallows and wipes her cheek. "It's not Ora."

"What?" Xena looks back down at the babies. "The baby isn't yours?"

Danae shakes her head. "Earlier we showed you Emit's mark and told you Ora has one as well."

Xena nods.

"Well, after Avi left, I changed Ora's sleeper gown. The mark is gone. This baby isn't the same one that left here hours ago."

Xena sits on the edge of the bed. "Are you sure?"

Danae nods.

"We are," Itra says.

"Why haven't you told the others?" Xena asks.

"We weren't sure until right before you knocked on the door." Danae pulls the blanket away from one of the sleeping babies, exposing only the ear.

"A changeling?" Xena whispers, running a finger along the edge of the pointed ear.

Danae sniffles. "It's not our Ora."

Xena stands. "We will get Ora back. I promise."

Danae and Itra nod.

Xena vanishes.

Kaly reads the page for a third time. She stands, running into Avi as she appears in the archives.

"Sorry," Avi says, stepping back. "Are you ok?"

Kaly shakes her head. "The forest, the fairies, the baby."

"What?" Avi asks. "I don't understand."

"I do," Xena says, walking up behind Kaly.

Kaly whirls to face her aunt.

"Avi, did you ever set down the baby?" Xena asks.

Kaly raises an eyebrow and slowly turns to face Avi.

"Yes," Avi says. "I inspected the baby when she appeared to confirm she was a girl."

"And in the forest?" Xena asks.

"For a second," Avi says. "I took off my cardigan to swaddle her." She looks from Kaly to Xena. "Something's wrong?"

Xena nods. "That baby isn't Ora."

"Oh, God!" Avi and Kaly whisper in unison.

"Whose baby is it?" Avi asks, backing into the reading chair where she sits.

"A changeling," Xena says.

Kaly gasps and thrusts the book towards Xena.

"What's this?" Xena asks, looking over the page.

"A passage about the bridge to nowhere—and time."

Xena clears her throat. "Enter a place between space and mine with time. An offering so divine the fairies will lose all realms of time. To cross and succeed will bring change indeed."

Avi places her head between her knees. She screams into her fist. She sits back up and swears as flecks of light fill her vision. She blinks a few times before speaking. "I tried to avoid the bridge but was forced on to it by that monster bird thing!"

"The usmu," Kaly and Xena say in unison.

"Whatever," Avi says, waving her hand. "I tried to hide in the forest but was chased out. I couldn't jump over the edge. My only option was the damn bridge."

"Avi," Xena kneels to her chair. "We aren't blaming you, but we need to find out if the switch happened before you walked onto the bridge. If it was before, then the realms of time for the fairies would not have been affected, but if the switch was after…"

"We could have unlocked time for the fairies?" Kaly asks.

Xena nods. "And triggered an extinction event written about in fairy folklore."

Avi shakes her head.

Xena continues. "Again, no real facts, just stories. Fairies live in an infinite time bubble. They don't age or evolve past early adulthood, but if they stray for too long outside the boundaries of time…" Xena bites the inside of her cheek. She sighs. "They age rapidly and eventually, die." She stands. "It's ancient folklore."

"But if the fairies swapped the babies," Kaly says. "And they know Ora is time, her life… is in danger."

Xena blows out a long breath. "Theoretically, if the fairies are real." She nods.

"I could use a little help up here!" Enyo shouts to all three of them, using the thought provoked communication.

Xena reaches for Enyo and Kaly. They take her hands and vanish from the archives.

19

Kaly, Xena, and Avi appear behind Leon while he is helping Hermes off the floor.

The large table is cracked down the middle, and several chairs are turned over. Some are broken, having been tossed from one end of the room to the other.

"What happened in here?" Xena asks.

Leon jumps.

"Enyo needs your help!" Hermes says, panting.

"She called for us," Xena says, trying to right a chair but giving up when she notices a leg is missing.

"She went after Junior," Leon says. He whispers the sequence to open the portal and points. "She shoved him through when we were fighting."

"What?" Avi steps beside Leon to look through the open portal. "Why are you fighting with Junior?"

"He tried to burn a message from Ember that gave us a direct order to get Teuta back," Hermes says.

"Leon," Kaly says, gripping his arm and turning him to meet her eyes. "Ora is still missing." Leon lurches back as if struck. "The baby is a changeling." He shakes his head. "We will go after Enyo, but we also need to get Ora back."

Hermes jumps through the portal, and Avi follows.

"Call Enyo back," Leon says. "Junior can rot in hell for all I care."

Xena nods. She steps through and the portal closes.

Kaly curses.

"I want to explain what happened here and get more information from Danae," Leon says.

Kaly nods and takes his hand.

Leon knocks on Itra's bedroom door.

"Come in," Itra calls.

Leon pushes the door open and Kaly follows him in.

"Xena, let us know about the baby," Kaly says, kneeling next to Danae, rocking the changeling baby.

Danae nods, not looking up from the bundle.

She takes Danae's free hand. "What can we do?"

"Find our girl," Danae whispers.

"We will," Leon says, "but we have some other news."

Itra comes to Danae's side with Emit.

"Junior attempted to burn a message from Ember," Leon says. Itra opens his mouth. Leon holds up a finger. "Hermes found it burning on a plate in the other war room."

Danae and Itra exchange a glance.

"What other war room?" Danae asks.

"The door that goes to Ivan's study has an iron spiral staircase to an open loft, the Mui family war room," Leon explains.

Danae and Itra nod.

"Hermes, Enyo, and I confronted Junior about the parchment. And well, it got a little out of hand."

Kaly snorts. "The room looks like a small tornado tore through it."

Itra frowns. "Why would he burn something from Ember?"

"We never got an answer," Leon says, holding up his thumb with the gold ring. "Junior broke the table with Hermes. Enyo opened a portal and tripped Junior through."

"He has always been a hothead," Itra says, "but this sounds extreme."

"He was on a high horse about being the one in charge and was insulted that we would even question this." Leon shakes his head. "There is more—Junior made a threat to dissolve the alliance and take back what is rightfully his."

"Son of a—" Itra mumbles. "What the hell is rightfully his?"

Danae places a hand on Itra's arm. He relaxes and looks down at the sleeping baby.

"Are Dita and Ana still here?" Danae asks.

"Ana's here?" Elis says from the open door.

Anton appears behind Elis, a sheet line across his cheek and his hair standing on end.

"You can't just bolt from the room," Anton says, patting Elis on the head.

"You were snoring!" Elis laughs and skips into the room. "There are two again, look dad!"

Elis looks over the chair at the baby in Danae's arms. "Who is this?"

Anton kneels next to Elis. "What do you mean?"

"That's not Emit or Ora, dad," Elis says.

Anton stands. "What's going on?"

Kaly kneels next to Elis. "Are you ready to eat?"

Elis jumps up and down. "Yes! I'm starving!"

Kaly leads Elis away from the room with a nod to Anton. When they exit the room, she closes the door behind them. She hears the murmur of Itra's voice, then Anton's startled gasp.

Elis runs down the corridor and into the suite's living area. He pulls out a chair and sits at the table. A giant pizza appears.

He laughs. "Look Kaly!"

"All of this for you?" Kaly laughs.

He picks off a slice of pepperoni and grins. "I might share." He wiggles both eyebrows.

"You're too much!" Kaly laughs.

"What's the plan?" Anton asks, pacing the room between Leon and Itra.

"Once the ladies and Hermes get back," Leon says, "I hope we can return to the City of Time and search for Ora." He sighs. "And free Teuta."

"And if you can't find either of them?" Anton says.

"One step at a time, Anton," Danae says, standing from the chair. "I can't go beyond that."

He nods. "And Ana?"

"Showed up about two hours ago with Dita," Leon says.

Anton stops pacing and his face drains of color. "Dita, the one who failed to save Iana."

Leon nods.

"Where are they now?" Anton asks, moving for the open door.

"Keeping watch," Leon says, nodding up.

"Can they be trusted?" Anton asks, pausing at the door.

"I think so," Itra says, walking toward Anton.

"Ana said she would avoid any interaction with Elis to prevent any confusion while you two were here," Kaly says, stepping back into the room.

Anton moves past her to the corridor. He can see Elis at the table.

"Elis is busy devouring a giant pizza," Kaly says, patting his shoulder.

Anton leans against the doorframe, watching Elis.

"Just before we showed up in the war room," Kaly says, "we found a worrying passage about the bridge."

Danae nods to Kaly.

"It's a bridge to nowhere," Kaly says, wringing her hands. "According to legends, the bridge is in an infinite loop. But the passage in the book I found is what's alarming." The book appears in her hands. She opens the book and recites. "Enter a place between space and mine with time. An offering so divine the fairies will lose all realms of time. To cross and succeed will bring change indeed."

Itra moves closer to read the passage again.

Kaly looks over the book at Danae. "If Avi crossed with Ora, infinite time in the fairy world is gone."

Danae gasps.

"Xena said that the extinction event for fairies was related to time in ancient folklore," Kaly says.

Danae sits on the edge of the bed. "But if they took Ora before she…" Danae trails off, tears coming to her eyes.

Itra kneels in front of Danae. "We can't think like that."

Danae leans over the bassinet and places the baby down. She stands and heads for the washroom. "I need a moment."

The door clicks shut.

Leon bends, taking Emit from Itra.

Kaly helps Itra to his feet. "We will do everything we can to find her."

Itra slumps and sits on the bed.

Leon lays the baby in the bassinet.

"We need to go." Leon bends, meeting the teary eyes of Itra. "Are you good to stay here with Danae?"

Itra sucks in a breath and nods.

Kaly and Leon nod and vanish.

Anton sighs. "Elis and I will stay until we get Ora back."

Itra looks over at Anton as he moves away from the door and towards Elis.

The washroom door opens and Danae stumbles out.

"They'll find her." Itra stands and wraps his arms around her shoulders and pulls her close.

She remains silent.

He gently pushes her hair to the side. "You're burning up!"

"I'm beyond blood boiling mad," Danae whispers into his chest.

He strokes her cheek. "I understand."

Kaly and Leon appear in the Zeus family war room near the wardrobe with the feathered cloaks. Leon takes two cloaks out and drapes one over Kaly.

"Did you find anything in the archives about the keeper's cuff?" Leon asks.

"Nothing useful," Kaly says, draping the other cloak over Leon. "Just a few lines about the essence of its bond to the owner's will."

A crash of bodies appears in a heap on the floor near Kaly. She jumps back into Leon.

Hermes stands and helps Avi and Xena to their feet.

"Where's Enyo?" Kaly asks, picking a leaf out of Avi's hair.

"She used the cloak to hide her appearance and shoved us through a portal," Xena says, brushing off the grass and dirt from her pants.

"And Junior?" Leon asks, shifting side to side.

"Gone," Hermes says, shaking his head. "By the time we went through, he was too far to catch on foot. I flew ahead and cut him off. The ladies and I surrounded him."

"He just kept muttering something over and over," Xena says. Then she points to her forearm. "I think he may be bound like Teuta."

"Just as we started to advance, a man appeared next to him and they both vanished," Avi explains. "I only saw him from the back, but he looked like Pax."

"Teuta's brother?" Leon asks.

Xena nods. "A version of him, at least. I only saw him in profile, but the resemblance was there."

Hermes shrugs. "I couldn't tell, to be honest. Junior was blocking my view of the man."

"Ok," Leon says, dragging a hand down his face. "But if they vanished, why didn't Enyo come back with you?"

"I think she is trying to follow them," Avi says.

"Following him was useless," Enyo says, walking in from the dining hall. "I only landed in the other war room."

"Does that mean they are here in the castle?" Leon asks, calling and double tapping his staff. The scythe glows a little too close to Hermes.

Hermes steps away. "I'll check every nook and corner. I was great at hide and seek here back in the day."

Leon nods. "Take Enyo." He gestures to Avi, Xena, and Kaly. "We'll find Dita and Ana."

20

Elis skips down the corridor. "Uncle Itra?" he asks from the open doorway to the nursery. Itra leans forward in the rocking chair and opens his arms. Elis runs forward and climbs onto Itra's lap.

"Hey buddy," Itra says, sniffing his hair. "You smell like breadsticks."

Elis giggles. "Duh!" He pats his belly. "What did you eat today?"

"Does coffee count as eating?"

"No!" Elis says, looking up at Itra. "You look sad."

"I am sad." Itra's frown deepens. "We lost Ora and Danae is very upset."

"But it's ok," Elis says, placing a finger on each side of Itra's mouth and pushing his frown up.

"Not this time, buddy," Itra says, hugging him closer and rocking back.

"Ember said this would happen," Elis whispers.

Itra stops rocking. "What did Ember say exactly?" He stares straight ahead, too scared to look down at his nephew's face.

Elis squirms on Itra's lap. "Emit will be time here and Ora will be time there."

"Where is here and there?" Itra asks.

"Our time is here," Elis says. "Ora will live in the City of Time."

"When did Ember tell you this?" Itra asks, trying to keep the tremble from his tone.

"Last night after I got to the castle with Leon and Hermy."

Itra continues rocking until Anton appears in the doorway.

"Let's give Uncle Itra time to shower and eat," Anton says, gesturing to Elis.

Elis hops down and skips to the door. "Her name is Zana."

Anton kneels to Elis's level. "Who is Zana?"

"The baby with Emit."

"How do you know her name?" Itra asks, standing to look over at the crib.

"She can talk to me," Elis says, pointing to his head. "Up here."

Anton glances at Itra before standing. "Can she tell you where Ora is?"

Itra turns to face Elis and Anton.

Elis shrugs. "Zana is a gift from the fairies."

Anton barks out a laugh. He covers his mouth and shakes his head. "Sorry, I think I might need a drink. Does this place provide a stream of whiskey?"

Itra nods to the changing table. Two glasses and a bottle of amber liquid appear. Anton pours two fingers in each and hands one to Itra. They clink and throw it all back at once.

"I'll fill Danae in with the latest details," Itra says, nodding towards the adjoining door.

Anton nods and leads Elis away from the nursery, back to the suite's living area.

Itra quietly walks through the door.

Danae is sitting up with an eyebrow raised. "Zana?"

"You weren't asleep?"

"Nah."

"Well, there is good news," Itra says, sitting on the edge of the bed. "We at least think we know where Ora is."

"What do we do with Zana?" Danae asks.

"Keep her?" Itra suggests.

"Instant family of five," Danae laughs, and then chokes up. "What about her parents?"

"I don't know," Itra says, standing. He walks towards the washroom. "Maybe a shower will provide clarity."

A pile of books appears on the bed beside Danae. She opens the one with a gold and blue cover first. The first page has a simple drawing of a family tree. She scans the branches, finding Mui, Junior, Dita, Ivan, Iana and Itra's names.

She turns the page and finds the Mui family crest with a bird in the center. She recalls seeing it on the backs of chairs and on various doors during their first visits to the castle. The first time Teuta sent Leon and her via portal from the dining hall to the archives, they had to open a door with this large crest. Teuta pretended to be a man to test Leon. The thread of that conversation with Teuta replays in an instant.

"Leon, the term keeper is not new!" Danae shouts through thought.

Leon stops mid step. Kaly runs into him. *"Danae?"*

"Yes! Do you remember when we were in the archives, the first time Teuta disguised herself as Zarek? She called him the keeper."

"What's going on?" Kaly asks, looking at Leon's face and knitted brow.

"Danae remembered something that I hope is useful," Leon says, climbing the final steps up to the square glass tower overlooking the clearing.

"I'm going to research Zarek," Danae says.

"Ok, keep me posted," Leon says, scanning the clearing. *"We are searching for Dita and Ana. We think Junior may be under the same will bond as Teuta."*

"Shit!" Danae curses. *"Elis is pretty certain Ora is in the City of Time."*

"Screw Dita and Ana!" Leon states, bolting down the steps. Kaly follows. *"We'll go now! Just keep Elis close until we return."*

21

"Leon," Kaly says, breathless behind him. "What's going on?"

"Elis thinks Ora is in the City of Time." Leon slows his pace. "Call the ladies to the war room and I'll get Hermes."

"Avi!" Kaly says. *"Meet us in the war room."*

Avi stops mid step and pulls on Xena's arm. "Something's up. We need to head back to the war room."

"Do you want to check the present cavern first?" Xena asks. "I think it's close."

"Sure, but quick," Avi says, following Xena down the spiral stone steps.

They stop a few minutes later at a tall wood and iron door blocking their entry.

"Open says me," Xena says, and the door glides open with ease.

Xena steps over the threshold and is met with a strong cool breeze from the large opening. The afternoon sun is past noon and nearly level with the cave. Xena scans the space.

"It's empty."

Avi points to the floor. "Are these drag marks in the dirt?" She traces the marks near the entrance and follows them behind a stalagmite in the corner. "Ana!"

Xena runs over to Avi, kneeling next to Ana's slumped figure.

"Ana, can you hear me?" Avi shakes Ana's shoulders gently. She doesn't respond. Avi places two fingers on Ana's wrist. "She's alive."

"Kaly, we found Ana," Avi says, *"but she is unconscious."*

"Where?" Kaly asks, heading for the dining hall door. "They found Ana unconscious."

Leon follows her.

"We're in the present cavern."

Hermes and Enyo sprint through the door from the conservatory to the dining hall. Kaly sidesteps Enyo and barely misses the impact of Hermes.

"Whoa!" Hermes shouts, skidding to a stop.

"What are you running from?" Leon asks, grabbing Hermes by the shoulders.

"The hedge maze with the fairy statue," Hermes says. "All the passageways are open, including the one in the middle."

"The vault!" Leon says, running past Hermes.

"Wait!" Kaly shouts. "What about Ana?"

"Take Hermes and Enyo!" Leon shouts back.

"On our way!" Kaly says, gesturing to Hermes and Enyo to follow. "Avi and Xena found Ana unconscious in the present cavern."

"We are icing a pretty big knot on her head," Avi says, gently adjusting Ana onto her back and resting her head on an ice pack.

"Show me, Pem," Xena says, standing by Ana's side.

An image flickers to life near the center of the cavern. Pem is stirring a pot on the stove.

"Pem, can you hear me?" Xena calls out.

Pem drops the wooden spoon inside the pot. She curses, trying to fish it out. "Mom?"

"Yes darling," Xena says. "I'm in the present cavern. It's been a busy day. We may need an extra set of eyes. Are you up for it?"

Pem turns off the stove and places a few items back in the fridge. "I'll just lock up and put on some shoes." She goes to the back door, lowers the blinds and turns the dead bolt. "Meet you in the present cavern, ok?"

"Ok," Xena says, watching Pem lock the front door and bend to lace up her shoes. She stands and her image flickers. "Pem?"

Pem steps through the image and into the present cavern.

22

Leon bolts up the first flight of steps near the main foyer. He slides across the marble landing to the window overlooking the hedge maze.

The fairy statue holding the stone heads of Medusa and Athena is off center, exposing the steps to the vault Danae once described.

"Ember, I need a little help here," Leon says.

He vanishes from the landing and appears in the center of the hedge maze. He calls his staff and taps once. The warm ember glow grows in size. He holds it over his head.

"Close says me!"

The light from his staff illuminates the entire maze. The twelve open doorways close all at once. The light dims and he blinks a few times before starting a quick staccato pace down the spiral stone steps. Racing footsteps echo up. He increases his speed, trying to keep his advance silent.

When light from below is visible, he releases his staff and listens. A murmur of conversation and scuffle of steps floats up. Leon moves down and peeks around the opening to a long corridor.

Junior and Dita have their arms raised and are standing with their backs to Leon. Junior is partially covering a man tapping on the stones.

Leon ducks back around the corner when he recognizes the man. *Pax, the devil himself.*

"I found Dita and Junior," Leon says to Kaly. *"And Pax."*

"Status?" Kaly asks, pausing at the entrance to the present cavern.

"Unknown, engaging the target," Leon says with a smirk, and he spins around the opening, calling his staff. *"Please stand by."*

He silently charges down the corridor, his thoughts on the present cavern as he reaches Dita. Before Junior or Pax can react, Leon wraps his hand around her arm and they vanish.

Leon and Dita appear in the present cavern.

"Oh geez," Pem says with a hand to her heart, stumbling into Hermes. "You two scared the crap out of me!"

Dita pushes Leon away. "Why the hell did you do that?"

"Whose side are you on?" Leon asks, standing between Dita and the others.

"What are you talking about?" Dita says, folding her arms across her chest and stiffening her posture.

"Junior?" Leon asks.

Kaly steps beside him, but he puts a protective arm out and pushes her behind him.

"Did it look like I was on a side down there?" Dita says, narrowing her eyes. "I had my hands raised in the air." She shakes her head. "Ana and I split up to check the caverns. I was in the future cavern when Junior came in with that man." She looks around. "Is Ana here?"

"She's unconscious," Xena says, "with a nasty bump on her head." She tilts her head to the corner.

Dita starts forward, but Leon cuts her off.

She sucks in a breath and stomps her foot. "I'm a healer! Let me at least check on her."

Kaly tugs on Leon's elbow.

He double taps his staff, and the glowing scythe appears inches from Dita's nose.

She doesn't flinch.

Kaly tightens her grip on Leon's elbow. He grunts and moves to the side.

Dita rushes past him and kneels next to Ana. She hovers her hands around Ana's head.

Ana coughs and opens her eyes.

"Don't move yet," Dita says, placing one hand on her shoulder and the other on the back of her head.

Ana clinches her fist and then sighs when Dita removes her hands.

"Ok, let's slowly get you up."

Avi and Dita help Ana sit up and then stand.

Ana scans the room. "What happened?" She looks from Kaly to Pem. "Were the twins here before?"

"Not twins," Kaly says with a laugh. "Pem is my cousin, Xena's daughter."

"Can you tell us the last thing you remember?" Xena asks.

"When I entered the cavern," Ana says, looking at the opening. "Junior was standing near the edge mumbling something under his breath. Then there was darkness."

"And you?" Leon asks, pointing his scythe at Dita.

"Junior came in," Dita says, "with the man you saw, just after I entered the future cavern. I've never seen him before." She sighs. "Junior said he needed my help. I followed without question at first. But like Ana's experience, Junior kept mumbling. I heard the same three words." She pauses for a breath. "Not my will."

"Damn it!" Enyo kicks a rock out the opening. "He's marked with a keeper's cuff."

"I found a burning parchment with a message to save Teuta in your war room," Hermes says, pointing at Dita. "We," he points to Enyo and Leon, "confronted Junior, and he flipped out."

Ana and Dita exchange a glance.

"Who is the man with Junior?" Dita asks.

"Father Time aka Chronos," Leon says, releasing his staff. "He is using the body of a man named Pax, Teuta's half-brother. It's a long story but we left him in the helix of Chronos six months ago."

Dita's mouth falls open. "The helix?"

"Yes," Hermes answers.

"Oh, no," Dita whispers.

"Do you know what Pax wants from the vault?" Leon asks.

"An engagement gift." Dita shrugs. "He was rambling about making her bow."

Kaly and Leon exchange a glance and nod.

"Danae," Leon calls. *"Junior is marked by the keeper's cuff. Father Time aka Chronos is Pax. He's here and trying to break into the vault for the ember amulet."*

"Shit!" Danae slams a book shut. *"Zarek was the first recorded, as marked by the keeper's cuff. Queen Teuta was his captain."*

"Evil wench finally gets a spoonful of her own medicine!" Leon says. He clears his throat, and all eyes fall on him. "Danae found a link to the keeper's cuff and Teuta. A man named Zarek was marked, and Queen Teuta was his captain."

"Anything about how to undo it?" Kaly asks.

"Nothing yet." Leon shrugs. "We need to go after Ora and prevent Pax from entering the vault."

"Hermes and I can go after Pax," Enyo volunteers.

"I'll go with you two," Pem says, pulling out her oval mirror charm from a gold chain tucked under her shirt.

Xena shakes her head. "No! Not a good idea."

"I can transform into any female here and that includes Teuta," Pem argues.

"She's right," Kaly says, patting Xena on the shoulder.

"Fine," Xena huffs, turning and pointing two fingers at Hermes and Enyo. "A hair missing from her head will be the death of you two."

Hermes nods. Enyo just shakes her head.

"Ember," Leon says.

All three vanish.

"What the hell was that?" Xena shouts at Leon.

"We don't have time to argue," Leon says, shaking his head. "Ana, go with Kaly to the archives. Dita, are you good at keeping watch from the tower?"

Dita nods and backs out of the cavern to the steps.

"I'm going with you!" Kaly protests.

"I need a resolution to the keeper's cuff," Leon says, kissing her cheek. "And you are the best researcher we have." Kaly sighs. "Keep an eye on Danae for me."

Kaly nods and takes Ana's hand. They vanish, leaving Avi, Leon, and Xena.

"What's your plan?" Avi asks Leon.

Leon holds up his thumb. "Protect time. Unite to fight. Ember of mine."

A portal fades and flickers. When the portal opens, a white bundle in a small wooden bassinet with curved legs is rocking on a worn path shaded by surrounding trees.

"Is that Ora?" Avi asks, stepping beside Leon.

"Only one way to find out," Leon says, starting forward.

Xena pulls on his arm. "Wait!"

A shadow falls on the bassinet, and a talon comes into view.

Leon shakes off Xena's grip with a glare. "And wait for that thing to take her?" He bounds forward and races through the portal.

"Shit!" Avi curses, following Leon.

Xena sighs and follows Avi.

23

The sun falls below the high open window. A cool breeze seeps into the small stone space.

Teuta climbs up to the window again. She rolls to her toes and can barely see past the edge to look down, but a flash of light from above makes her jump and she falls hard on her side.

"Ugh!" She stands, brushing off the dirt from her dress and straightening her ponytail.

"Teuta?" a voice calls out.

"I'm here!" She presses a foot on a protruding stone and reaches and grasps the corner of the window. "Can you hear me?"

A dark shadow flies by the window.

"Here, I'm right here!"

Teuta props her other foot on another hold, balancing her weight.

"Did I shrink or is this damn window higher?" Teuta mutters.

She reaches across the windowsill and grasps the outer edge. Her feet dangle and her grips slips. She grunts and tightens her hold, swinging her legs to the wall and kicks off her shoes. Her right foot finds a small crack and she wedges her toes in.

"Is anyone out there?"

The sun falls directly behind something large.

Teuta squints and gulps when the massive wings expand.

It flies level with the window.

"A bloody usmu!"

Both beaked heads turn towards Teuta and blink.

"What the hell is this?" Teuta mumbles, adjusting her sweaty grip.

"A ride," a female voice says. The two heads lower and expose a woman on the back of the bird. "Care to join me?"

"And you are?" Teuta says, wiping her brow again.

"Not stuck in a stone box," the woman says and laughs.

"Ha! Ha!" Teuta mocks.

"Are you coming or not?" the woman says, maneuvering the beast of a bird with one hand and extending the other to Teuta.

"Who are you?" Teuta asks again.

"Prende."

"Lady Prende, goddess of love, beauty, and fertility?" Teuta asks, noting the woman's gold garment, her golden wavy hair, and her round, flawless face.

Prende smiles and nods. "Take my hand."

Teuta eyes the two heads of the bird and the steep drop below the creature.

"I promise they're harmless," Prende says, leaning down to reach for Teuta's hand.

The white feathered head closest to Teuta opens its beak and snaps it shut.

Teuta flinches.

"She doesn't need any teasing from you!" Prende scolds the bird with a light tap.

Teuta blows out a breath and reaches for her hand.

Prende lifts her out of the small window with ease and places Teuta's tiny frame in front of her. "Hold on!" Prende loops a piece of her dress around Teuta.

24

Enyo appears a second before Hermes and Pem in an empty stone corridor. She pulls her dagger and motions them behind her.

"Where are we?" Pem whispers.

"I'm guessing below the hedge maze," Hermes says, receiving a glare from Enyo.

"But there's no entrance." Pem points ahead and behind them.

Hermes looks down the corridor in each direction and blows out a long, quiet whistle.

"Open says me," Enyo says, facing a wall.

A few steps down, the stones slide back and to the side.

No one moves or makes a sound.

Hermes wrinkles and then pinches his nose. "Is there something dead down there?"

Enyo doesn't hesitate and rushes in, blade pulled back to strike. She nearly trips on the uneven stone steps leading down into darkness.

Hermes throws up his light stone and follows Enyo.

Pem hesitates, shakes out her sweaty hands, and rolls her shoulders back before matching their pace.

Enyo holds up a hand and Hermes stops. Pem plows into his back, making him run into Enyo. She glares back at them.

Pem frowns and steps back. She mouths the word, 'Sorry.'

Enyo rolls her eyes.

"Move!" A man's voice surrounds them.

Hermes opens his palm and the light stone falls, bathing them in darkness.

Enyo draws her sword and silently moves further down. She strains to see through the next opening. She turns and places a hand on Pem's shoulder. She sends her command with a thought. *"Stay low and wait."*

Pem squats down and pulls Hermes to her level.

Enyo swiftly moves with both blades up and crossed through the opening into a dark cave. Water drips from the tips of the rock formations. She dances around the puddles to keep her approach silent. A shadow of movement stalls her progress about five paces ahead. She slinks behind a stalagmite and waits.

"The opening has to be here!" a man shouts and kicks a few rocks towards Enyo. One rock strikes the tip of her sword's blade.

Ping

"Who's there?" the man bellows.

Enyo sucks in a breath and listens for their steps, but it is silent. She shakes her head and steps out, weapons raised. The tip of her dagger is a hair from Junior's chest. She tries to spin low, but Junior is a move ahead. He wraps his giant arm around her neck, pinning one arm against his chest and the other with his hand.

"Drop the blades," Junior whispers, turning her towards the other man.

Pem stands and walks into the cave, slowly clapping. "You think you can stow me away and keep me there?" She stops a few paces from Junior's back.

Junior loosens his grip when he looks back. "Teuta!"

Enyo breaks free and lunges forward. She slashes her dagger down, tearing the fabric of Pax's sleeve and drawing blood. She swings her sword, but he moves and dodges her next assault. She backs up a step, thrusts a quick arc up with the dagger and a low swing with the sword. Her dagger misses him, and the long blade connects with stone.

Hermes creeps forward towards Pax, retreating from Enyo's assault and away from Junior charging towards Pem in Teuta's form.

Hermes hides behind a large stalagmite. He holds out his foot and trips Pax. He falls hard on his back. Enyo places a foot on his chest and rests the tip of her sword on the pulse jumping from his throat.

Hermes charges through the air towards Junior.

"Protect time," Pem says, dancing back and twirling. "Unite to fight. Ember of mine."

Junior lunges for her.

She darts just out of reach.

Hermes swoops down and shoves Junior through the portal she opened.

"No!" Pax shouts.

"Ember," Pem says in a high-pitched Teuta giggle. "We have a new head for the décor."

The man writhes under Enyo's foot. She pushes the blade closer, nicking the skin.

A warm ember glow fills the small cavern.

The man bucks again, but Enyo just smiles and shakes her head.

"Your fate is up to Ember," Pem says, skipping around a stalagmite.

"Illyria of mine," a woman sings.

Pem stops skipping.

"The heirs of time," the woman continues to sing. "Arise in your place."

The man pushes up against Enyo. She shakes her head, holding steady.

"Your trespass here is over, dear," the woman says with a low vibrato. The room brightens to a blinding white.

Enyo's foot falls to the floor. She whirls, but the light is blinding.

"Pem," Enyo whispers.

"Here!" Pem answers. "Just blind at the moment."

The room falls to darkness.

Enyo rapidly blinks and searches the space. "He's gone!"

Junior and Hermes fall onto the stone floor in the present cavern.

Hermes scrambles up. "Are you marked?" he asks, backing away from Junior.

Junior rolls back his sleeve and holds up his forearm with the gold cuff inked on his tan skin.

"When did he cuff you?" Hermes asks, taking small steps towards the large opening.

Junior stands and shakes his head. "You do not know the trouble we are in at the moment."

"Just answer the question!" Hermes says, stopping at the edge.

"We need—"

"There is no we," Hermes says, pointing at Junior and to himself. "You ruined that chance when you burned Ember's message."

"He has control," Junior says, holding up his arm.

"Quit stalling. Answer the question."

Junior takes an aggressive step toward Hermes.

Hermes pushes off and hovers over the edge. "So, your answer is violence?"

Junior glances at the drop to the lake and teeters back. "We need to stop them!"

"Stop who?" Hermes asks, flying out a little further from the edge.

"Enyo and her descendants."

"Why would I stop the line Ember assigned to protect time?" Hermes drops a few feet and Junior gasps. Hermes smiles and shakes his head. "For someone so tall, I find it funny that you are not a fan of heights."

Junior's forehead glistens with a layer of sweat. "Father Time will erase our bloodlines if they protect the heirs of time."

Hermes laughs. "Do you really think that man has any chance of surviving Ember after trespassing here?"

Enyo and Pem appear behind Junior. Enyo holds a finger to her lips.

"He will make Ember bow," Junior says.

Pem snorts.

Junior turns to face Enyo and Pem. Hermes can see his sweat-soaked shirt sticking to his back and the hilt of a small dagger in his waistband.

"Is he gone?" Junior asks. He reaches for the hilt of his dagger.

Hermes flies forward, landing a kick on the back of Junior's knee and snatching the blade.

Junior crumples to the floor.

"Ember," Enyo says. "We give you this traitor to punish or free, but we have a messenger to retrieve."

Junior looks up from the stone floor and raises his hands. "Wait!"

Pem waves bye.

Junior vanishes from the present cavern.

"What happened below?" Hermes asks, adding a holster with a thought to his right thigh to place the small dagger. He slides it in with ease.

"We can explain on the way," Enyo says. "Protect time. Unite to fight. Ember of mine." She walks through the portal.

Hermes and Pem follow her through.

26

"Leon!" Avi shouts, turning in a slow circle.

The late afternoon sun dances in through the tall, thin pine trees and glistens on freshly fallen snow.

Xena appears beside Avi. The snow blows off the trees above, leaving a sprinkle of flakes dotting their hair.

"Follow his tracks," Xena suggests, pointing down at the boot prints.

"An infant in the snow," Avi mutters, winding her way around a few rocky boulders and trees.

"We'll find Ora!" Xena says, following close behind Avi. She cautiously looks up, inspecting the sky and trips on a root.

Avi breaks her fall.

"Sorry," Xena apologizes.

Avi doesn't respond, but points to Leon kneeling in the snow with his head in his hands.

Xena moves past her.

"Leon," Xena calls out. "What's wrong?" He doesn't move or react to her call. "Leon." She moves around him. "Ah!"

The wooden bassinet is overturned with a gash of marks on the wood.

"Are… are those—?" Avi chokes up with a sob. "We're too late."

Leon stands and brushes the snow from his pants. He calls his staff and double taps to the scythe. He slices the air with four quick arcs. "Show me Ora."

The image flickers to a blue sky and mountains marking the horizon.

Leon spins around, looking for an opening in the dense forest. He turns back to the image, studying the changing landscape.

"There!" Avi points to a familiar peak. "This is near the bridge."

Leon releases his staff and pushes off, flying up above the tall trees. He looks down. "Are you coming?"

Avi nods and pushes off.

Xena watches the image fade before pushing off and joining Leon and Avi in the air.

Avi flies higher, looking for the peak.

Leon and Xena circle scanning the forest and horizon.

"This way!" Avi flies west.

They fly in a v formation.

The setting sun is nearly blinding until a cloud partially covers the unforgiving rays, revealing the usmu hovering above the bridge, clutching a white bundle in one of its talons.

They fan out and dive towards the bridge without a word.

The usmu notices Leon first and shrieks. It flies up but is met with a kick to one head by Avi. It shrieks again and lashes one talon towards Leon.

Xena flies just below and reaches for the bundle, but it's just the blanket. "She's not here!"

They fly away in three directions.

The usmu dives towards Leon and releases the white blanket. It floats down into the canyon.

Leon calls his staff and double taps it against his thigh. He flies, scythe raised, straight at the usmu.

It rolls left, missing the blade, shrieking, and flapping to circle Leon. It spots Xena circling over the bridge below and dives towards her, but Avi uses her amulet and conjures up Kaly, Pem, and Enyo as decoys. This slows the descent of the usmu as it tracks the three new arrivals hovering in his path.

Xena flies under the bridge, out of sight.

Leon catches up with the usmu and swings his scythe, slicing the tip of its wing.

Its cry shakes the snow on the bridge and sends a shower of snowflakes to the valley below.

Leon and Xena wince and cover their ears.

Avi spots a glimmer next to the usmu and dives feet first into the double-headed creature, sending it through the portal and creating a vacuum of silence.

Leon looks up and spins.

Avi floats down to his level and the conjures of the other ladies disappear.

"Any idea what you were thinking when you sliced that thing?" Avi asks with a smile.

Leon's eyes go wide. "Pretty sure it was something like I hope it goes straight to hell."

Xena peeks out from under the bridge. "All clear?"

"For now," Avi answers.

Xena flies up. "Where did it go?"

Avi and Leon answer in unison. "To hell."

Xena shakes her head. "There are no prints in the fresh snow on the bridge. I think this was a distraction."

"Any ideas on how to deal with a fairy?" Leon asks, nodding towards the opposite ridge near the bridge.

A tall figure with a hooded gold cloak is facing them.

Avi flanks Leon's left and Xena flank's his right as they fly towards the stranger.

Leon hovers above the canyon eye level with a woman. She has soft features and gold wavy hair blending in with her cloak.

He glances at Xena and Avi, they nod.

"My name is Leon. We are only here to find my infant niece, Ora. We mean no harm."

"I am Prende."

Avi and Xena both gasp.

Leon looks to each of them with his brows knitted.

"Goddess of beauty, love and fertility," Xena whispers.

"I have someone that you may want, but it isn't Ora," Prende says, waving a hand and Teuta materializes.

Leon flies towards Teuta with his scythe raised but is met with resistance, leaving him suspended in midair. He looks back to the straining faces of Avi and Xena, holding each of his legs.

116

"And you mentioned no harm," Prende says, shaking her head. "Tsk, tsk. No trust for a man that can't honor his word."

"She is the reason all of this is happening!" Leon spits towards Teuta.

"Oh?" Prende says, raising an eyebrow. She looks at the bulging veins on Leon's red face to Teuta's straight posture with her arms folded over her small chest, the gold ink of the cuff visible on her forearm.

"Tell me I'm wrong," Leon says, looking directly at Teuta.

She smiles. "You're not right."

"Where is Ora!" Leon points his staff at Teuta.

"Ask Avi," Teuta says, "she took her."

Avi lets go of Leon's leg and he wobbles. He pulls free of Xena's grip and faces Avi.

Avi shrugs. "I didn't take her from the castle. I helped her escape the room we were trapped in."

"So you say," Teuta says.

Avi frowns. "I left the stone walled room with a portal to protect, not harm time. The portal left me in the forest over there." She points to the other side of the bridge. "Maybe she can explain the changeling?" Avi gestures to Prende.

Prende laughs. "You think I'm a fairy?"

"Well, you're here and I don't see any tracks so," Xena says.

"Goodness," Prende says, nodding at each of them. "This is who is assigned to protect and serve Ember and the Castle of Teskom."

Teuta whirls and points her finger up at Prende. "You have no clue what that duty entails."

"You're defending their ignorance?"

"More like they are new." Teuta huffs. "They were called up six months ago. And they did just defeat an usmu. Give them some credit."

"And lost two children in less than forty-eight hours."

"More like they were kidnapped!" Leon growls.

"Why should we not suspect you?" Avi asks, pointing at Prende. "You show up high in the mountains where we are tracking Ora and with Teuta no less."

"You doubt my intentions, child," Prende says with a smile.

"Child?" Avi says with a frown. "You look fourteen."

Prende unhooks her cloak, revealing the curves of her chest, waist and hips. "I am not a teenager, but a goddess."

"We know your type," Avi says with sarcasm. "And their little heads too!"

Leon snorts a laugh.

Xena shakes her head. "We can't just wait around for you to explain." She hovers closer to Teuta but continues looking at Prende. "Either you tell us what you want in exchange for her now or we can come and get her later."

A portal opens behind Teuta and Enyo steps through.

Pem and Hermes step through behind Enyo.

"Restrain her," Enyo commands.

Hermes and Pem take Teuta by her arms and walk back through the portal.

Prende watches the entire exchange with her mouth ajar.

The portal closes, leaving Enyo with Xena facing Prende.

"Bravo," Prende says, clapping. "You just let a tiger loose in the castle."

Enyo smirks. "Prende."

"You two know each other?" Leon asks.

"Enyo and I go way back," Prende says, twirling a strand of her golden hair. "Isn't that right?"

"Seriously," Leon says, shaking his head. "I don't have time for this. Ora is still missing!" He flies through a thought provoked portal.

Avi flies over to Xena, and they land behind Enyo.

"The protectors of time," Prende says. "I told Ember your line would disappoint her and dear me. Was I right? One duty and failing already."

"Why are you even here?" Enyo says, ignoring her arrogance.

"We received a distress call from the usmu," Prende says. "And my pets always report back."

"That thing was your pet?" Avi asks.

"One of many." She whistles, and another usmu descends from the clouds.

"Why would one attack me and an infant?" Avi asks, folding her arms in front of her chest.

Xena's feet leave the ground, but she remains behind Enyo beside Avi.

"Fairies are tricky creatures," Prende says, gesturing towards the bridge. "They are only seen when they reveal themselves. And you are currently surrounded, just like you were on the bridge. My usmu can see past their glamor. It was not attacking you. Only defending time."

"The talons in my back would suggest another scenario," Xena says.

"You got in its way, allowing the fairies time to make the switch."

Xena shakes her head. "You're lying."

"I wish," Prende says with a nod. The usmu hovering above flies lower and extends a talon. She raises her hand, grasping the dark curve and flipping herself on to its back with practiced ease. "Good luck making it out of here."

Enyo unsheathes her blades.

A blur of wild white hair attached to rotting grey and gaunt faces suddenly appears out of the snow, surrounding them, at least four fairies deep and several dozen appearing with each passing second.

Avi and Xena turn back-to-back with Enyo.

The first distinguishable features are the seething sharp teeth of the nearest fairies, crouching low. They snarl and snap their jaws.

"These are not the pretty faces I imagined," Avi whispers nervously.

"No kidding," Xena responds out of the corner of her mouth. "Enyo, what's the plan here?"

"Bargain," Enyo says with a smile. "Who here has a bargain I can't pass up?"

The fairies closest to the ladies stand at attention and the sea of decaying faces part, allowing a small woman to walk down an open path.

"A bargain you seek, what a treat," the young woman says, reaching Enyo. Her face is full and bright, a stark contrast to the withered, bony creatures standing behind her.

"We will walk free, with baby and all three," Enyo responds.

"The price will be high for the trespass to fly and free with baby and all three."

Enyo nods. "A real deal will be as you feel." She smiles. "The usmu is gone. Am I wrong?"

The young woman smiles and laughs. "Oh, that price too high is less to pay for they did save the day." She points to Avi and Xena. "But you are new."

Avi manages a glance at Xena. Her mouth is hanging wide open, watching the exchange.

"Fair to assess," Enyo responds. "Don't stress. I'm like you a young but true. An original line to these divines."

"The truth you tell will do you well."

The young woman whirls in a circle to face the fairies. They nod in unison. "The bargain to be free, with baby and all three. The usmu talon you keep and a pint of your line for our divines."

Xena pats her jacket and sighs with relief. A piece of the talon Dita removed from her shoulder is still in her pocket from earlier.

"A good bargain indeed with baby and all three to be free," Enyo says, feeling Xena nudge her hip.

Enyo kneels in the snow. She forms and packs a snowball. She sticks the hilt of her sword in the center, forming a small well. She drags the tip of her dagger across her palm and drips her blood into the well. "Bring the baby and we three will open our door and place the talon before."

The young woman doesn't respond. All eyes are fixed on the blood filling the snow. Small pink veins appear after each drop.

Enyo clears her throat and repeats the rhyme. "Bring the baby and we three will open our door and place the talon before." She packs the top of the well and adds a layer of fresh snow. She stands and tosses the blood marbled snowball in the air.

Enyo vanishes.

The young fairy dives forward and is met with a blade to her throat. Enyo appears behind the fairy and spins them to face the crowd.

Enyo catches the snowball and meets the stunned gazes of the front lines. "Bring the baby and we three will open our door and place the talon before."

Xena removes the talon from her pocket. And waves it over her head, drawing the attention of the other fairies, now seething again.

A wicker basket appears between Avi and Xena. Avi kneels and uncovers the basket. A pair of brown eyes meets hers. She inspects the infant's ears, peeks down the back of her gown and spots the mark like Emit's. Avi taps Xena's leg.

Xena looks down and nods.

Avi covers the baby, keeping a hand on her as she opens a portal.

Xena winks at Enyo.

Enyo glances at the snowball. Xena nods and tosses the talon in the air. Enyo throws the snowball in the young fairy's face and falls back through the open portal before the first fairies reach her.

27

Kaly knocks on the door to the archive suite. Itra answers and swings the door open.

Elis looks up from his drawing. He has paper scattered all over the floor and stacks of crayons in every color.

"Hey Kaly!" Elis hops up and picks up a drawing. "It's you and Leon with me and Zana." He runs over and hands Kaly the drawing. Kaly kneels next to Elis.

"Is this my farmhouse?" Kaly asks, tracing the outline of the roof and the open front porch. The details are eerily accurate.

Elis nods. "Zana said this is her new home."

Kaly looks up at Itra and over at Anton, now standing up from the couch. "Why would Zana live here with me and Leon?"

"She will need you and you will need her," Elis says. He skips to another drawing and resumes coloring.

Kaly stands clutching the paper to her chest.

Itra nods towards the corridor.

Anton and Kaly follow him.

"Who is Zana?" Kaly whispers once they're further away from Elis.

"The baby we thought was Ora," Itra answers. He peeks his head in the door. Danae is asleep with one hand resting on Emit in the bassinet beside the bed. He motions them to the other bedroom and closes the door.

Kaly presses a hand to her chest, glancing down at the drawing. "The baby, the name, how?"

"Elis can hear her, the baby," Itra says. "But that was a whopper of a surprise about living with you and Leon."

"Elis made the paper and crayons appear," Anton says. "He was quiet, only humming on and off." He shakes his head. "I don't understand his ability, or rather abilities at this point."

"My father's name was Zano," Kaly says, wiping a tear from the corner of her eye.

"Has Elis ever heard you talk about him?" Anton asks.

"No," Kaly says, shaking her head. "He died when I was a kid."

"Leon mentioned something about an accident on a dig site in northern Albania," Itra says.

Kaly nods. "His crew found him one morning with a machete at the bottom of some stone steps they uncovered during the dig. It was ruled an accident."

"I'm so sorry, Kaly," Anton says, placing a hand on her shoulder. She nods and pats his hand.

"Do you think this is another connection between this castle and him?" Itra asks.

"Maybe," Kaly says, "but I can worry about that later. We have an update from Enyo. She said Ember made Chronos—disguised as Pax—disappear. Same with Junior."

"Danae mentioned that Junior may have been marked with a keeper's cuff," Itra says.

"Hermes confirmed the mark before he was taken," Kaly says. "Dita and I found a text that may be helpful for reversing the cuff, but we need a translator." Kaly smiles. "Any chance we can convince him to come?"

"Him?" Itra asks. "You mean Uncle Vincent."

"Yes," Kaly says.

Anton runs a hand through his hair and blows out a breath. "Your call!" He opens the door to check on Elis. He is standing in the corridor. "Hey buddy." Elis turns. "Why do you have a baby?"

"She was lonely," Elis says. Anton goes to him and kneels down. He opens his arms and Elis hands over Zana. Her eyes are wide open.

"My word, your green eyes are beautiful," Anton whispers, stroking her cheek.

Kaly peeks over his shoulder. "She's very alert."

Itra kneels next to Elis. "She was sleeping in the crib. How did you get her out?"

Elis stands. "Ember helped me." He skips back down the corridor to his drawings.

Anton looks up from Zana. "This is weird, right?"

"Ha!" Itra stands. "Beyond weird." He drapes an arm around Kaly. "You have my blessing to make a house call to Uncle Vincent."

Kaly pulls him into a hug. "Thank you!"

"Maybe we skip the part about my missing child?" Itra suggests.

Kaly frowns. "You want me to lie to the old man?" She laughs. "Not a chance. I want his help and not a scolding."

"Ok," Itra says, scuffing the floor. "Good luck."

Kaly opens the portal without speaking. "I guess it's thought activated now." She waves and steps through.

"If Iana saw all of this in her visions," Anton says, looking down at Zana. "I understand why she had a panic attack. I'm barely hanging on in real time."

28

"Duke!" Vincent grumbles. "What are you barking at?" He walks down the hall, and a figure back-lit by the sun is standing at the front door.

"Uncle Vincent!" Kaly calls through the door. "It's Kaly. Can I come in?"

"Duke, sit!"

The dog submits and sits with one final bark.

"Come in."

Kaly opens the door and steps in. Vincent moves past her, looking for her car in the drive.

"Did you fly here or something?"

"Or something," Kaly says, holding up her left thumb. The sun pings off the gold ring. She places her left hand on Vincent's shoulder.

His pupils double, and he lets out a long sigh. "Ember."

Kaly smiles with a wink. "We could use your help."

Vincent nods. "Let me call the neighbors. They can watch Duke for a bit." He turns towards the kitchen and says over his shoulder. "They owe me a favor."

Kaly bends and pets Duke's head. "I'll bring him right back," she whispers to Duke while waiting for Vincent.

He returns with a leash.

"All set." Vincent opens the door. Kaly walks out and he leans down and clicks the leash in place. "We need to walk Duke over to the gate in the pasture."

Kaly nods and watches him lock the door and pocket the keys.

"Are you ready to hear the news?" Kaly asks. "Or do you want to wait?"

"Only if you have any good news to share," Vincent says, lifting an eyebrow.

"You are officially a great uncle to beautiful twins." Kaly smiles at his smile, reaching the corners of his crow's feet. "Danae had them last night."

"Are they well?" Vincent asks, pulling back on Duke's leash as they approach the bordering fence.

A chocolate quarter horse is grazing nearby. It bobs its head as they approach and trots over.

"She's beautiful," Kaly says, reaching across the fence as the horse approaches.

Vincent stiffens, watching Kaly interact with the horse and avoiding his eye contact as the neighbor approaches.

"Thanks for watching Duke," Vincent says to his neighbor.

"No problem," the neighbor says, unlatching the gate. Vincent hands the leash over and the neighbor unclips it. "Go on Duke! Millie has fresh bacon."

Duke sprints across the open pasture towards the farmhouse in the distance. The neighbor chuckles and waves his hat. The horse follows him away from the gate.

Kaly laughs. "Bacon wins all day, every day."

Vincent smirks, but studies her. "Something's wrong."

She nods. "It's been hell the last twenty-four hours. I don't know where to begin."

He nods, turning his back to Kaly and extending his arms.

Kaly bites her knuckle, recognizing the action of him waiting on a cloak. She opens the portal to the archives and taps him on the shoulder.

He turns and gapes at the open door.

She holds up her thumb. "Remember?"

He laughs. "When you said 'or something' I thought you actually flew here."

Kaly takes his hand and walks him through.

29

Vincent and Kaly arrive in the archives to a cacophony of noise.

Hermes is standing between Teuta and Leon, who are shouting over each other.

Vincent releases a long, ear-piercing whistle that instantly quiets the room.

All eyes fall on Kaly and Vincent.

"Great," Vincent says. "Now that I have your attention, can you two go cool off in separate corners?" He points to Leon and Teuta. "I'll get caught up on what the hell has happened here. Then we can sit down like adults and have a civilized conversation." He raises a single eyebrow and waits.

Teuta opens her mouth, but she shuts it and stomps off with her hands still looped together with a small rope.

Hermes shrugs, tightens his grip on the rope, and follows her.

Leon frowns but doesn't protest. He sits down hard on a chair nearby.

Vincent turns to face Kaly and spots a familiar face. "Ana?"

Ana smiles. "Hi Vincent, glad you could make it."

He nods once. "Kaly, can you give me a quick highlight reel of events? I'll get the details later if needed."

Kaly blows out a long breath but starts in chronological order. "Elis was taken by Chronos yesterday evening. Teuta summoned the Protectors of Time. Danae delivered Ora and Emit. Teuta came to the delivery center and took the babies without permission. Leon and I came to aid Anton and then came here after the babies were stolen." Vincent glares at Teuta. "We recovered Elis late last night from a place we think is the City of Time."

"Is Elis ok?" Vincent asks.

Kaly nods and continues. "Teuta encountered Pax aka Chronos. He marked her with a keeper's cuff and took her. And this morning Avi and Ora were taken to some place near Teuta. Avi escaped with the baby but wound up high in the mountains near the bridge to nowhere. And we thought we had rescued both of them from an usmu, but the baby was switched to a changeling instead of Ora."

Vincent stumbles back, clutching his chest.

Ana helps him sit in a chair across from Leon.

He wheezes and coughs.

"Dita!" Ana shouts.

Dita appears next to her in an instant. She places her hands above Vincent's chest.

He inhales and waves her away.

"The fairies took Ora," Vincent whispers.

Leon leans forward. "We don't know for sure, but there is more. Junior was marked like Teuta by Chronos. He attempted to break into the vault, but Ember made them vanish."

"To where?" Vincent asks.

"We aren't sure yet. That was part of the argument with Teuta you witnessed when you arrived." Leon stands. "We encountered Prende, on the far side of the bridge to nowhere, when we went back to look for Ora. Apparently, she rescued Teuta."

"Lady Prende?" Vincent asks.

"Yes, but she is an arrogant witch," Teuta says, walking around the stacks with Hermes.

"I'm not so sure her role in today's rescue was innocent," Teuta says. "Ember said that when my line took over after Zeus, there was another blood line wanting to take over. I always assumed it was Enyo's father, Phorcys. But Prende's arrival in the mix has me second guessing that assumption."

A book flies from a shelf and opens in front of Teuta's face. Hermes holds the book.

"She is of Ember's line, a true divine," Teuta says.

Hermes turns the book around for Vincent and the others to trace the line from Ember to Prende.

128

"Does that mean she has full access to the castle?" Kaly asks, looping an arm around Leon's waist.

Another book lifts from the stacks and floats towards Kaly. She holds out her hands, but it remains hovering in the air and then crashes to the floor.

"Yikes!" Kaly jumps back.

Footsteps race through the stacks.

Leon calls his staff and pushes Kaly behind him.

"She's back!" Anton says, racing out of the stacks.

"Who?" Leon and Kaly ask in unison.

"Ora!" Anton grins. He catches Ana's face in the corner of his eye and turns. His grin falls fast. He sucks in a shaking breath and jogs back to the suite.

Leon turns to Teuta. "Hermes stay with Teuta. She is not allowed anywhere near Danae or her family."

Hermes nods and places a firm hand on Teuta's shoulder.

"Ana, can you replace me up there to keep watch?" Dita asks, pointing up.

Ana nods and vanishes.

Leon bursts through Itra and Danae's bedroom door.

Elis is leaning over the bed next to Danae, stroking a baby's hair.

Itra's holding two babies sitting on the bed on the other side of Danae.

Danae meets Leon's eyes. Tears are dripping off her chin.

"Is she ok?" Leon asks, falling to his knees beside Elis.

Danae nods and rolls the baby to her side, exposing the birthmark on her right shoulder blade.

Kaly claps excitedly from the open door. She hugs Xena and Avi. Enyo nods at her.

"Make way," Vincent says, entering with his hands out and fingers waving. "Give this old timer some baby snuggles."

Elis skips across the room and hugs Vincent's waist. "When did you get here?"

"Just in time!" Vincent says, hugging him back.

Itra lays Zana down next to Ora and stands with Emit. He side hugs Vincent and places Emit in Vincent's arms. "Emit, meet your great-uncle, Vincent."

Emit opens his eyes and gazes up at Vincent.

Vincent smiles and sniffles. He moves over to the rocking chair and carefully sits. He gently strokes Emit's cheek.

Dita walks from the open door to Danae's side of the bed. "Do you mind if I check the babies?"

Leon stands, putting himself in the space between Dita and Danae.

Danae narrows her eyes. "Can you show me your forearms?"

Dita nods and rolls up her sleeves. She turns her tan unmarked arms over.

Danae nods and nudges Leon aside. She picks up Zana first and hands her over.

Kaly joins Leon, watching Dita assess Zana. "Elis drew a picture of her with us at the farm."

Leon slowly turns to Kaly. "Come again?"

"Elis can hear her," Kaly says. "He drew her with us at the farm."

Dita hands Zana back to Danae, but Leon intercepts.

"May I?" Leon asks Danae.

Danae nods and asks Dita, "Is she well?"

"Yes," Dita says. "Her vitals are strong, and there are no abnormalities other than the slight point to the helices of her ears."

Leon slides up the small pink cap, exposing her ears and hair. She has light-brown wispy curls. He traces the point of the ear and strokes her cheek, admiring her dark, long eyelashes. She opens her green eyes and puckers her mouth.

Leon gasps. "She's beautiful."

Kaly pokes his side. "You're smitten."

Leon frowns at her for a second but then breaks and smiles down at Zana. "Well, I appreciate pretty girls."

"He was always a sucker for girls in general," Danae says, smiling at Kaly.

Dita shifts and hands Ora back to Danae. "She is well, but running a little warm. It's not a fever."

Danae frowns.

"Some babies just run warmer than others," Dita adds.

Xena steps closer to the bed. "Pem was a hot baby. It freaked the nurses out initially. Don't worry." Xena does a slow turn. "Speaking of my daughter…"

"She went to check the statue in the hedge maze for a new head." Enyo says.

Xena smiles. She reaches over and pats Danae's knee. "I'll go check on her."

"Thank you for bringing Ora home," Danae says to Xena and looks over her shoulder at Avi and Enyo. "I know it wasn't easy."

Enyo pushes away from the wall. "We managed, but we have a few loose ends that need to be managed now. Avi and I will be in the archives if you need us."

Avi nods and follows Enyo.

30

Teuta looks up from the book on her lap when Enyo and Avi emerge from the stacks.

Enyo pulls her dagger out and casually tilts it from side to side.

"Do I want to know whose blood that is?" Hermes asks, tightening the rope tethered to Teuta's wrists.

Enyo smirks. "Let's just say it was a bargain."

"Did you kill Prende?" Teuta asks, looking past Enyo to assess Avi.

"Now why would you assume that?" Enyo asks, stopping inches from Teuta.

"She took Ora and you brought her back," Teuta says, meeting Enyo's eyes.

"Why would she do that?" Enyo challenges her, staring her down.

"To leverage time for a place at the table," Teuta says.

"Oh, but you are so wrong." Enyo laughs and steps back, facing Hermes. "Did Kaly find a resolution to the keeper's cuff?"

Hermes shrugs. "Vincent needs to translate the text, but he only got here a few minutes before you returned."

"This is more time sensitive than infant coddling," Enyo says, looking through the stack of books on the table to her right. "Do you recall which book he was supposed to translate?"

A book floats above the table next to Avi.

Avi takes the book. "I'll run this back to Vincent."

No one protests.

Avi traces her way back through the stacks, recalling the maze to the suite door. *It's open.* But they had closed it behind them. She stops and turns in a slow circle. She feels someone watching.

"Somebody is hiding in the stacks." Avi pushes the thought to Hermes and Enyo.

Enyo and Hermes nod.

Hermes puts a hand on Teuta's shoulder and vanishes with her.

Enyo listens and moves through the stacks, tracking the soft footfall of the intruder. She pauses at the end of a row and waits. A shadow falls ahead of the person. She darts out with her blood-stained dagger.

"Ah, no!" Avi screams.

Elis stands frozen with his mouth open and eyes wide.

Avi runs over to Elis and kneels to his level, blocking the sight of Enyo and her bloody dagger.

"Hey kid," Avi says. "You can't be out here without a parent or an adult."

"But you're an adult."

"True, but we didn't know it was you in here and we are still on high alert." Avi stands and takes his hand. "We should get you back to the suite. They'll be worried."

"Elis!" Anton shouts.

"He's here," Avi answers.

Anton turns towards Avi's voice and finds the break in the stacks. "Elis!" He runs forward and swoops him up, looking over Avi's shoulder at Enyo, still in the strike ready pose. "Are you ok? What happened?"

"I'm good," Elis says and giggles. "I think I broke Enyo."

Enyo shifts and blinks at the mention of her name. She drops her hand gripping the dagger and shakes her head. "I could have…"

"But you didn't," Avi says, looking at Enyo.

"You can't just run off, son." Anton turns back towards the suite.

"Did you find him?" Vincent shouts and then rounds the corner. "Boy! You know how to scare an old man."

"Oops," Elis whispers, and his cheeks redden. He ducks his head into Anton's shoulder. "Sorry."

"We're just glad you're safe," Vincent says, patting him on the back.

"We'll be in a time out if you need us," Anton says.

Elis groans.

They silently watch Elis and Anton leave the hall.

Avi coughs. "I was just coming to see you," she says, standing next to Vincent. She holds up a book. "We really shouldn't delay this any longer."

"I agree," Vincent says, patting his pocket. He pulls out a pair of reading glasses.

Avi hands over the book.

"It should be marked," Kaly says from behind Enyo.

Enyo jumps and swings with her dagger as she whirls to face her.

Kaly ducks, but the blade slices a few hairs from her ponytail.

"Shit!" Enyo curses. "Sorry! I think I may need a time out too. And hopefully let my nerves settle a bit."

Kaly straightens and pats her ponytail. She shrugs. "I was due for a trim."

"Enyo," Kaly says, reaching out to touch her shoulder. "You're very pale and sweaty. Maybe you should let Dita check you over before resting?"

"I'm not ill," Enyo whispers. "Just hungry and tired."

"And reckless," Avi says. "Go on! We'll call if anything changes." She taps her necklace.

Enyo vanishes.

"When he is done translating," Kaly says, looping her arm around Avi, "I want to hear what happened out there that got Ora home."

"If you ever need a poem written, Enyo would be my first choice."

Kaly and Vincent laugh.

"She spit out rhymes without a second thought," Avi says, keeping her face neutral.

"Oh, you're serious?" Kaly asks.

"Very," Avi says. "She saved Ora and us."

"Only to nearly take out Elis and Kaly," Vincent mumbles.

"It's been a rough few hours," Avi says, nodding towards the book. "What language is that text in?"

"A new one for me," Vincent says, "but it's actually coded in ancient Illyrian."

"Coded?" Kaly asks, looking over his shoulder. "Your gift allows you to unravel coded language?"

"Part of the loophole," Vincent says, grinning. "I can understand, read, write, and speak any language. Since the code is written in letters and not numbers, I can translate it like reading a newspaper."

"Remarkable," Kaly whispers. "So does this text provide an undo for the keeper's cuff?"

Vincent shakes his head. "More like a transfer. If we can find the key to the cuff, we can transfer the mark of a person to another." He sighs. "But the problem remains only with a new person."

"Junior and Teuta are marked with the same cuff?" Avi asks.

"Unfortunately, yes," Vincent answers.

"Is the keeper's cuff infinite?" Kaly asks, eyes wide.

"If the will of the owner dies," Vincent explains. "The bond breaks, releasing the marked."

"Ok, so find the key and transfer the mark to who, Ember?" Kaly says, holding up one finger. "Or kill Chronos?" She drags a finger across her neck.

Avi barks out a laugh. "Technically, does Ember have a will if she isn't human?"

Vincent chuckles. "Neither option will work in this case. Chronos isn't human either."

Avi and Kaly glance at each other with their eyebrows raised.

"Chronos is the essence of time," Vincent explains. "His human form is just a shell of his power, not the actual source. You can't actually kill Chronos, you can only kill the host."

"To counter that," Kaly says, pacing away and back, "is the will of a person a human trait or a manifestation of energy?"

Avi shakes her head. "I think my brain just exploded with a billion 'what if' scenarios!"

"We can call a family meeting and discuss our options," Vincent says, closing the book.

Avi's stomach growls. "Maybe over dinner." Her eyes drift up to the darkness veiling the dome. "Meet in the dining hall?"

"Sounds good," Kaly says. "I'll gather the family and find Xena and the other ladies. Do you want to wake up Enyo?"

"Is there a suit of armor here somewhere?" Avi asks.

Vincent pats Avi's shoulder. "Maybe just knock on her door."

31

Hermes and Teuta are the last to join the others at the table, currently covered in plates of food and bottles of wine.

Kaly taps her spoon on her wineglass. "Let's start with a toast to Danae and Itra and the beautiful twins." She raises her glass. "To time."

"To time," the others salute in unison.

Itra nods and raises his glass before sipping. He's alone at the end of the table. Danae refuses to leave the archive suite with the babies unless it's to return home. And Anton and Elis have promised to keep watch.

"Can we start with a recap of the events on the mountain this afternoon?" Kaly asks, nodding to Avi.

Avi glances at Xena and Enyo.

Xena nods.

Enyo tilts her glass to Avi before draining the red wine. It refills instantly. She smirks.

Xena shakes her head.

Avi spends the next twenty minutes explaining the overturned bassinet, the usmu, and the confrontation with Prende. She finishes with their recovery of Ora from the decaying fairies.

"What will Enyo's blood provide for them?" Dita asks.

"A delay to their decay," Xena says. All eyes shift towards her. "It's a working theory, so I could be wrong. If Ora broke the time realm and they are actually dying, Enyo's blood could save a few from the rapid decay."

"How?" Leon asks.

"I am a direct descendant of Gaea," Enyo says.

Leon shakes his head. "And?"

Kaly places a hand on his arm. "Gaea could spontaneously reproduce."

Leon scowls. "You gave them the ability to multiply."

"I dumped my blood into a snowball and smashed it in the queen's face," Enyo says with a smirk. "If they can use it more power to them but it would be highly unlikely."

Dita shakes her head. "You actually preserved the cells by using the snow."

Enyo frowns. "I don't actually think they will have time to figure it out. They all looked pretty far gone except the young queen."

"And we are positive that the infant you recovered this time is actually Ora?" Teuta asks, leaning her elbows on the table. The rope slides loose, but is still bound around her wrists.

Itra nods. "It's Ora. The mark on her shoulder is enough to confirm it for me. And her nose. It's the same as Danae's and nearly identical to her baby photos. Also, Danae discovered a small dip in her left ear last night, and the baby returned has the same."

"Why do you ask?" Xena narrows her eyes at Teuta.

"After Avi left, the ground gave way and I fell into a pit." Teuta pauses and tilts her head. "Although it may have all been a vivid dream."

"Just finish," Enyo says, stabbing a bite of chicken.

"I landed in a dark pit with a single stream of light. I was greeted by a young lady. She said welcome to the City of Time. At first, I thought she was Ember, but on closer inspection, it was Ora. She confirmed it before pointing to a large, dark dome with twelve shimmering lines. It shifted clockwise. When I looked back, she was gone, and the room was normal again."

Leon coughs, holding his fist over his mouth. "Bull shit," he coughs.

Teuta glares at him. "Is that really so hard to believe after everything you have witnessed here?"

Kaly squeezes Leon's knee under the table. "If that was Ora, hypothetically. Did she share any other details like when, where or how she arrived there?"

"No, my recount included the extent of our conversation," Teuta says. "But when Prende pulled me out of there, I caught sight of something too new to be that far in the past." She points at Leon. "A man with a black cloak in the village below. He had a watch like the one you wear."

All eyes turn towards Leon.

"A watch," Leon says with a chuckle, "is a common accessory. Why would this stick out?"

"Not in ancient Illyria," Kaly says. "Vincent, did the text confirm what the key to the keeper's cuff looks like?"

"There is a key?" Teuta asks.

"Like you don't know that already!" Itra scoffs. Teuta frowns. "Danae found a reference to your abuse of this very power. You cuffed a man named Zarek. How many others did you control?"

Teuta opens her mouth and then closes it, shaking her head.

"Please everyone," Leon says, pointing at Teuta. "Take note, she is officially speechless."

Dita leans forward. "You've used the keeper's cuff before?"

Teuta nods but refuses to look up from the table. "I didn't know what it was when we found it." She blows out a long breath. "My crew and I captured a trade ship that had several chests full of odd trinkets, including the keeper's cuff. I kept a few for my own personal collection. When we were boarded by Roman pirates, I hid the collection. We had a false wall built in between my room and my first mate's."

Teuta leans back in the chair and looks at the gold ink on her forearm. "After the pirates left with only a few coins and pieces of jewelry, I knew we would be boarded again. When we ported, I removed the treasure and made arrangements in the village to hide it until we returned. I found the cuff wedged between my sleeping rack and the hidden wall right after we pulled the anchor. I handed it to my first mate, Zarek, to hide below deck. But the cuff vanished on contact but then appeared again a second later."

"It was an accident?" Avi asks.

Teuta nods. "I did not know what it was. And before I knew it, half my crew had passed it around, watching it vanish and then reappear. Each man was marked with the same gold ink I bare."

"But if you didn't have the key," Kaly says, "were they under your will or someone else?"

"Someone else," Teuta says, shaking her head. "Nothing happened at first. But then, three days later, the crew that were marked abruptly stopped what they were doing and jumped overboard. They swam towards a small inlet off the coast near Durres. The only people left on board were me and the cook. We tried to raise the anchor and go after them, but there was no wind and we paddled too slow. When we finally ran the boat ashore, the crew was gone."

"If you handled the cuff," Itra asks, raising an eyebrow. "Why weren't you marked?"

"I wore gloves on board to hide my feminine hands." Teuta holds up her hands, the rope slides down a little off her wrists. "I always dressed like a man when sailing."

"Did they take the cuff?" Pem asks.

"I never found it. And trust me, I tore the entire ship apart. I thought they took it." Teuta tilts her head. "Or it was at the bottom of the sea."

"Did you ever see your crew again?" Xena asks.

"Four months later, I received a message from a local that the men had returned and were attempting to board my newest ship. We went to the docks with my new officers and arrested the men for mutiny. Zarek pleaded for forgiveness, saying they had no choice. The gold ink on his forearm was gone. Most of the men stated the same thing. They were tending to their duties one moment, and then followed a command to jump overboard the next. Their memory between that moment and arriving on my shores was sketchy. A few could recall digging and building something, but no one had any clue what or where."

Kaly claps and the room's attention shifts from Teuta to her. "I think I know what they were building!"

"How?" Dita asks.

"I've studied the period when Teuta was queen," Kaly says, pointing at Teuta. "Do you recall the year this took place?"

Teuta thinks for a moment. "After the death of my husband, King Agron. Between 231 and 230 BC."

Two journals appear in front of Kaly. She anxiously thumbs through the first one.

"Are those my brother's journals?" Xena asks, leaning closer to inspect the handwriting.

"Yes," Kaly says. "Bingo!" She pounds a fist on the table and the plates rattle. "Sorry, a little excited. In the nineteen sixties, excavation started on the Durres Amphitheater. It was dated back to the second century, but my father noted a tunnel was added right before the Roman invasion that toppled Teuta's reign." She points down to the page. "The folklore passed down stated that the workers completed the build as if they were choreographed puppets. Some entries even reference them as devils or zombies."

"How is a tunnel helpful?" Hermes asks.

"That tunnel led to a cavern that was never completed because of a cave in, leaving several men trapped underground." Kaly smiles. "The site was recently excavated, and the artifacts were taken for further assessment."

"Wow," Pem whispers.

Leon smiles. "Ladies and gentlemen, my wife and brainy champion."

"If we find the key to the cuff," Vincent explains, "we can transfer the mark to a new person." He sighs. "But the problem remains. A marked person is tied to the keeper's will."

"It's not actually a key to undo, just to transfer?" Teuta asks.

"Correct," Vincent says. "The only way to sever the marked bond to the keeper is the death of the keeper."

"Is there any other alternative?" Teuta asks.

"Attempt to kill Chronos?" Leon suggests.

"That is where it gets tricky," Vincent says. "The host in this case is Pax, but Chronos is the essence of time, and is not human. If we kill Pax, will that kill time's will?"

"Or is will a manifestation of energy?" Kaly adds.

"Or," Pem says, bouncing her eyebrows, "we find and transfer the mark to someone who will die soon, severing the bond?"

"Pem!" Xena scolds.

Pem shrugs.

"Not bad!" Hermes laughs.

On the far side of the dining hall, the middle door of three opens to a small library, where a fraction of the books from the archive are held. A large man steps out with a book.

Enyo pulls the sword from her sheathe and reaches for the dagger.

Dita turns and gasps. "Dad?" She pushes her chair back and runs towards the man. The man bends and wraps her into a hug.

Itra stands with his mouth hanging open.

Ana smiles.

Kaly leans towards Ana and whispers, "You saw this reunion?"

Ana nods.

Itra walks towards the giant and nervously wipes his hand on his shirt before he extends it towards the man. "Mui, sir, my name is Itra."

Mui releases Dita and smiles down at Itra. "I know who you are, son. It's nice to finally meet you." His hand covers Itra's hand and forearm. He shakes it gently. The entire table is standing now except for Teuta.

Vincent's face is beaming like Itra's.

Mui greets each person but saves Teuta for last. He removes the ropes from her wrists and holds his hand over the gold ink. Teuta's eyes go wide, and she lets out a soft cry. He releases her forearm. She inspects her skin. The ink is gone.

"How?" she whispers, looking up at Mui.

"Ember knew this day would come, as did Ana," Mui explains, taking a seat at the head of the table. The chair resizes itself automatically to fit his large frame. "The transfer of the keeper's cuff is not anything physical." He holds up his forearm, gold ink reflecting on his tan skin. The entire table gasps in unison. "It's mental. I am now bound to the keeper's will along with my son, Junior. A burden I choose with my free will to carry to protect Ember and the Castle of Teskom."

"You knew he was coming?" Dita asks, looking at Ana. She nods. "A little warning would have been appropriate."

Ana shrugs.

"Young lady," Mui says, looking at Dita. "My arrival here at this moment has been planned for centuries."

"Teuta is free of the mark?" Itra asks.

Mui nods.

Teuta transforms from fairy to queen in an instant with a large grin.

Itra narrows his eyes. "But that means Chronos has control of your will along with Junior's?"

"Yes and no," Mui says, nodding. "Chronos, Father Time, or Pax, whatever you want to call him, is currently suspended in time. Thanks to the recovery of an ancient artifact made during the battle six months ago."

"I don't understand," Itra says. "What recovery?"

"A few ships that attacked the castle had artifacts from the Library of Alexandria onboard," Junior explains from the open doorway.

Enyo stands, pulling out her sword.

Junior holds up his hands. "I'm marked but under my control and free will at the moment."

Enyo watches him circle the table to an open seat.

Vincent and Junior nod in greeting as he sits.

"The items we pulled from this ship were mostly texts, a few pieces of pottery, and two carved statues, all dating back to Illyria," says Junior. "But one piece was a gift Ember gave to Chronos before their failed engagement."

"An infinite suspension of time," Mui says with a grin.

"The bridge to nowhere?" Xena asks.

"Almost," Junior says. "The artifact is a tiny version of the bridge and the fairy realm's bubble. Similar to the castle's shield, it reflects an infinite loop when inside."

Vincent nods and chuckles. "The Medusa shield we recovered protects the castle and this dimension from the outside world." Mui nods. "But this protects the fairies and their realm?"

"Traps more than protects," Junior answers with a grin. "If only all fairies were so lucky." He winks at Teuta.

She tosses a piece of bread in his direction but misses.

Mui shakes his head. "Seriously? You two have never kissed and made up?"

Leon barks out a laugh. "You two… liked each other?"

"More like childhood best friends turned teenage drama," Dita says, laughing at the scowling frowns and glares from Junior and Teuta.

"Can we get back to the threat?" Enyo asks, rolling her eyes.

Mui smiles and nods. "Ember trapped Chronos in an hourglass. It's safely stored in the vault."

"How does a man fit in an hourglass?" Dita asks.

Mui wipes a finger on the table and blows. "His essence."

Dita's face pales. "Dust to dust, ash to ash…"

Mui nods.

Avi fingers her infinity pendant. "How long will he be trapped?"

Junior and Mui look down at the table.

"Well?" Teuta says.

"We don't honestly know," Mui says, patting the book he brought out of the library. "But I'm hoping this group can figure that out."

The book opens and the pages flip to the center of an illustration captioned City of Time. The lights dim in the dining hall, and the illustration fills the room in full scale and three dimensions.

"Cool," Hermes whispers.

The table and chairs are in the center of a village surrounded by stone buildings and a sandy square. A sundial stands in the center of the square. In relation to the room, it hovers near the center of their table.

Enyo turns in a slow circle. "This is the square near the market in Illyria." She points to the door leading to the conservatory, the illusion showing an open market with street vendors lining each side.

Itra chuckles. "The original time square?"

Kaly laughs, but Leon nudges her. "Is that Pax?" A figure in a black cloak appears on the far side of the illusion, opposite the market.

Teuta looks in the direction Leon is staring. "That's the man I saw with the watch."

The man slinks forward, keeping his head low. He slows and circles the sun dial, making Pem and Xena move away from the table. The others stand, backing away from the table and watch.

He places his wrist down on the center of the sundial and it opens. An hourglass rises from the center. He removes the hourglass and turns it upside down. The movement in the square around the man stops.

Itra walks around to face the man and clasps a hand over his own mouth.

Vincent joins Itra. He whispers, "It's Elis."

The illusion fades immediately, and the hall lights lift.

Itra falls to his knees. "Is he… is he releasing Chronos?"

"I don't think we can assume that based on what we saw." Vincent states, scanning the faces staring back, some with disbelief, others with horror or sadness. "Right?"

A book floats out from the library and stops in front of Vincent. A compass is embossed on the cover with gold and silver flecks. He takes the book, and it opens to the first page.

He removes his glasses from his pocket and puts them on. He reads with a shaky voice. "He will guide time to defeat and complete the key to thee. A true fight a birth right for time the heir to prepare."

Itra shakes his head and pounds a fist to the floor. "No! For the love of my sister, hell no!"

Mui raises his hands. "I know this seems overwhelming."

"Seems?" Itra stands and marches to Mui. He points a finger up in his face. "My sister died, my nephew was kidnapped, my newborns were taken by Ember's messenger."

Teuta winces.

"Jesus! They were barely out of the womb, not even an hour old! Then my daughter was snatched out of my arms and held by the fairies!" He shoves Mui in the chest. Mui doesn't waver, just frowns. "And we have a third infant now without her parents."

Itra vanishes.

32

Itra lands in the future cavern to an image of the teenage version of the Elis he just witnessed turning the hourglass. Elis is talking with another boy.

"Emit," Itra whispers.

The scene moves to face the young boy. Itra reaches forward to touch the boy's face, so similar to his own. His hand goes through the image and the scene swirls into a darker room with a small window. A young girl comes into the frame and her profile is barely visible from the light streaming in.

"Ora?"

The young girl turns away from the light and sings. "Hear us call for the fate of us all. We must bring time's end to start again."

The tilt of her voice fades to a hum of the same melody before the room brightens to a blinding white. A dark, hooded figure stands in the center. He points towards Itra.

Itra takes a hesitant step back.

"You must free the young, for it has begun. Ember's divine are the true lines to all time."

Itra gulps and closes his eyes. When he opens them, he is standing in the center of the archives. He exhales and holds a hand to his chest to slow his racing pulse. Once his pulse is steady, he wanders back through the stacks to the archive suite.

He enters the living area. Elis and Anton are cuddled together, asleep on the couch. He softly closes and secures the door from the suite to the archives. He walks down the hall to their room and enters without knocking.

Danae smiles at his intrusion. "Your footsteps, even when quiet, are familiar." She rocks forward and stands from the rocking chair. "You just missed their first choir performance." She hums and Itra stiffens.

"That melody is from what?" Itra asks.

"Their crying harmony." Danae lays Ora down between Emit and Zana. "Why?"

"Our daughter just sang this melody to me in the future cavern."

Danae turns too fast to face him and has to grasp the side of the bed for balance. "What do you mean?"

Itra sings, "Hear us call for the fate of us all. We must bring time's end to start again."

"Tell me everything."

Itra spends the next hour explaining their dinner conversation. He tells her everything about the rescue of Ora, Teuta's story about Ora and the keeper's cuff, Mui's arrival, Elis as a teenager with the hourglass, and the time in the future cavern.

Danae's face transforms from confused, curious, sad, and furious in a few seconds once he finishes. "Itra, we need to leave and go as far away from here as soon as possible."

He sits on the bed closest to the bassinet and stares at the trio. "And go where?" He turns towards Danae. "Ember will just show up one day and take them again." He shakes his head. "They looked maybe the same age as Elis is right now. So maybe seven years of peace before they are called to action."

Danae picks up a pillow from the bed and screams into it.

Itra tosses the pillow aside and wraps his arms around her. She is stiff. He kisses her forehead. She softens and folds her arms around him. They remain embraced until Danae cries out. Itra feels warmth against his chest and looks down.

"It appears my milk has come after all." Danae pulls her soaked shirt away from her and looks up at the two wet spots on Itra's shirt. She laughs.

Itra smiles at her joy and pulls off his shirt.

Their door bursts open to a wild-eyed Elis. He points and laughs at Danae's wet top. "Do you need a bib like the babies?"

Danae frowns at him and turns away from the door. "Elis, some day you will learn how to knock." She changes her top with a thought.

"No time for knocking," he says, jumping up and down. "There is a real-life giant requesting to speak to you two."

Danae and Itra freeze.

A giant shadow hovers behind Elis.

Itra motions for Danae to stand behind him, shielding her and the babies with his arms out.

"May I come in?" Mui asks from the hallway.

Elis skips in the room.

Danae reaches for the ember amulet on instinct, only to recall it's no longer around her neck. She curses under her breath.

"No, you may not." Itra states, to Danae's surprise. "You are marked by the keeper. I would prefer to keep this conversation as far away from the babies as possible."

"I understand," Mui says. "Can you and Danae join me in Ivan's study?"

Itra turns to Danae. She nods. "Give us ten minutes."

"Thank you," Mui states, retreating down the hallway.

"Leon!" Danae shouts.

"Yes," Leon answers, toweling off from a shower.

"We need you and Kaly to watch the babies while we talk with Mui."

"On our way," Leon says in thought and aloud as he dresses.

"On our way where?" Kaly asks, stepping out of the shower.

"Danae and Itra need to speak to Mui." Leon admires her curves as she dries off. "She asked us to come down to watch the babies."

She flicks the towel at him and immediately dresses with a thought.

He frowns.

Kaly smiles and takes his hand.

33

Itra knocks once on the door. He squeezes Danae's hand.

She squeezes back once.

Vincent answers the door. "Have a seat." He gestures to the blue sofa. "Mui is grabbing a few items from the war room."

Itra and Danae step inside the study.

The deep blue walls contrast with the bright gold spines of the books lining the built-in shelves of various heights and widths scattered across the walls.

Danae's eyes linger over the chaotic design. She squeezes her eyes shut and shudders.

"Do you know if Ivan will join us?" Itra asks, helping Danae get comfortable on the sofa.

"Not likely," Vincent says, sitting in a gold chair across from them. "Teuta didn't complete her message delivery before she was taken."

Mui slides open the pocket door and steps in with two loose parchments and a book. He sets them down on the marble coffee table but remains standing. He opens his arms. "Thank you!"

Itra and Danae crane their necks to look at his face.

"For what?" Itra asks.

"Merging our lines and giving us time."

"We never realized what heart aches this merger would give my family."

Mui frowns. "It's an honor to serve and protect Ember and the Castle of Teskom."

"At the cost of my sister's life," Itra says, standing up. "And my children being snatched away. Where is the honor in that?"

Mui nods. "I understand the loss but the gift of this place—"

Itra waves a hand, cutting him off. "Means nothing without Iana or the safety of my family."

Vincent stands. "Maybe we should discuss only business." He motions for Itra and Mui to sit.

Mui nods and sits, the chair expanding to fit his size.

Itra sighs and sits back down on the sofa.

Danae reaches for Itra's hand and laces her fingers through his before speaking. "What business requires a meeting at nearly midnight?"

Mui leans forward and flips a parchment over. "This is the signed alliance between Zeus and I to serve and protect Ember and the Castle of Teskom."

Danae's skin prickles. She looks around the room. "Teuta, I can feel you in here."

"Come out or get out!" Itra says, inspecting the frown on Danae's face.

"It isn't Teuta," Mui says, rolling up his sleeve. "You're feeling the keeper's will. Is perception your gift from Ember?"

Danae nods and rubs her arms, fighting the chill.

"I assure you he cannot affect Junior or I at the moment." Mui flips over the second parchment. "This is a contract to sever the alliance and dissolve the descendants' obligation to protect and serve, but at the sacrifice of the compass and time."

Danae stands and still has to look up at Mui. She points her finger. "You want us to forfeit our children and Elis to Ember to get out of this life sentence of servitude?" She picks up the parchments and crumples them up. "You may be something out of a fairytale for some, but you're a freaking nightmare of a human if you think it's even an option!" She tosses them at Mui's face.

Mui catches the parchments. "I'm obliged to give you a choice," he whispers.

"Now we have a choice?" Danae folds her arms across her middle. "Why now?"

"Time," Mui says. "And Ember has the heir to her divine."

Itra leans forward. "What do you mean, divine?"

150

Vincent clears his throat. "A pure blood." Danae and Itra frown at him. He holds up his hands. "A divine in ancient Illyrian translates to 'of the origin.'"

"How are the children an heir to Ember?" Itra asks.

Vincent nods to Mui.

Mui nods to the book. "Her heir is the changeling."

The book opens to an illustration of Prende holding an infant.

Danae sits down hard. She scans the page and finds the caption. "Zana is Prende's baby?"

"We believe so," Vincent says. "After Itra vanished from the dining hall, Teuta received a message from Ember. It was to pull this book and provide you two the choice. We believe that if you signed the contract to sever the alliance, Zana's line would be the next to serve."

Itra looks up from the text to meet Vincent's eyes. "We can't give them up."

Vincent nods. "We know and we support that decision."

"And Zana?" Danae whispers. "What will happen to her?"

Vincent and Mui glance at each other. "According to Ana, Zana will live with Leon and Kaly."

Itra nods. "Elis drew Zana with them at their house." He shakes his head. "Does Elis have Iana's gift of visions like Ana?"

"He has her essence of the visions," Mui says. "It may fade with time. All descendants receive a small essence of their parent's gift upon their death."

Itra squeezes Danae's hand. "So we just take Zana without Prende's blessing or consent?"

"According to the text, she gave up Zana for a chance to live here in your place," Mui says.

"How could she possibly choose this over her own daughter?" Danae asks, staring down at the illustration. "Why would she do this?"

"She is the goddess of love, beauty and fertility," Mui says. "A mother to many."

Danae shakes her head.

Itra wraps an arm around Danae. "What else are you holding back?" Itra says to Mui.

Mui grins. "If you choose to leave the Castle of Teskom,... " Itra opens his mouth, but Mui holds up his giant hand. "... the twins may not return unless summoned by Ember. If they cross through the ember archways, time will stop in every dimension."

"You mean when we leave," Itra says.

"Ember would prefer if you raised the twins here," Mui says.

"Ha!" Danae laughs. "She can't protect them here, as evidenced by Ora's kidnapping this morning. We are returning home."

"Are we done here," Itra asks, "or is there more?"

"One last item," Mui says, looking at Vincent.

Vincent frowns.

"We need Elis," Mui says.

"Hell no!" Itra points at Vincent. "You agreed to this?"

"No," Vincent says. "I objected, but was defeated in a house vote."

"Why do you need Elis?" Danae asks.

"To open the sundial to place the hourglass inside," Mui says.

"And keep it out in the open like that? No!" Itra says. "It stays here in the vault."

"But you two so kindly pointed out that here is not as secure as we once thought," Mui says, opening his arms.

"You think you can twist our words against us?" Danae asks.

Mui shakes his head. "Just making an observation."

"Elis will not take part in this or any future side missions," Itra states, grasping Danae's hand. They vanish from the sofa.

Vincent leans forward, resting his face in his hands.

"It could have gone worse." Mui states.

"Are you mad?" Vincent asks, speaking through his hands.

"According to some," Mui says and laughs. "We will let them sleep on it. It's late and your family has had a few rough days."

"He will not bend on this decision," Vincent says. He stands and yawns. Then he levels a glare at Mui. "And I support that decision."

Mui nods. "We need an alternative by tomorrow evening. Enyo and Avi have volunteered to take the first shift protecting the hourglass in the vault. Pem and Xena will take over in a few hours."

"Will Dita and Ana remain here to assist?" Vincent asks, turning for the door.

"Yes, until Ember sends them home." Mui stands. "And you?"

"Until the kids are safe at home," Vincent says, sliding open the door. "I'm not going anywhere. Are the Mui suites available?"

"Yes, the wall barricading the corridor is gone."

"Very well," Vincent says. "Good night, Mui." He walks down the corridor to the dining hall without waiting for a response.

Junior pushes his chair back from the dining hall table when Vincent enters. "Did they…?"

"Sacrifice their children?" Vincent shakes his head. "Hell no!" He slams the conservatory door on his exit.

Junior winces at the clatter of noise and stands.

"He is not happy with our approach," Mui says.

Junior turns to face him as he walks to the table.

"And it went the way we expected. Three questions, three answers, all no."

"And the alternative?" Junior asks.

"To be determined," Mui answers. "Did you learn anything from Chronos?"

Junior shakes his head. "His sole focus was to retrieve the stone he gave to Ember." He laughs. "I think he chose me because of my past with Teuta, expecting we still shared some love towards each other."

"What happened between you and Teuta?" Mui asks.

"A broken promise," Junior says, looking up at the dome. "I said I would return without a summons and my love would be enough to keep my memories intact, but Ember had another plan. She made me not only forget the Castle of Teskom but forget my relationship all together. Six months ago, we returned to face the rogue descendants led by Medusa and Poseidon. On the third day, after the morning battle that killed Iana, I finally recalled my promise to Teuta. I was searching for her when I crossed paths with Medusa and was turned to stone."

"And after you were released from stone?"

"All hell broke loose," Junior says, facing his father. "A lot of finger pointing over whose fault it was about the breach of the castle, the issues with the future archway, and the missing shields.”

“And now?” Mui asks.

Junior shrugs. “It’s been over a decade since I broke my original promise. She is angry and I am indifferent.”

“Indifferent doesn’t travel back in time and find and convince his father to take on the burden of the keeper’s cuff.”

Junior rolls his eyes, but his cheeks redden.

Mui smiles and pats his shoulder. “Get some sleep, son.”

Leon and Kaly linger over the three babies snuggled in soft blankets in the crib.

"Do you really think we can take Zana home?" Kaly whispers.

"We have the space," Leon says, fighting a full grin. His heart is pounding so loud he doesn't hear the door open from the hallway.

Kaly turns and waves Danae over. "They just fell asleep again. All three woke with wet diapers."

"How did it go?" Leon asks, turning to face Itra's frown. "That good?" He raises a single eyebrow.

"I don't trust Mui," Itra states.

Danae places a hand on Itra's arm. "We need sleep." She smiles at Kaly. "Thank you for watching the littles. Can you come back down for breakfast?"

Kaly nods and takes Leon's hand. "I'll be up early in the archives researching the sundial. Come find me if you need a hand in here."

Danae nods. "Good night."

"Good night," Leon says, and winks at Kaly before they vanish from the nursery.

Itra turns for the door.

"Where are you going?" Danae asks.

"To check on Elis and Anton."

Danae sighs and leans over the crib. She gently touches each one on the nose. "He's a protective poppa bear."

Itra returns a moment later. He wraps his arms around her waist and nuzzles her neck. "Anton is snoring loud enough to raise the foundations."

Danae chuckles.

"Elis is sprawled out next to him fast asleep." He kisses her just below her ear. "Do you want to shower?"

She turns to face him. "I'll shower alone, my dear."

He kisses her nose. "I'll be here," Itra whispers.

35

The expanse of the vault's warehouse tall ceilings and never-ending row of stuff makes Avi feel tiny. She inspects the vault's art collection near the hourglass. "Enyo, these pieces and signatures are from what dimension?"

"What part of my appearance suggests art expert?" Enyo taps the hilt to her sword. She loosens one of three braids and her dark curls spring free.

Avi sighs. "What is it like in your time?"

"Peaceful most days," Enyo says, releasing the second braid.

Avi reaches a hand up to tug one of Enyo's curls.

Enyo bats her hand away.

"So you don't dress like a warrior heading to battle every day?"

"No," Enyo says, tugging out the last braid.

Avi laughs and gestures to a mirror a few steps away.

"And your sisters," Avi says, watching Enyo frown at her reflection. "Do they know how to fight like you?"

"Yes," Enyo says, finger combing the ends of her massive mane. "We were trained to protect our abilities from a young age."

"What abilities?" Avi asks, stepping into her line of sight.

"I can communicate with inanimate objects." Enyo grins at Avi's scrunched brow. "When Medusa was turned to stone, I could hear her. Same with Kaly before she was freed."

"And this?" Avi points to a miniature marble sculpture of a harp.

Enyo laughs. "If it has a soul that can speak." She walks over and plucks one of the sculpted strings.

Ping

A high note echoes through the space.

Avi plucks the same string.

Silence.

Enyo plucks two more strings.

Ping, ping

The harmony of the notes blend, matching the faint echo of the first note.

"Do you hear words or just music?" Avi asks, studying Enyo's face.

"Both," Enyo says. "Bind the line."

"That's what the harp said?" Avi asks.

Enyo nods.

"Odd," Avi says, tilting her head. "And your sisters?"

"Pemphredo can see the future through her dreams, but it's never clear when it will apply." Enyo moves away from the harp. "Deino can bring a forbidding sense of dread to a soul that crosses her path."

Avi frowns. "Note to self." She fingers her infinity charm. "Never call on Deino for assistance when in a pinch."

"Not unless your pinch needs to shake in their boots!"

Avi chuckles and studies the hourglass. The pedestal comes up to her hip and the iron swirls caging the yellowed tinted glass levels with her chest. The dark sandy like essence fills the bottom half of the hourglass.

"Do you think this vault is secure enough?" Avi asks, bending to look through the top half of the hourglass towards Enyo.

"After you and Ora were taken," Enyo says, circling the pedestal, "I question everything. Including how Chronos got in and cuffed Teuta."

"And Junior," Avi says. "Did you know about him and Teuta?"

"No." Enyo shrugs. "Not surprised, the fight over the future ember archway issue they uncovered during our last visit was full of drama."

Avi nods. "True, that was a viral worthy event."

"Viral?"

158

"It's a term when a video hits millions of views in a short amount of time."

"What's a video?"

Avi palms her forehead. "Oy!"

Enyo shrugs.

"Best explanation, um, ok… like the images you've seen in the future caverns or like tonight, with the City of Time display of the buildings and the sundial."

"There is magic like that in your time?"

Avi laughs. "More like smart phones with the ability to record."

Enyo shakes her head. "What do you do when you are not here?"

"I'm studying at a university in the city of London," Avi says. "After my visit here, I changed my thesis to ancient history with an emphasis on folklore in the Balkans." She laughs. "I'm studying you and your family."

"You mean our family," Enyo says. "You're a descendant of our line."

Avi smiles. "Hermes mentioned I look like Deino and Teuta said I am a descendant of Deino's line. Do we really resemble each other?"

"Scary identical," Enyo says. "She wears her hair down and parted in the middle like you and has the same olive complexion, oval face, and full eyebrows. Your height and slimmer curves are a dead ringer for her too."

Avi pulls her hair to the side and looks down. "It's odd because I look nothing like my parents minus our complexion. There is an old family photo we kept after my grandmother died that has an aunt that looks like me… and I guess Deino. Maybe the likeness skips a few generations."

"It's possible," Enyo says. "Xena reminds me of Pemphredo, but Kaly and Pem's likeness of each other is quite something."

Avi nods. "If it wasn't for the white stripe in Pem's hair, I wouldn't be able to tell them apart."

"Were you talking about me?" Pem asks, appearing behind Avi.

Avi jumps and bumps into the pedestal. The hourglass teeters.

Enyo dives forward to steady it in place, only knocking it further off balance. It falls to its side.

The iron cage protects the glass from shattering, but the essence inside shifts. A few granules fall through to the other side.

"Shit!" Avi squeaks.

"Uh, sorry," Pem says, stepping beside Avi.

Enyo's face goes pale, and her hands tremble over the hourglass.

"Do we just set it back up or what?" Pem asks.

"Thinking," Enyo whispers.

"Don't move it!" Teuta shouts, appearing next to Enyo.

Enyo draws her dagger in one swift move, angling the blade just below Teuta's chin.

Teuta holds up her hands and mumbles, "Just the messenger."

"Ember sent you?" Enyo asks.

"Yes," Teuta says, glancing at the hourglass.

Enyo lowers her dagger.

"The hourglass is sensitive to movement of any kind."

"What did I just do?" Avi asks.

"Tipped the balance," Teuta states, dancing nervously from foot to foot. "The urtar stone was part of Chronos. And he is trapped inside the hourglass. The dust you see is part of him and part of the urtar stone. Any granule could be a piece of the stone of judgement."

"What will happen if we move it?" Pem asks.

"You can't tip the hourglass again." Teuta takes a step towards it, but Enyo cuts her off.

"Why?" Enyo asks, raising her dagger again with her back to the hourglass.

"I didn't receive an instruction guide." Teuta puts a hand on her cocked hip. "It's your job to protect time, not mine." She smiles and vanishes.

"Damn her!" Enyo mumbles, turning to face Avi and Pem. They take a few steps away from the pedestal. Enyo points the dagger towards Pem. "Why did you pop in?"

"My mom was talking in her sleep," Pem says with a shrug. "After I woke up, I couldn't fall back to sleep. I thought I could relieve one of you from watch duty."

160

Enyo frowns.

"What time is it?" Avi asks.

"Nearly three in the morning," Xena answers, appearing next to Pem.

Avi squeaks out another curse.

"What's happened?" Xena asks, focusing on Enyo's drawn dagger.

Pem rounds her shoulders forward and stares at the floor. "I accidentally startled Avi and she bumped the pedestal holding the hourglass."

"And why is that a problem?"

Enyo moves away from the pedestal, allowing Xena to see the damage.

She rushes forward. "Is it broken?"

"No, just off balance," Enyo says.

Xena frowns and faces Enyo.

"The dust is from the urtar stone and Chronos. He had it on him."

"The literal stone of judgement," Xena whispers.

All three nod in unison.

"Will this ever be easy?"

They shake their heads.

"How do we balance it?"

"Teuta was so kind to point out that we are the protectors of time," Enyo says. "And it's our job, not hers, to answer that question."

"Damn fairy," Xena mutters.

Enyo chuckles. "My thoughts precisely."

"Avi and you should get some rest," Xena says. "We'll be no good half dead on our feet. Pem and I will keep watch and wake Kaly in a few hours to research how to balance this thing."

"Are the other ladies still here?" Avi asks.

Xena nods. "Dita and Ana agreed to stay until we permanently secure the hourglass. They will take over for us in the morning."

"Can we trust them with this?" Avi asks, biting the corner of her lip.

Pem looks up and meets Xena's worried eyes when she doesn't respond. "Mom?"

"Their family ties to Mui and Junior make me hesitant, but I believe Ana has a connection with Itra and Elis, so I trust her to keep them safe. As far as Dita is concerned, if it comes to duty before father… I'm not sure."

"Maybe Hermes and Ana?" Enyo suggests.

"Hermes has been on night watch," Pem says.

"Just go rest," Xena says, wrapping an arm around Pem's shoulders. "We can figure out the rest later."

Enyo and Avi nod and vanish from the vault.

"Why did you leave the suite?" Xena asks, squeezing Pem closer.

"You were talking in your sleep."

"I was talking to Pemphredo."

Pem looks up to meet Xena's eyes.

"At least I think that is who she was."

Pem's eyebrows knit together.

"We are going to have a visitor this afternoon or it was all just a dream."

"Who is coming?" Pem asks, stepping away to face her.

"Princess Danae."

36

Knock, knock

"Just a minute," Kaly calls out. She wiggles out from under Leon's embrace and tucks the blanket back around him. He stirs but doesn't wake. She dresses with a thought into a pair of leggings and a baggy sweater before she opens the door, stepping out, and closing it quietly behind her.

"Good morning," Xena says.

Kaly examines her aunt's puffy eyes and pale skin. "Did you sleep at all?"

"A few hours," Xena says, brushing a few stray hairs away from Kaly's brow. "We need to research the urtar stone before you dive into the sundial."

"What's happened?"

"The dust inside the hourglass is not just Chronos but the urtar stone." Xena sighs. "And it was tipped on its side a few hours ago. According to Teuta, it can't be moved until the urtar stone is balanced."

Kaly opens her mouth to speak but hesitates. Her eyes grow wide.

Xena looks behind herself, but the corridor is empty. She looks back at Kaly's frozen expression.

"What is it, Kaly?" Xena asks, touching her shoulder.

Kaly swallows. "After we left here six months ago, I did what I always do."

"Research every fine detail?"

Kaly nods. "One area I focused on was the urtar stone. Xena, if the stone of judgement is here in the castle and not intact, we are all in danger."

Xena furrows her brow.

"One of the recurring passages about the stone includes the necessity for balance."

"And if it is off balance?"

"The scale drops." Kaly blows out a breath and pulls her hair up into a high ponytail. "The only way to balance it again is with human contact."

"And if left as is?" Xena whispers.

"Think concentration camps, the great depression, plagues, but worse."

Xena takes a few steps back, the air knocked from her lungs. She gasps, trying to inhale, but panics.

Kaly pushes her to the floor. "Put your head between your knees and concentrate on slowing your heart rate." She looks up and finds Leon hovering behind her.

"What happened?" Leon asks, scanning the corridor.

"It's a panic attack," Kaly says. "Can you find Dita?"

Leon nods and jogs down the corridor. He runs in to Hermes on the stairs. "Sorry man. Have you seen Dita?"

"Dining hall. Why?"

"Xena," Leon says jogging past him towards the dining hall.

Hermes sprints up the stairs and slides to a stop beside Kaly.

"Is she ok?" Hermes whispers.

Xena inhales and coughs.

Dita and Leon race down the corridor.

Kaly and Hermes stand back, giving Dita space to examine Xena.

"Why did she have a panic attack?" Leon asks, watching Kaly's face soften as Xena stands with Dita's help.

"We need to have an emergency family meeting," Xena says. "Gather everyone in the dining hall."

37

The aroma of coffee and tea fills the air in the dining hall as they gather. Mui and Junior sit at one end with Dita, Ana and Vincent. Leon, Kaly, Itra and Hermes sit in the middle. Pem, Xena, Enyo and Avi remain standing.

Mui counts the faces in the room. "Who is watching the hourglass?"

"Teuta," Kaly answers. She nods to Xena.

"Last night, the hourglass fell on its side." Xena holds her hands up to quiet the burst of questions from Junior and Mui. She continues. "It was an accident, but we now have an issue outranking its security." Xena pauses. "The urtar stone is part of the dust inside the hourglass with Chronos, and it is now off balance."

The color drains from Ana's face. "Doomsday."

"Pardon?" Itra says, looking from Ana to Xena.

Kaly stands. "After our last visit, I researched every viable text outside of the castle about the urtar stone." She takes a breath, trying to slow her rapid speech. "Ana's comment isn't wrong. It is the fuel for conscious behavior. If the urtar stone is left off balance for long, a series of very catastrophic events could occur."

"How do you balance an urtar stone?" Itra asks, clenching and unclenching his fists.

"Human contact," Kaly says.

"If you release the stone," Dita panics, looking at Mui. "You release Chronos!"

"And this is where it gets complicated," Kaly says. "It has to be a divine—not just any human."

Avi gasps and her knees go soft.

Enyo and Pem guide her to a chair.

Avi murmurs, "No, no, no!"

"And someone inno—" Kaly chokes up.

"Innocent?" Itra finishes for her and stands. "Are you serious?"

Kaly nods and wipes a tear.

"Zana," Leon whispers, looking up at Kaly.

Kaly fights a sob. Leon pulls her down and wraps his arms around her.

"No!" Enyo protests. "If Chronos took the urtar stone, it doesn't have to be someone innocent."

"He took it as a new human," Vincent says. "Pax was a new divine, a clean slate."

Enyo sits down next to Avi.

"What will happen to Zana?" Pem asks.

Kaly unfolds from Leon's embrace. "Physically, no harm, but the burden she will carry is permanent."

"What do you mean by burden?" Itra asks.

"She will be a peacekeeper," Ana answers. "Her childhood will be short. She will be thrust into action to keep the balance of right and wrong."

"You've seen this?" Junior asks Ana.

"A version of this, yes."

"Speaking of seeing things," Xena says, shifting the glaring attention away from Ana. "We may have a visitor this afternoon." She hesitates for a breath but continues. "Princess Danae."

Hermes stands. "She's coming here?" He rolls up on his toes. "With Zeus?"

Xena shrugs. "Not sure if he is also coming."

"What does she want?" Mui asks, leaning forward, resting his elbows on the table.

"An infant," Xena whispers.

Itra curses.

"Zana?" Kaly asks.

"Pemphredo couldn't decipher the dream just that she arrives and leaves with one infant."

"It could be a good thing," Hermes says. "The day I met Leon and Danae in the hedge maze, I saw Danae's reflection in the bronze mirror shield with a crown." He chuckles, looking at Leon. "I know that you two are descendants of Zeus through Perseus. If she is coming here, that could only mean one thing." He grins and pauses, holding out his arms. He searches the blank stares.

No one answers.

He continues. "Protection."

Nearly everyone shakes their head except Enyo.

"Explain," Enyo says.

"She protected Perseus from her father. If a child is in danger or needs assistance, she is exactly who I would call."

"Did you call her?" Mui asks.

Hermes shakes his head. "No, I haven't returned home."

"We can ask her if she arrives," Xena says. "First things first. How do we remove the urtar stone without releasing Chronos?"

Ana stands. "We don't."

"What have you seen?" Itra asks, meeting her eyes.

Her lips tighten in a straight line. "Zana goes in the hourglass with Chronos."

"Are you insane?" Leon shouts, kicking his chair back.

Ana flinches.

"Is it the only way to keep him in and achieve balance?" Vincent asks.

Ana nods.

"Why are we even discussing this?" Leon asks. "This is not an option."

"Well then," Ana says, scooting her chair in and walking to the conservatory door. "You can come up with another idea because I am only telling you what I see."

"Fine!" Leon shakes his head. "Kaly, can you help?" He extends his hand to her.

She takes his hand and stands.

"We'll be in the archives until we find an alternative," Kaly says, before vanishing with Leon.

"One last question," Itra says. "Where is the keeper's cuff at present?"

Mui and Junior stare at each other.

Vincent laughs. "Is it in the hourglass too?"

Junior nods. "I know he had it on him right before he and Enyo fought near the vault." He looks towards Enyo.

She holds up her hands. "I never saw it."

"Then I believe I can speak for Danae and myself," Itra says, straightening his posture, "when I say there will be no plan that includes any of the children, ever." He vanishes from the dining hall.

Xena, Enyo, Pem and Avi nod to Hermes and Vincent before heading to the war room.

"That's how your family resolves an issue?" Dita asks before the ladies exit. "You state your thoughts and run?"

Xena turns to face Dita, standing at the table with her arms crossed. Enyo pulls her sword.

Xena puts her arm out to stop the action as Junior and Mui stand.

"We are not running from anything," Xena says, keeping her tone level. "We are seeking an alternative solution." She gestures to the table. "And you? What are you doing?"

Dita stiffens. "We remain at this table until we can agree on a solution."

"Our options at the moment aren't solutions," Avi says, pushing her way past Xena. "They are barbaric. It may be ok in your time to sacrifice a child for the common good, but we grew a conscious in the last three hundred years."

"I never…," Dita whispers, going pale. "… I would never harm a child. Or anyone. I'm a healer."

"Tell that to Elis," Pem snaps. She throws open the door to the Zeus family war room and marches through.

The ladies follow her.

When the doors close behind them, Xena pulls on Pem's arm. "You realize Dita has healed me twice and Ana too, since we arrived."

Pem shrugs off Xena's hand.

"She is not the enemy," Xena reiterates.

"I know," Pem says, scuffing her shoe on the floor.

"Then why throw her under the bus like that?"

168

"I snapped, I'm sorry."

Xena puts a finger under Pem's chin and tilts her head up so their eyes meet. "It's not me who should hear the apology."

Vincent steps into the room and raises a hand. "Hermes needs to sleep, and I want to help Kaly with the archives. Does that leave anyone available to patrol the grounds?"

"Make them do it," Enyo says, gesturing to the doorway leading to the dining hall.

Vincent chuckles. "Junior volunteered, but I think it would be best if we monitored him and Mui until the keeper's cuff is no longer a threat."

"Check with Leon," Xena suggests. "I'm almost certain he needs to blow off some steam and stalking Junior may just do the trick."

Vincent nods and vanishes.

Hermes salutes and lopes over to the stairwell.

"Do you want us to wake you if the princess arrives?" Avi asks.

Hermes pauses, foot raised over the first step, and nods.

"Xena, you and Pem should try to sleep a few hours." Avi nods her head to the stairwell. "Enyo and I will go to the vault."

"I make zero promises on sleep but will attempt, too." Xena tugs on Pem's arm.

Pem resists. "I need to burn off some energy."

Enyo tilts her chin up. "Go run the arrows loop."

Pem cocks her head in question.

"The top floor above Mui's suites before the glass turret. The stones are worn and easy to run on."

Pem nods. "Great, thanks."

Xena purses her lips. "You sure?"

Pem pats Xena's shoulder. "Yes, mother." She winks and jogs out of the war room.

Xena sighs and looks back at Avi and Enyo. "Wake me if you need anything at all."

Itra rounds the corner of the stacks and finds a high ponytail peeking out from the top of a large pile of books.

"Kaly?" Itra says.

"Just a second," Kaly says, holding up a hand. "Is Vincent with you?"

"I'm here," Vincent says, coming out of the stacks across from Itra.

"Great, look at this." Kaly stands and hands him an open book. She turns around to face Itra. "Where's Leon?"

"Babysitting Junior on watch duty," Vincent says without looking up from the page.

"I have one other note to add to the research list," Itra says. "They think the keeper's cuff is inside the hourglass with Chronos and the urtar stone."

Kaly goes pale and dives for a book on the chair next to her. She mumbles and thumbs through the book. "Trifecta."

Vincent looks up from the book and gapes at Kaly.

"What does that mean?" Itra asks.

"Three gifted babies, three great powers, all inside the castle." Kaly shoves the book at Itra. "Balance!"

"Explain," Itra says, looking at the text with an illustration of a gold scale.

"We have the compass plus time, equaling three." Kaly states, now pacing between Vincent and Itra. "And the hourglass has Chronos, the urtar stone, and the keeper's cuff. Three for three!"

"Hold up." Itra sets the book down. "You said inside the castle."

Kaly stops mid pace and frowns. "As long as they and the hourglass remain here, the catastrophic event threat is basically zero."

"Great theory," Vincent says, shaking his head. "But we have no way of knowing if the cuff is actually inside."

Itra shakes his head. "Mui and Junior said last night that their mark is no longer a threat as long as Chronos stays inside."

"The keeper's cuff mark is an infinite bond to the owner's will, but the actual cuff is still a physical object." Kaly states, tightening her ponytail. "Unlike the key."

"I'm still not clear on how one takes possession of the cuff as the keeper," Itra says.

A book from the pile next to Kaly slides out and opens.

"A keeper must give to possess the essence of the cuff and control those who behold." Kaly looks up from the text. "Give what?" The pages flip to a detailed illustration of the cuff. She thought provokes a magnify glass and holds it over the captions. She looks up with a grin. "Take a look."

Itra bends over the page reading the caption above a pointed tip on a gold embellishment. "Drip the line with divine." He looks up and repeats. "Drip the line with divine."

Vincent nods. "Divine in this case is blood." He snaps the book shut. "If we can find the cuff without marking ourselves, we can create a new keeper."

"Did you translate the text?" Kaly asks, pointing to the book in Vincent's grip.

"The divine you mentioned from your research of the urtar stone is also mentioned in this text." Vincent raises the book. "But the transfer from dust to stone to divine might be impossible."

Kaly gapes at Vincent.

"The urtar stone is like your feathered-cloaks. It vanishes on contact with a person but is still present." Vincent looks down at the book. "But unlike the cloaks, it's not taken off but created again by the person carrying the burden."

"You're saying it has to be created by Chronos?" Itra asks.

"Yes, according to the text here," Vincent says, handing the book back to Kaly.

"Will the shield we used to return Kaly back from stone work in reverse?" Itra asks.

Vincent claps and smiles.

Kaly ducks as a book with the bronze shield on the cover flies just over her head and hovers in front of Itra. He takes the book and shrugs at Kaly's frown.

"Sorry," Itra says with a smile. He stares down at the book. "Show me answers."

The book opens and the pages flip to an illustration of the bronze shield and a drawing of the mirror. A small caption is written between the two. Kaly looks over his shoulder and places the magnify glass over the text.

Itra reads it aloud. "To see the truth of what's inside, reflect or hide, a truth to breathe or thoughts to die. Or a shield will decide." He sighs. "Is anyone else ready to never hear or see another rhyming phrase?"

Vincent chuckles. "I find them elegant and whimsical."

Itra flares his nostrils and frowns.

Vincent laughs.

Itra gives the book to Kaly and sits down. "I just want answers, not more damn riddles."

Kaly turns the page to inspect a new passage. She scans the text and frowns. "It's written backwards."

Vincent looks over her shoulder. "We need a mirror to read it."

Kaly looks up from the page and pats his cheek. "And here I thought you could translate any language."

Vincent laughs again. "I could, but why take the fun away from the author that spent the time writing this to only display in a mirror?"

"I need to check on Danae and the babies," Itra says, standing and nodding towards the suite. "You can use the mirror in the hall bath." He pats his stomach. "I'm ordering breakfast."

Kaly smiles and nudges Vincent to follow Itra to the suite.

"I could eat," Vincent says.

Elis is licking the syrup off of a plate next to a stack of empty ones at the table in the corner.

"Did you order and eat all of those?" Itra asks, counting seven plates.

Elis lowers the plate and grins. "Almost. Dad had two."

Itra leans over and kisses his hair. "When is the last time you showered?"

Elis frowns. "I don't know."

"It's time!" Itra says, wrinkling his nose. "Bath or shower?"

"Bath. No wait, shower!" Elis says, jumping from the chair and bolting towards the washroom. He skids to a stop at the open door. Kaly and Vincent are standing there, holding a book up to the mirror. "What are you doing?"

"Kaly is reading the text on the page." Vincent glances over his shoulder to look at Elis. "The person wrote it backwards. Do you want to see it?"

Elis nods.

Vincent bends and picks him up. "Ugh! How much did you eat?"

Elis laughs and pats his belly. "So much!"

Kaly turns the book for Elis to see the text.

"I can't read it," Elis says, frowning.

Kaly moves the page closer to the mirror.

Elis leans over the book, still looking at the page.

Kaly taps the mirror.

His eyes freeze on the text in the mirror. "Wow."

"Pretty cool, right?" Kaly asks, watching his eyes dance over the text.

"A window to those who seek," Elis reads.

"Very good," Vincent says, giving him a squeeze before setting him down.

Elis stands on his tiptoes. "What does the rest of it say?"

"A window to those who seek, a peek to find the truth inside, is a divine to your regal line." Kaly looks past the text and notices

Danae's reflection with Itra and pauses. She turns to face her, but Danae is gone. Itra is standing alone.

"What's wrong?" Itra asks, watching Kaly's smile fall to a frown.

"I just saw Danae standing next to you," Kaly says, handing the book to Vincent. She sticks her head out the door and inspects the hallway.

"She's nursing Emit at the moment," Itra says.

"Odd," Kaly says. She turns back to Vincent. "Did you see her?"

Vincent shakes his head. "Sorry dear."

Elis starts for the door.

"Oh no," Itra says, blocking his exit. "You need to shower, remember?"

Elis groans.

Anton walks down the hall from the nursery with a baby. "Did you say shower?"

Itra nods.

"Good," Anton says. "I can take care of it and clean up after him."

"But dad!" Elis pleads.

"But nothing," Anton says, handing Itra the baby. "Your uncle even noticed how bad you smell. It is time!"

Ora wiggles in Itra's arm. He snuggles her closer.

Vincent and Kaly file out of the washroom.

Anton closes the door, softening the whining from Elis.

Kaly and Vincent laugh and walk to the table.

The dirty plates vanish, and several new platters appear with sliced fruits, cheese, dried meats, jams, and bread. A pot of coffee and three mugs appear last.

Kaly pulls out a chair but looks back at Itra. He is still standing in the hallway, gazing at the baby.

"Itra?" Kaly asks. "You good?"

He swallows a lump in his throat and sucks in a breath. He doesn't take his eyes off Ora. "What if they take her again?"

Kaly walks over to him. "We will tread carefully and make sure we know the outcome before acting. I promise."

174

39

"Were you tapping on the glass?" Avi asks.

Teuta twirls to face Avi.

"How long have you been standing there?" Teuta bounces from foot to foot.

"Long enough to watch you tap on the glass." Avi folds her arms across her chest and raises an eyebrow.

"Well then, why did you ask?" Teuta tilts her chin up.

"Seriously?" Enyo says from behind Teuta.

Teuta jumps several feet in the air.

Avi barks out a laugh, pulling Teuta towards her. They stumble away from the artifact.

"You two are sneaky!" Teuta huffs out a short breath. She places her hand over her heart. "What has happened?"

"You mean the family meeting?" Avi asks.

"Just more layers of doom and gloom." Enyo bends to inspect the hourglass. "Did you try to move this while we were gone?"

Teuta straightens. "Absolutely not." She walks closer and points. "There are words printed on the glass. And I wasn't tapping it. I was trying to clean it to see what it said."

Avi and Enyo lean over the hourglass and follow Teuta's finger over the loopy text. Avi stands and looks around the vault. "Do you think there is a blue light down here?"

Teuta's light stone turns blue.

"Great!" Avi opens her hand, and her light stone falls dark and into her palm. "Enyo, drop your light, too."

Enyo opens her hand. Her stone fades and drops into her palm. The vault falls dark, besides the dim glow of Teuta's stone.

Avi nudges Teuta. "Bring your light closer to the hourglass."

Teuta steps closer and drops the light directly over it.

Avi tilts her head, attempting to make out the text as it slowly lights up letter by letter in a purple hue.

"Bind my line with thine time." Enyo reads, tossing her light stone back up.

The room shifts back to a normal daylight hue and the text vanishes again.

"How did you know it would light up like that?" Enyo asks.

"I think I saw it in a movie once," Avi says.

Enyo shakes her head. "Odd."

Teuta paces away from them, mumbling.

"Do the words etched in the glass mean anything?" Avi asks, looking from Enyo to Teuta.

Teuta marches back towards them and stops. "Ember used this to trap him, right?"

Enyo and Avi shrug.

"If she did, there is a reason," Teuta says, pointing up. "Otherwise, she could have banished him back to the helix."

"She did that?" Enyo asks.

"Who else has that kind of power?" Teuta asks, looking Enyo up and down.

"No, I'm just surprised she didn't banish him further away. Fort Kelmend isn't that far."

"Keep your friends close and your enemies closer," Teuta says. She twirls and vanishes.

Avi laughs. "If I wrote a tell-all book about this place, I would either end up famous or locked up for psychosis."

Enyo rolls her eyes. "Are you good here alone for a minute?"

Avi nods.

"I'm going to relay the etched message to Kaly and Vincent." Enyo steps back away from the pedestal and vanishes.

"Or you could just tell her with a thought," Avi says to no one. She spins in a slow circle. Her eyes wander up past the full pallets stacked at least thirty high over to the large tanks and airplanes on the far side of the endless space.

176

"Alone in a giant vault."

She smirks and walks over to the stone harp. She plucks a few of the sculpted strings before checking out the shields in the glass cases. She recoils at the three-dimensional snakes on the Medusa shield. She stops in front of the bronze shield that Xena, Enyo, and Noel recovered.

"Leon, any word if Noel will join us?"

"Avi?"

"Yes."

"I thought you were in the vault."

"I am."

"How did you know that my doppelganger just arrived?"

"I didn't know that Noel was here."

"Hmm, ok. I can relay the message that you would like to see him."

Avi's cheeks redden. *"No need."*

Enyo appears next to Avi. "Are you blushing?"

"No!" Avi says, frowning at Enyo. "What did they say about the message?"

"They have an interesting theory," Enyo says, pointing to the bronze shield in front of them. "They think this shield may uncover what is actually inside the hourglass."

"Really?" Avi walks towards the shield.

"Hold on," Enyo says, standing between Avi and the shield. "Kaly promised Itra we wouldn't try or do anything until we were sure of the outcome while the children are here."

Avi nods. "We are proceeding with caution and not jumping knee deep before asking, cool."

Enyo laughs. "You have some interesting phrases."

"Leon said Noel just arrived. Do you know if anyone else is here?"

Enyo furrows her brow. "Noel? The one that looks like Leon."

Avi nods.

"He's less of a brute than Leon." Enyo smiles. "What dimension was he from?"

"Ottoman." Avi states. "Do you think there is anything down here from your time?"

Enyo laughs. "You just changed the subject."

Avi turns away from her, focusing on a few old chests.

"There is likely something down here from every time." Enyo turns in a slow circle. "What do you call this thing?" She walks over to a white metal object with wheels.

"A car," Avi says. "Although, this make and model must be from a different dimension. I don't recognize the T on the front."

"Interesting. And what does your dimension call that?" Enyo points to a gold sculpture.

"A scale," Avi says, admiring the craftsmanship. A gold rod at the center curves out to balance two gold half domes hanging from three small gold rods.

Avi leans over the domes and spots a tiny inscription visible inside the half domes. "Do you recognize these symbols?" She waves Enyo over and points down.

Enyo squints and touches the half dome to tilt it forward and freezes.

Avi frowns. "What's wrong?"

Enyo doesn't respond or blink.

"Enyo?" Avi snaps her fingers in front of her.

Enyo remains frozen with a blank stare.

Avi pulls Enyo's hand away from the scale.

Enyo exhales and blinks when the dome swings away.

"What in the hell?" Avi asks, checking Enyo's eyes and hand.

"The inscription is Illyrian symbols for end and time," Enyo says, rubbing her fingers. "When I touched the dome, my vision faded to darkness."

Avi steps away from the scale. "I think that is enough curious exploration of the items down here."

"Hints why they are locked away from the world," Enyo says, backing away from the scale. She shakes her head. "Are you ready to hear what the scale said?"

"It spoke to you?" Avi whirls to face Enyo.

"Yes, its name is Anubis," Enyo says, biting the inside of her cheek.

Avi's mouth falls open.

"You recognize the name?" Enyo asks.

"In ancient Egyptian mythology, he's the god of death, a man with a dog's head. But in Greek mythology, he is a guardian of the tomb."

"That makes his message a little darker." Enyo pulls out her dagger and tosses it from hand to hand.

"What did he say?" Avi asks.

"Stack the stone against your own," Enyo recites. "A compass to guide is near inside. To begin again or tip the end. You must decide."

"Elis," Avi whispers.

Enyo nods. "I'll go warn Itra and Anton." She vanishes.

40

Enyo lands in the center of the archives. She listens for any movement. *It's quiet, too quiet.*

She rushes through the stacks to the archive suite. The door is open. She pulls her sword and charges in.

The furniture is overturned.

She sprints down the hall and pounds on Itra and Danae's bedroom door.

"Danae! Itra!"

She twists the handle and shoulders the door. It flies open. The bed is tossed, pieces of shredded fabric still hanging in the air, pillows are torn open and tossed on the floor, and the rocking chair is smashed on its side. She checks the washroom and the entry to the nursery. All are vacant but in complete disarray.

She runs out of the nursery and shoulders open the other bedroom door. It's intact but vacant.

"Wake up!" Enyo shakes Xena.

Xena's eyes fly open. She quickly sits up, barely missing Enyo's head hovering near hers.

"What's wrong?" Xena says, massaging her neck. She clears her throat and swings her legs over the edge of the bed.

"Chaos!" Enyo says, gripping her arm.

Avi jumps back when Enyo and Xena land beside her in the vault.

"A little warn…" Avi says but stops, looking Enyo over. "What's happened?"

"The archive suite looks like a battleground."

"What do you mean?" Xena asks.

"The archive suite door was open," Enyo shakes her head. "The suite was trashed."

"Pem!" Xena paces, waiting for a response.

"Mom, you're safe?" Pem answers.

Xena swallows. *"Yes, come to the vault!"*

"A little busy," Pem says. *"With decaying fairies!"*

"Shit!" Xena grabs Enyo's arm and reaches for Avi. "The damn fairies are here!"

Avi holds her amulet and conjures the soul of Deino. Deino appears to Avi's left. She nods to her and gestures to the hourglass. Deino smiles and nods in return.

Avi takes Xena's hand.

Xena tightens her grip on Avi and Enyo and they disappear.

"Noel, can you shield Pem and Ana until I return?" Leon asks.

Noel glances over his shoulder as Leon swipes his scythe through three charging fairies. They vanish to dust.

Leon looks back. Noel nods.

Leon sprints through the conservatory to the main foyer. He curses, looking out over the clearing. It's full of mangled fairies running towards the castle.

Junior and Mui are back-to-back on the first step, fending off the attack of a dozen seething grey faced creatures.

Leon's spine tingles. He rolls to his toes and charges out, closing the castle doors with a thought on his exit.

The whoosh of air and loud crash of the door slamming shut startles the fairies surrounding Junior and Mui long enough for Leon to swing through half of them.

Junior and Mui react and cut through the others.

Leon pushes past Mui and shoves Junior. "Stay back and close your eyes!" He taps his staff back to the ember glow. He mumbles, "Cheer's to winging it."

Leon balances on the edge of the bottom step. He closes his eyes and lowers the ember glow to the clearing. "Burn!"

A burst of hot air pushes him back.

A shrieking chorus roars in unison.

Leon winces and slowly opens his eyes to inspect the damage. The clearing is vacant of life under the clear sky. The sun at its peak erasing any shadows.

"What sorcery was that?" Mui asks, extending a hand to Leon.

"Ember's gift," Leon says, taking his hand and standing. "We need to ensure the castle is clear. Are you coming?"

Junior bends to inspect a pile of dust. "I need to check how they breached the archways. Dad, go with Leon."

The castle door opens behind them.

The men turn, weapons raised.

Enyo points her blades down at them, flanked by Avi and Xena. "What did you morons do?"

Leon frowns. "Saved the castle. You?"

Enyo shakes her head. "Where are Itra and Danae?"

"In the archive suite," Leon says, climbing up the steps.

"Wrong!" Enyo twirls her sword into a defensive stance.

Leon stumbles, catching his toe on the last step. "What?"

"The suite was attacked. It's vacant."

Leon's face falls and his red cheeks pale. "Kaly and the children?"

"Gone!" Enyo presses the tip of her sword to his chest. "How could you let anyone in? Weren't you on watch duty with that fool?" She points her dagger at Junior.

"They appeared all at once," Junior says from the bottom step. "We had no time to cut them off."

"You idiots!" Enyo shakes her head. "Fairies use glamor to shield their appearance. They were the distraction while someone attacked the suite. Why didn't you send anyone to the suite to check?"

"Mom!" Pem rushes past Noel to Xena.

"We need to find the others," Xena says, hugging her close. "Where is Dita?" She looks past Noel and Ana.

Pem leans back to face Xena. "I haven't seen Dita since the dining hall." She turns to face Ana. "You?"

"Same," Ana answers. "Not since I left the dining hall this morning."

Hermes appears beside Leon, hair shifted to one side and a sheet line crease on his cheek. "Did I hear somebody scream?"

41

"Danae," Itra whispers, blinking in the darkness. He struggles to sit up and pats the surface beneath him. Sand falls through his fingers. He scrambles up and hits his head.

"Danae!"

He crouches low and extends his hands out in all directions. His eyes slowly adjust to the darkness. He makes out the staggered stones on a wall a foot away. He turns and finds another wall. He reaches back, feeling the resistance of a third wall.

"No, no, no!"

He quickly pats the wall and finds an opening. He creeps forward and stubs his toe. He reaches down and feels a step. He follows the smooth stone up and finds another.

"Stairs from hell?"

He climbs the steps, and the air above his head chills his scalp.

"Anton! Vincent!"

His voice echoes back, making him pause and shake his head.

"Can anyone hear me? Anyone!"

The echo of his call sends a prickle of fear up his spine. He climbs up faster and the space widens above his head after a few minutes. He straightens from his crouch and stretches his back. He counts the steps from that point, but gives up when he reaches fifty.

"Why would Ember send me here?"

Itra starts his ascent again, skipping up two at a time. He pauses, catches his breath. A bright glow fills the stairwell. He feels the air go from cool to hot in an instant. A shriek roars down from above.

Itra covers his ears and shrinks down on a step.

"Hey there, don't cry," Kaly coos, staring down at Zana. She bounces the baby against her chest.

Zana quiets to a sniffle. Kaly looks up and takes in the space for the first time. The cave opening appears a few paces ahead. She carefully steps over a few large cracks to the ledge. *Where am I?*

The sun glistens over the lake below. Her eyes follow a large crane lifting off from the shore. A loud cry from above fills the air. Kaly cowers back away from the edge and covers her and Zana's ears.

Zana goes still, and her eyes go wide. A large shadow falls over them, darkening the cave.

Kaly straightens and backs further away as an usmu wing covers the opening. It slowly turns, exposing the rider.

Kaly recognizes Prende from Avi's description.

"What have you done?" Kaly asks.

"Me?" Prende says, placing a hand to her chest. "I'm only here to save you and Zana, of course."

"Save us?" Kaly covers Zana and holds her tighter. "You're the reason we are in danger!"

"Why would I ever harm my own child?" Prende twirls a piece of her long hair. "Come along, we have little time."

"No, ma'am. I don't trust you or that thing."

Prende raises an eyebrow and flexes her hand around the reins.

Kaly turns and darts around a few stalagmites.

"Stop!" Prende's shrill voice echoes all around.

Kaly hops over several large crevices and stops at the edge of a dark pit. She spins around and loses her balance. She teeters, flailing out with her free arm.

A large hand grasps her arm and steadies her away from the edge.

She exhales and turns to face a door. She hops through and into the arms of Leon.

"Are you hurt?" Leon asks, patting her and Zana down.

"No," Kaly says, catching her breath. "Prende, she was there."

Xena follows a dark shadow near the horizon. "And so were her pets. Everyone inside the castle, now!"

The caw of an usmu echoes down the stairwells near the front foyer. Junior and Mui make it inside just before the front entrance slams shut and the iron bar lifts into place.

"Go to the war room!" Leon commands.

Enyo thrusts her dagger's hilt at Xena. "Protect the vault with Avi and Pem."

Xena nods and takes the dagger. The three of them vanish in a blink.

Noel takes the lead.

They jog from the entrance foyer. The pinging of beaks on the tinted glass overhead makes them duck in alarm and the shadows waver as the flying beasts block the sun, darkening the path through the plants.

Enyo and Leon move back-to-back. He double taps his staff to the scythe, following Ana, Hermes, and Kaly, who shields Zana. Junior and Mui are not far behind them.

Noel opens the dining hall door hidden behind the climbing vines. He hesitates, inspecting the hall, and motions for the others to follow.

Enyo pulls her sword out when Mui and Junior quicken their pace.

They file in, but the door slams shut before Junior and Mui can enter.

An ember glow seals the door.

"I think they're no longer in control of their own free will," Enyo comments as Leon attempts to open the door. *"Avi, is the hourglass still intact?"*

"Yes, why?" Avi answers, inspecting the hourglass on the pedestal.

"Ember just sealed us in the dining hall away from Mui and Junior."

Avi curses and relays the message to Xena and Pem.

"What does it mean?" Enyo says to Kaly.

"We were wrong," Kaly says. "Chronos isn't the owner of the keeper's cuff."

43

Danae pulls Ora and Emit closer, taking in her bedroom.

"We're home!" She fumbles the knob on the bedroom door. "Itra, a little help here." She finally twists and pulls the door open. "Itra?"

She wanders through the house, checking their converted guest bedroom turned nursery, the kitchen, living room, and bathroom. She sighs and opens the front door.

The front porch is blinding in the warm afternoon sun. She squints past the brightness and looks out over the vineyard.

"Itra!"

Ora squirms. Danae snuggles her closer.

"Hungry?" Danae whispers. "Hopefully, your dad will come home soon."

Ora coos in response as Danae walks back into the nursery.

Danae lays Emit down in the crib and sits in the soft rocker. She positions Ora, stroking the side of her cheek until she latches.

"Do you recall how we got home from the castle?" Danae asks, admiring Ora's long, dark eyelashes. She rocks back but freezes. Her hair rises along her arms. She searches the room for anything hard.

Knock, knock

Danae covers her chest and Ora with a blanket. "Who is it?"

"A friend."

A woman?

The woman cracks open the door.

Danae's face falls into a deep grimace. She stares at the strangely familiar face and her eyes fall to the gold and ruby embellishments under the bust of a blue silk gown.

"I apologize for my delay," the woman says.

Danae tilts her head, trying to place the accent of the woman. "And you are?"

The woman bows low in a curtsy. "My full title is Princess Roslyn Danae. You may call me Roslyn."

"Roslyn." Danae blinks and laughs. "Seriously?"

A shiny gold wreath with rubies appears on top of her brown curls as she straightens. She nods with a grin.

Danae's jaw falls open.

"My son only received the message from Ember this morning," Roslyn says. "I came as soon as I could. The children and your safety are of grave concern. The danger you face could be catastrophic."

Danae closes her mouth and swallows. "Where is Itra?"

"Safe."

Danae shakes her head. "Safe where?"

"Out of reach."

Danae stares her down.

Roslyn's face remains neutral.

"Anton and Elis?"

Roslyn tucks in her chin and glances at the floor. "We've hidden the compass."

"Hidden where?" Danae stiffens.

"With Perseus."

"Safe from harm?" Danae asks.

"Yes."

"And Anton, his father?"

"Safe at home." Roslyn smiles.

"Kaly and Zana?" Danae shifts Ora to her other arm.

Roslyn's smile falls flat. "I don't know their fate."

Danae's voice shakes. "And Vincent?"

"Not sure."

Danae adjusts her top. She raises Ora to her shoulder and gently pats her back. "Why were we ejected from the castle?"

"The archive suite was compromised."

190

Emit lets out a sharp cry.

"May I hold him?" Roslyn gestures towards the crib.

Danae stands, adjusting Ora. She puts herself between Roslyn and the crib. "Can you show me your forearms?" She reaches in the crib and strokes his soft head, soothing Emit.

Roslyn raises an eyebrow. "The rumor of the keeper's cuff is true?" She raises both arms and tilts her wrists from side to side.

The skin is tan but unmarked.

"What rumors?" Danae hesitantly moves aside, allowing Roslyn to bend over the crib and pick up Emit.

"Pemphredo, a grey sister, had a vision of the keeper's cuff impacting the alliance with the return of Prende."

"Prende?" Danae's eyes go wide. "She is the owner of the cuff?"

Roslyn nods, but doesn't look up from Emit. "Does he look like Itra?"

"Yes," Danae answers, still turning over the idea of Prende as the keeper. "Are you sure Chronos isn't the keeper?"

"He couldn't be a keeper, he isn't human." Roslyn meets Danae's eyes.

Danae frowns. "But isn't Prende a goddess?"

"Ha, ha. In some folklore, yes. But she is mortal and therefore human."

Danae shakes her head. "Why would Teuta and Junior say that Chronos cuffed them?"

"Because like Zeus, he too had an alliance."

"With Prende?" Danae's pulse pounds, deafening her ears.

Roslyn's head bobs, and Danae's vision goes dark.

44

Itra climbs the final five steps and falls to the ground. He closes his eyes, his vision still spotty from the invasion of the blinding light in the stairwell. He takes in a big breath, attempting to slow his racing heart by slowly exhaling. He repeats his breathing but feels a hand press on his shoulder.

He rolls away and stands. He blinks twice at his childhood best friend dressed in uniform.

"Ermal?" Itra says, his voice husky.

Ermal nods and hands Itra a canteen. His face is covered with a three-day-old beard.

Itra swallows three large sips and wipes his mouth.

"Why are you here?" Itra asks, handing him back the water.

"Really?" Ermal laughs. "Twins go missing at a birthing center right after I get a long message from Danae that Elis is missing. And then you two vanish along with Anton. Where else would I go when people vanish or weird shit happens?"

Itra turns around, taking in his surroundings for the first time. He spots the archway and the large boulder a few feet away where the path bends. He shakes his head.

"Do you want to explain why I just watched you crawl up out of the ground?" Ermal asks.

Itra looks down and spins in a slow circle. *The stairwell is gone.* He laughs. "Do you recall Danae's experience with the steps from hell?"

Ermal frowns and his eyes widen.

"Well, she isn't making it up." Itra places a hand on Ermal's shoulder. "Can you call our land line?"

Ermal laughs. "Who has a land line these days?"

"We do after replacing several useless cell phones in the last six months." Itra nods to the archway. "And with the babies we wanted to call or be called without depending on scrambled phones."

Ermal hands him his phone. "It's only got a little juice, so it may die soon."

Itra dials their number and hits call. It rings three times.

"Hello?" a voice answers.

Itra holds the phone out to look at the number. *It's correct.*

"Danae, are you ok?"

"Is this Itra?"

The woman's accented voice is clear, but it is definitely not his wife.

"Is my wife there?" Itra says, looking at Ermal's radio clipped to his shoulder.

Ermal nods and steps away.

"She is but resting at the moment."

Itra's hand trembles. He tightens his grip on the phone.

"Wake her up, it's important!"

He hears the faint ping, a warning that the battery is low, before the phone lights up and powers down. He jogs over to Ermal.

"I have a unit heading over now to do a wellness check," Ermal says, taking the dead phone from Itra.

Ermal continues. "The dispatcher called your neighbor, Franc. He said there were no vehicles onsite, but a light was on inside. He offered to check but we declined until the officer clears the house."

"I don't know who answered. Her accent…" Itra says, shaking his head. "It was familiar, almost ancient, like Hermes." He turns to the archway. "I'll be right back!"

"Wait!" Ermal calls out, but Itra doesn't pause before he ducks under the archway. "Be careful!" Ermal takes a long swig from the canteen and shoulders his pack.

His radio crackles. "Ten one, ten eighty-four, ten ninety u. Permission to breach."

"Ten four," Ermal responds. "Granted." He chews on the inside of his lip and paces back and forth.

"Ten one," the officer calls.

"Ten four," Ermal responds.

"Home is vacant, light on in the nursery. No sign of a struggle or disturbance. The phone is off the hook in the kitchen."

"Ten four," Ermal answers. "Check with the neighbor for any movement since the first call."

"Ten six."

Itra sprints back under the archway.

Ermal nearly draws his pistol. "You should know better than to surprise me by now."

Itra shakes his head and sucks in a big breath. "The castle is gone!"

45

"What do you mean, gone?" Ermal asks, dropping his pack and placing his hands on Itra's shoulders.

"I ran under," Itra says, sucking in a breath. He points to the archway. "It's just the clearing. I check the other archways and it's the same. No castle!"

"You were cut off?" Ermal asks, looking over Itra's shoulder. The once warm ember glow of the archway is void of any color. He shakes his head. "Man, your house is empty."

Itra's knees buckle and Ermal helps lower him to the ground.

"What?" he whispers.

Ermal sits down and leans against his pack, facing him. "When my officer arrived, the gate was locked. I gave him permission to enter. He inspected the house and found a light on in the nursery and the phone off the hook in the kitchen, but no signs of a struggle or major disturbance."

"Ten one," the officer calls.

Ermal taps the radio. "Go ahead."

"The neighbor had eyes on the house since the call from dispatch. No sighting of anyone but myself entering and exiting the house. But he mentioned a flash of light, like a camera, inside the home moments before I arrived."

Itra's frown deepens.

"Ten four," Ermal responds. "Officer ten ninety-seven."

"Ten four."

The crackle of the radio goes silent.

"Can you tell me what happened in there?" Ermal asks, lifting his chin to the archway.

"Teuta took the twins from the birthing center. Danae used her gold ring to follow the twins to the archive suite. We have been there ever since. There has been a mess of mishaps since we arrived. But Elis was recovered from the ancient City of Time."

"Elis is safe?" Ermal asks.

"He was."

Ermal opens his mouth to ask another question, but Itra shakes his head.

"Anton and Elis were in the living room of the archive suite with Kaly, Vincent, and Zana."

"Wait, when did Kaly and Vincent arrive?" Ermal's brow furrows.

"Kaly and Leon came to help Anton when Danae went into labor and Elis was missing. Vincent came to help this morning."

"And you said someone else, Zana?" Ermal asks. "One of the grey sisters?"

"A changeling baby recovered after my daughter, Ora, was taken and held by the fairies."

Ermal clasps a hand over his own mouth.

Itra's bottom lip quivers. "We recovered, Ora, but now I don't know. It all happened so fast."

"Try to recall the events leading up to you being here." Ermal leans forward.

Itra nods and bites down on his bottom lip. "I was helping Danae with the twins in the nursery and there was a loud crash and shouting coming from the living room." Itra pounds a fist to the ground. "I wasn't thinking, just reacting. I shoved Emit and Ora into Danae's arms and got them to the large mirror in the bedroom." Itra pauses at Ermal's raised hand. "It's an exit only portal Gjeto showed me when Danae was taken to the suite the first time." Ermal nods. "I opened it and she stepped through just before the door to our room burst open. The glass of the mirror shattered when the rocking chair smashed against it. I ducked and ran to the bathroom. I locked the door but the air outside was heaving like a tornado was inside the suite." Itra stands. "One minute I was placing all of my weight against the door and the next I was on my knees at the bottom of the steps."

Ermal stands. "And the others?"

"I honestly have no clue."

"Let's assume Ember ejected you for safety," Ermal says. "The others may be safe, too."

"Dita, where are you?" Ana asks, watching Noel, Leon and Enyo try every door in the dining hall, but they are all sealed shut except one. "Thanks Ember."

"Why are you thanking her?" Kaly asks, gently rocking Zana in her arms.

"She left us access to the washrooms at least." Ana nods towards the only open door. *"Dita!"*

"Stop yelling!" Dita responds. *"I am working on Vincent. He's injured."*

"Where are you?" Ana asks. *"How serious are his injuries?"*

"Ivan's study and he is nearly stable. He had a large cut and lump on his head when he appeared in here."

"Ember has sealed us in the dining hall. The usmu and Prende are attacking the castle and your brother and father are no longer in control of their own free will."

Hermes lands after inspecting the dome. He tilts his head and frowns, watching Ana's frown deepen. He nudges Kaly.

Kaly furrows her brows. "Ana, what do you see?"

Ana shakes her head. "It's Dita. She is in Ivan's study with Vincent. He appeared there with a head injury."

Leon sprints to the door leading to Ivan's study. "Ember, let me through. I need to check on Vincent."

The door releases, and Leon sprints down the corridor.

Dita is helping Vincent sit up as he steps inside the study.

"Are you good?" Leon asks, moving level with Vincent's face. He examines the healing wound and streaks of blood in contrast with his white hair.

"I will be fine," Vincent says. "Help this old man up."

"You shouldn't stand yet." Dita scolds.

"Pish posh." Vincent grasps Leon's arms and stands. His vision fades a little, but then he finds his balance. "It took Elis and Kaly with Zana."

"We found Kaly and Zana." Leon holds on to his arm as they amble towards the dining hall. Dita frowns but takes his other arm. "Have a seat and we'll all get caught up on the last hour."

Noel pulls out a chair for him at the dining table, and Vincent does a double take. "When did you get here?"

"Like I said, a lot went down in the last hour." Leon pats his shoulder. He rounds the table and pulls out a chair for Kaly, facing Vincent.

Kaly cradles Zana as she sits, and Leon sits next to her.

Enyo remains standing behind them.

Ana and Dita take a seat with Hermes on the other end of the table near Noel.

"Kaly," Leon says. "Can you explain what happened in the archive suite?"

Kaly nods. "Right after Enyo left, we were hit by a tornado like force. It came in without a warning. I didn't see a person, just a blur of wind and furniture moving."

"Why were you there?" Ana asks, pointing at Enyo.

Enyo shifts from side to side under the scrutiny of Ana and the others.

"Teuta found letters etched on the hourglass." Enyo shakes her head. "I went to the archive suite to explain the text we found."

"What did it say?" Dita asks, leaning forward.

"Bind my line with thine time." Kaly states.

Tuck, tuck, tuck

Every eye shoots up at the glass dome. Hermes flies up to inspect and cowers at the dual heads of the usmu violently pecking on the glass.

Tuck, tuck, tuck

"Not sure if you want to hear this, but this thing is trying to peck its way in!"

"Is the glass holding?" Leon asks, looking up.

Tuck, tuck, tuck

"I don't see any cracks, yet."

"Tani!" Leon yells.

A shrieking *caw* cries out. The shadow of the usmu vanishes from the dome.

Hermes looks down at Leon. "Where did you just send them?"

"To the bottom of the ocean." Leon shakes his head. "I honestly didn't think it would work, but if it did, then Teuta is gone or worse."

"Who was the last to see Teuta?" Vincent asks, leaning forward, resting his elbows on the table.

"She vanished from the vault after we made the discovery of the text and never showed back up," Enyo says. She paces the length of the table. "I'll ask the ladies in the vault."

"Has anyone seen Teuta in the last hour?" Enyo asks, pushing her thought to Avi, Xena and Pem.

"No," they answer in unison.

"They haven't seen Teuta." Enyo states. "Anyone else?"

Everyone shakes their head and shrugs.

"Can we back up a minute?" Noel asks, pointing to Kaly. "You said after Enyo left the suite, it was attacked."

Kaly nods. "I had just started walking down the hallway to tell Itra and Danae about their find, but the door from the archive burst open and I crouched down with Zana. Anton and Elis were in the washroom. Vincent was at the table."

"I'm pretty sure I was struck by a chair," Vincent says, tapping the non-wounded side of his head. "When the air settled, Kaly was gone. I didn't find Elis or Anton before I collapsed and appeared on the sofa in Ivan's study."

"Do you know if Itra or Danae made it out with the twins?" Leon asks.

"I don't know," Kaly whispers.

"Nor I," Vincent responds.

"And Anton and Elis are where?" Ana asks.

"I was going to check for them next before Kaly warned us of Prende's arrival." Leon says, tapping his gold thumb ring on the table.

"How were you taken if you didn't see anyone?" Dita asks Kaly.

"I felt no hands on me," Kaly says. "I was crouching in the suite and then inside a cave. It wasn't the present or future caverns. There were large crevices and cracks all over, including a huge, dark pit." She shivers. "I ran from Prende, and I nearly fell in the pit. Leon reached me just in time."

"And Prende was in the cave?" Dita asks.

"No," Kaly says. "She was on the back of an usmu that flew to the entry of the cave right after I heard a loud scream from above. What happened up here?"

"Noel arrived much to the confusion of Mui who was standing in the front foyer." Leon states with a half-smile. "I had just spoken with him and went upstairs to join Junior."

"Who summoned you?" Ana asks Noel.

"I found this in my tent." Noel pulls a small piece of parchment with purple loopy text from his back pocket. "I'm not sure who, but this was notification enough to come and check."

Ana holds out her hand. Noel hands over the parchment. She inspects the text.

Dita leans over and reads it aloud. "Do you remember?"

Vincent chuckles. "Same message as always."

"Shortly after Noel arrived and the confusion about who he is was cleared up," Leon says. "We battled a clearing full of decaying fairies. I used my staff's ember glow to…"

Kaly's mouth falls open.

"You burned them?" Vincent asks.

"More like abolished," Leon says, frowning. He leans closer to Kaly and whispers. "Sorry dear."

A single tear falls down Kaly's cheek and lands on Zana's forehead.

Leon points to Enyo. "She came to us shortly after the fairy attack and let us know about the destruction of the archive suite. We did not know the fairies were only a distraction."

"Why did you return to the suite?" Ana asks Enyo.

"Avi and I were looking at a few of the artifacts in the vault and found a gold scale with two ancient symbols of end and time. When I touched the scale, I went blind. Anubis spoke to me." She swallows. "Stack the stone against your own. A compass to guide is near inside. To begin again or tip the end. You must decide."

"You heard it?" Dita asks.

"I can hear and speak to inanimate objects that have a soul," Enyo says, looking at Kaly.

"It's true." Kaly nods. "She spoke to and heard me while I was stuck in stone."

"Who is Anubis?" Noel asks.

"Anubis was the god of death in Egyptian folklore." Kaly states.

"What do you think the message means?" Noel asks.

"The compass near inside is referencing Elis." Leon pushes back away from the table and stands. He calls his staff and double taps to the scythe. He swings the blade in four quick moves and a dark square frame hovers in front of him. "Show me Elis."

Elis's soft brown curls appear in the frame. It slowly zooms out.

Hermes and Enyo gasp. "Perseus," they say in unison.

"He is in Zeus's castle." Hermes lands beside Leon, pointing to a desk and window behind Elis. "This is a study in the south wing." Elis looks up and smiles. "Princess Danae must have shielded him from the attack, maybe she has Danae and Itra too."

"Show me Anton," Leon says.

Elis's face fades, replaced with a frazzled Anton pacing in the living room of his home. Nada comes into the frame carrying a drink.

"Why would she separate the father from his son?" Ana asks, studying the live image. "Who is she?"

"Itra's cousin, Nada." Leon answers. "Show me, Danae."

The frame goes dark.

Leon repeats. "Show me, Danae!"

It remains dark.

"Show me, Itra!"

An image of Ermal and Itra standing near a stone archway appears.

"Does anyone else notice that the ember glow is missing from the archway?" Hermes asks, staring at the frame.

Kaly stands and inspects the landscape. "It's the same path we take." She points. "Look at the boulder over Ermal's shoulder at the bend."

Vincent leans forward and nods. "She's right."

"If the ember glow is gone?" Leon asks Vincent.

"Itra can't see the castle if he walks under." Vincent states.

"Why would Ember block Itra and why can't we find Danae?" Leon asks. His pulse jumps and his right eye twitches.

"I can't answer the first part," Hermes says, "but if the princess is shielding Danae and the twins, it would hide them from everyone, including her own brother."

"The twins!" Leon says. "Show me Ora and Emit."

The frame goes dark.

"Ember would only eject Itra for two reasons." Vincent says, glancing up at the dome. "Protection or rejection of our line." He shakes his head. "And since I am still here, it was for protection."

"And Junior and Mui," Enyo says, but doesn't finish as Kaly blurts out.

"Could Prende and Chronos be working together?" Kaly asks.

Dita shakes her head. "I saw Chronos with Junior."

Enyo laughs. "Hermes, when we surprised Chronos and Junior near the vault. Junior didn't follow Chronos orders and attacked Pem in Teuta's form, right?"

"You're right!" Hermes nods. "Junior ignored him and released you."

"Why do you think it's Prende?" Ana asks Kaly.

"She keeps showing up and she's human." Kaly paces a few steps and then turns back to face the awaiting group. "Vincent, in the translated text about the keeper's cuff, we were perplexed about how Chronos could possess the cuff with the whole immortal factor, right?" Vincent nods. "Well, if they are working together…"

Vincent stands a little too fast. He leans down on the table until his vision clears. "We never considered that Chronos would have an alliance."

Junior and Mui stare at the woman motionless, face down in the middle of the clearing.

"Who is she?" Junior asks, sheathing his sword.

"More likely who was she," Mui answers. "She fell at least a hundred feet."

Junior turns to face his father and looks up at him. "Was she riding an usmu when they vanished?"

Mui nods and sheathes his blade. "Do you feel free?" He rolls up his sleeve and inspects his arm. The gold mark is still present.

Junior shakes his head. "I still feel a pull on my will."

The woman coughs.

Junior startles and draws his sword again. "She's alive!" He jumps off the last large step leading to the castle entrance, but Mui reaches down and grabs his shoulder.

"And the owner of this!" Mui whispers, pointing to his forearm.

"No," Junior protests. "She isn't Chronos."

"Can't you feel her call for help?" Mui asks.

"No. It's just the right thing to do." Junior frowns and tries to fight the compulsion to help. He feels his airway close off and struggles to suck in a breath. His face turns red, and he drops his sword, reaching his hands to his throat. He falls to his knees and pounds a fist to his chest.

The woman sits up and smiles at them.

Mui catches her wicked grin and kneels to Junior. "She is controlling your breath. Fight it! Breathe!"

"I can't!" Junior wheezes.

"What do you want?" Mui stands and points his blade at her.

She laughs.

Mui charges towards her, but his knee gives. He stumbles and falls down hard.

"My new pets." She muses and stands. "You are quite the surprise. Two giants under my control. For what, to protect the little fairy?"

Mui attempts to stand.

Thump

He looks back. Junior is face forward in the dirt but breathing again with the gentle rise of his chest.

"What do you want?" Mui snarls at her limping but confident stride. He stands, tests and bends his knee. He raises his sword.

"To show you who is in charge." She stops just out of striking distance, smiles, and picks a few stray leaves from her hair. "Tsk, tsk."

Mui's hand holding the sword swings to his right and the tip of his blade strikes the dirt next to Junior's neck. Mui fights to pull his sword back.

Junior stirs and coughs.

"Son, don't move!" Mui grunts and pulls again. He doesn't take his eyes off Junior, but can sense her circling. "What is this? What do you want?"

"Somebody will have to pay for my pets. Who could be so powerful to abolish an usmu or ten of them?"

"Ember," Mui answers. His grip slick with sweat and patience nearly out.

"Now, now," the woman says. "I don't think she would harm a divine creature. Try again."

"We were blocked from the dining hall," Mui explains.

Junior's eyes open.

"Son, don't move an inch." Mui risks a look up and spots the woman mindlessly twirling a lock of her honey-colored hair. "You know we didn't do it."

He nods up to the castle entrance that is closed again. They were compelled to open it after they were denied entry to the dining hall.

"Very well." She waves her hand and releases her hold on Mui. He falls back away from Junior.

Hermes appears hovering beside Junior.

Junior glances at the hilt still strapped to Hermes and glances at the woman.

Hermes doesn't hesitate and throws a small dagger straight for her. It strikes and sinks into her chest. She looks down at the hilt and wraps her hand around it.

"I wouldn't pull that out," Mui warns.

"Kill him!" she commands, pointing at Hermes.

Mui swings his sword in a wide arc.

Hermes flies straight up out of the blade's reach and hovers with a smile.

Mui grunts.

Enyo appears behind the woman and raises her dagger to her throat.

"You will pay for this!" Prende mutters.

"I think Ember has another plan," Enyo whispers in her ear.

"My husband will banish you and your line for eternity!"

Junior stands holding his throat and raises a brow to Mui. He croaks out a hoarse whisper. "Chronos?"

Prende spits on the ground. "You fool!"

The sky above them darkens. A rumble of thunder clammers down.

Junior looks up.

Mui doesn't take his eyes off Hermes.

Prende throws her head back and slams it into Enyo's nose.

Enyo tightens her grip on her. "Tani!"

A blinding flash falls and strikes the ground near Mui.

Mui's feet leave the ground, and he falls back hard, striking his head on the edge of the stone steps to the castle.

Junior looks around, his vision spotty. He blinks until his vision returns and hesitantly looks up.

Hermes is gone.

He scans the clearing. "Dad!" He runs over to Mui's side.

"Watch out!" Mui faintly whispers.

Junior turns as another bolt of lightning strikes.

"Shh," Danae softly whispers to Ora. She rocks back and stands. She walks the room and hums.

Ora quiets.

Danae goes to the window and looks out over the lake. She glances down at the bustling village below and spots a sundial in the center of a small square. She studies the layout of the surrounding buildings, and her eyes fall to movement on an adjacent balcony.

A door swings open, and a head bobs out with brown curls. Danae sucks in a breath. Tiny hands reach over the edge as Elis's precious face peeks over the stone railing.

A large man fills the open doorway, shadowing her nephew.

"Elis!" Danae shouts. Her voice startles Ora.

Elis turns towards her. He squints and rolls higher on his toes. The man in the doorway advances towards Elis. He stops in full view and Danae's mouth falls open. He's as tall as he is broad, and his tight purple tunic reveals a very defined physique.

Danae swallows. "Elis, sweety, look over here."

Elis turns and tugs on the man's tunic. He looks down at Elis and then makes eye contact with Danae for a brief second and then kneels beside Elis.

"He can't see you," Roslyn says, walking up behind Danae.

Danae turns to face her. "How? I can see him and the village below? And he heard me call his name!"

"Have you heard of glamor?" the queen asks, circling the room to watch over Emit resting in the crib.

"Like the fairies hid from Avi?" Danae asks, laying Ora down next to her brother.

She nods.

The setting sunlight streams in the window, dancing over her jewels fixed around her crown.

"You see a window, everyone else can only see a stone wall."

"Why is Elis here without Anton or Itra?" Danae squares her shoulders, folds her arms, and narrows her eyes.

"I barely got Elis out." She shutters. "He is dangerous."

"That giant with Elis?"

The princess smiles. "No, that giant is my son, Perseus."

"Ok," Danae says, blowing a hair from her eye. "Who is dangerous?"

"The man that attacked the suite has several names, but is mostly known as Perendi."

Danae raises her brows and shrugs her shoulders.

"He is married to Prende."

Danae takes a step back and covers her mouth with the back of her hand. "Why?"

"Prende is an Ember divine. She's barred from the Castle of Teskom and cannot serve and protect Ember. After she struck a deal with Chronos."

"You mean he… that monster has allies?" Danae bends forward. "I might be sick." She sucks in a breath and slowly exhales. She unfolds and meets Roslyn's gaze. "Why would she harm us?" She points to the crib. "Or my family?"

"An ancient loophole." She walks towards a small desk in the corner. "What do you know about my history?"

"According to Kaly, an oracle told your father that your son would one day kill him. He locked you in a bronze chamber when you were still childless. Zeus still found his way to you." Danae nods towards the window. "And thus, the giant lives."

Roslyn smiles. "Interesting summary, and nearly correct. The bronze chamber had a single mirror built in the wall. A portal for Zeus to enter and leave unnoticed." She opens the drawer and pulls out a worn oil hide bound parcel with thin ties. "My father, King Akrisios, banished us from the castle after my son was born. He feared the wrath of the gods, otherwise I am sure he would have killed Perseus." She gently unties the hide and reveals a tiny gold cuff.

Danae gasps. "Is that a keeper's cuff?"

She nods. "His parting gift to my son."

Danae leans forward to inspect the detailed engravings. "The king actually cuffed him?"

"Yes."

"As an infant?"

"Yes."

"To prevent your son from ever killing him?"

"Yes, however, his plan was flawed." She gently wraps the cuff back up. "He was using his control over Perseus during events at the funeral games in Larissa. He intended to make Perseus imbalanced and appear weak. The effect made my son throw a discus off target and strike the side of my father's head, killing him instantly."

"Fulfilling the oracle's prophecy," Danae whispers.

"He was devastated. Perseus knew of this destined fate as a young boy and vowed to change the future." Roslyn opens the drawer and places the parcel back inside. "Once marked by a keeper's cuff, it alters a person for life, including their children born after the marking. They're immune and cannot be controlled by the owner."

"Leon and I are descendants of you and Perseus." Danae states and glances at the twins. "So, we are immune and they're safe too?"

"Yes, but Itra's line is not." She frowns. "Including Elis."

"Ok," Danae says. "I understand our immunity, but why is this vital. What am I missing?"

"The same oracle my father spoke with told Prende that the only way she would ever gain access to the Castle of Teskom is if she controls time."

"Time." Danae raises a brow. "As in Chronos or my babies?"

Roslyn glances over at the crib and shuts the drawer.

"But you just said they are immune to that thing." Danae points at the desk.

"Elis is their guide. Their compass."

Danae shakes her head. "If she cuffs Elis, she controls time."

"Elis is already marked by the keeper's cuff."

"What!" Danae shouts. Emit stirs. She takes in a breath. "When?"

"When Chronos took him, Prende was waiting."

"Anton checked him over." Danae shakes her head. "There are no visible markings."

"Perseus's mark didn't appear until his fourteenth birthday."

"But you said he was cuffed as an infant."

She shrugs. "I can't explain the magic or the curse, just the history of experience."

Danae chews on her thumbnail. "Why would they leave him alone and unguarded?"

"They thought they hid him well in the ancient City of Time."

Danae walks to the window. "Isn't that where we are now?"

"No, this is Illyria." She joins Danae at the window. "Illyria was built on the ruins of the ancient city." She points to the sundial in the square below. "And that is the only remaining piece."

"Ember showed the family a vision of this square with a teenage version of Elis removing an hourglass from the center of the sundial."

Roslyn stiffens. "An hourglass."

"Ember trapped Chronos in an hourglass after we caught him near the vault."

The princess nervously laughs. "It can't be?"

"What can't be?" Danae brushes her hair away from her brows to look at Roslyn directly.

"A prophecy of a young man, sliding the urtar scale to reset time." Roslyn turns her back to the window. "Ember would never be so reckless."

"Explain."

"Did you see the hourglass?" Roslyn asks. Her face pales.

"No, it's secured in the vault. The hourglass was one of many artifacts we recovered during the battle with the rogue descendants."

"Was there anything etched on the glass?"

"I overheard Enyo speaking to Kaly about the glass and a light before the suite was ambushed."

She pushes off the wall and heads directly for the door.

"You can't just leave." Danae states, moving quickly to block the door. "What's going on?"

"I am sending a messenger to bring a grey sister here." She moves past Danae. "Do the protectors of time have the infinity amulet?"

"Yes, Avi." Danae places a hand against the door. "Why?"

"They can speak to Avi. Has she seen the hourglass?"

Danae nods.

"We can confirm the hourglass and—"

"And then what?" Danae asks, keeping a firm hand on the door.

"To begin again or tip the end. You must decide."

49

A bowl appears beside Pem.

"Popcorn?" Xena says, sniffing the air before she turns to see Pem throw a few pieces in the air, tilt her head back and open her mouth. She catches each kernel and grins. "We are on guard duty, not watching a movie."

Pem swallows. "Want some?" She extends the bowl to Xena.

Xena takes a handful and pops a few in her mouth.

Avi laughs. "Why do you call it popcorn?"

Xena and Pem freeze mid chew.

Pem looks down at the bowl and back up to Avi. "What do you call it?" She extends the bowl to Avi.

Avi picks a white kernel from the bowl. "This is kokoshka."

Xena and Pem laugh in unison.

"I thought Leon said you lived in London?" Xena asks, quieting her laughter.

"I do!" Avi sticks her tongue out. "Honest, that is what they call this." She tosses a piece at Pem.

Pem transforms into Avi. "Kokoshka."

Avi blinks.

Xena laughs.

Pem transforms back to herself.

"Not cool," Avi says, glaring at Pem.

"Ah, noted." Pem states and winks. She pops in a few more pieces and talks with a full mouth. "We'll have to ask Noel what the Ottoman dimension calls this."

"Manners!" Xena says, shaking her head at Pem.

Avi laughs and abruptly stops. Her necklace vibrates under her top. Two women in purple gowns with drawn hoods appear behind Xena and Pem. Her face pales.

"Avi, are you ok?" Xena asks, a chill runs down her spine when Avi points behind her. She slowly turns and takes in the two women.

Pem turns and drops the bowl of popcorn. "Where did you two come from?" She examines their tall, shapely figures but gasps as they lower their hoods, revealing their familiar faces. She looks from her mom to the one on the right—the likeness is like Kaly and herself—they're nearly identical. And the woman on the left to Avi, almost the same minus a few wrinkles near the stranger's eyes. "Wow. Our genes are strong!"

"Deino?" Xena asks. The woman on the left nods. "And Pemphredo, we've met this is my daughter and your namesake. Pem, these are Enyo's sisters."

"Did Enyo call you?" Avi asks, looking down at her amulet.

"We come on behalf of Princess Danae." Pemphredo answers with a smile.

"Why?" Pem asks.

"A threat to time," Deino says. "Does the artifact have any words etched on the glass?"

"Yes, why?" Avi steps closer to the pedestal, blocking their view. "Is that important?"

"What does it say?" Pemphredo asks, stepping towards the pedestal.

"Bind my line with thine time." Avi answers, stepping in front of Pemphredo. "Do you know what it means?"

Pemphredo ignores her question and asks. "Why are you blocking me?"

"Show me your forearms."

Pemphredo wrinkles her nose and looks over at Deino.

Deino shrugs.

They push back their sleeves and hold up their forearms.

Avi inspects Pemphredo's unmarked olive skin.

Xena steps closer to Deino.

"Clear," Xena says.

Avi steps aside.

Pemphredo leans over the hourglass.

"Danae and the twins are with the princess." Deino states, moving beside Pemphredo. "And the boy with the curls is with Perseus."

"Elis!" Xena says, her brows rise to her hairline. "Why?"

"Safety," Deino says, stepping closer to the pedestal.

"Where are Anton and Itra?" Pem asks.

"Not sure," Deino says, reaching to touch the hourglass.

"Stop!" Xena and Avi shout in unison.

Deino and Pemphredo turn towards them, hands raised.

"We can't move the hourglass." Xena explains. "It was tipped over by accident. Teuta warned us that the few grains fallen to the other side cannot be mixed again."

Deino and Pemphredo glance at each other and then look down.

"Can you show us the text?" Pemphredo asks.

Avi nods. "Xena and Pem drop your light stones."

They open their palms; their stones dim and fall into their hands.

Avi looks up at her light stone, and it turns blue. She moves her light over the artifact.

A word appears on the glass. She moves it again and the entire phrase appears.

"Do you know what this means?" Avi asks.

Pemphredo nods.

"Can you move the light to this side?" Deino says, pointing to the side closest to her.

Avi adjusts the light and Deino mumbles a few words.

"What did you say?" Avi asks.

"There are three symbols etched here." Deino steps back.

Pemphredo circles the pedestal and bends level with the hourglass.

"Kaly! I need you and Vincent here now." Xena says, looking at the crease between Pemphredo's brows.

"What's up?" Kaly whispers from behind Xena.

Xena and Pem jump.

Vincent chuckles.

"We have visitors." Xena nods towards Enyo's sisters. "And there are symbols on the glass we missed before."

Vincent pulls on his glasses and walks to Deino and Pemphredo. "May I?"

They step aside.

He bends to read the new symbols. "Ancient Illyrian, wait no, maybe Egyptian. The first one here, a small plant in combination with the triangle and these few lines, means to begin or start a destiny. The next one with the straight line with a second askew on top is tip or bend. And the last one the staff of Anubis, meaning death or end."

Avi clears her throat. The others turn to face her. "To begin again or tip the end."

Vincent holds a finger in the air. "Ah yes, that's it." His smile falls to a frown. "I've seen that phrase somewhere before."

A book appears in front of Vincent. He grins and reaches for the book, but it flies to Avi. His grin falls to a frown.

"It wasn't me," Avi says, holding up her hands. "But this is the book Teuta gave me when I first arrived." She reaches for the book. The book falls softly in her grasp. The blue light reveals a second image of an hourglass under the image of the three haggard women on the cover. She looks at the other ladies. "Open it?"

They nod in unison.

"Hapur," Avi whispers.

The book opens near the middle. The blue light over her head hovers closer to the pages. An image lights up of three women holding hands standing in a circle around a young man. "Bind his line, to save time." Avi reads aloud, pointing to the tiny caption.

"Who is he that it is referencing?" Kaly asks, stepping closer to Avi to inspect the drawing, but the pages flip to the family tree of Ember.

Kaly and Avi scan the page and gasp in unison.

"Elis and Zana." Avi states, turning the book towards the others. "Married."

"Who is Zana?" Deino asks.

"The changeling baby we accidentally brought back when Ora was taken," Avi explains. "What does their union mean?"

Deino and Pemphredo exchange a glance.

216

"An old prophecy." Pemphredo takes the book from Avi. The pages flutter to a page with faded text.

Avi adjusts her light back to yellow and increases the brightness.

Vincent leans over and scans the page. "It's written in Illyrian."

Pemphredo nods. "A day will come when this world is one. A divine bride will lead the guide inside to begin again. He must tip the end. Four worlds will bend and fold to derive a world untold."

"How?" Avi and Pem ask in unison.

"Ember." Pemphredo and Deino answer in unison.

"She wouldn't?" Xena asks.

"It's a prophecy told for centuries," Vincent says. "It's not likely a fact, but what I can't figure out is why this passage is in this book."

"We share an oath to protect time," Deino explains. "This prophecy if fulfilled essentially breaks time."

Avi walks to the gold scale. "Please share the message from Anubis with the princess." She looks over her shoulder. "Stack the stone against your own. A compass to guide is near inside. To begin again or tip the end. You must decide."

"What does this mean for Elis?" Xena asks.

"His fate is spoken." Pemphredo states and holds up the book.

Avi stiffens. "Excuse me!"

"What the hell is that supposed to mean?" Kaly asks, stepping between Avi and Pemphredo.

Deino steps beside Pemphredo. "His union with Zana."

"We are the protectors of time." Pemphredo states. "We need to do what we can to protect time and their guide. We will pass the messages to the princess."

"Can we bring the family back here?" Xena asks.

"It's not safe until this is out of the picture," Deino says, pointing to the hourglass. "And we don't know if Prende had any additional allies."

"And what are Anton and Itra supposed to do?" Vincent asks, the crease between his brows deepens.

"We can't assume to know the princess's plan to keep them safe," Pemphredo says, making eye contact with Vincent and facing Xena's frown. "But we'll ask."

Avi purses her lips. "Why is she, the princess, the safest bet?"

"Her gift from Ember," Deino says. "She can shield any living being from anyone."

"Avi," Pemphredo says, reaching up to her chest. "Just tap the amulet."

Avi reaches up and hovers her finger above the ember infinity amulet. It vibrates. "Is there anything you're withholding?"

Deino glances at Pemphredo and winks.

"A ruby stone embedded in pointed gold can balance the scale with the weight of the divine." Pemphredo pulls her hood up. "It's a dream I have seen without former context, but it applies now considering Anubis's message and the inscription on the hourglass."

"Where is the ruby stone?" Pem asks.

"I haven't seen the location in my dream, but I've seen your mother with it." Pemphredo smiles at Xena. "See you soon."

"Safe travels," Avi says. She taps her amulet, and the ladies vanish on either side of Enyo.

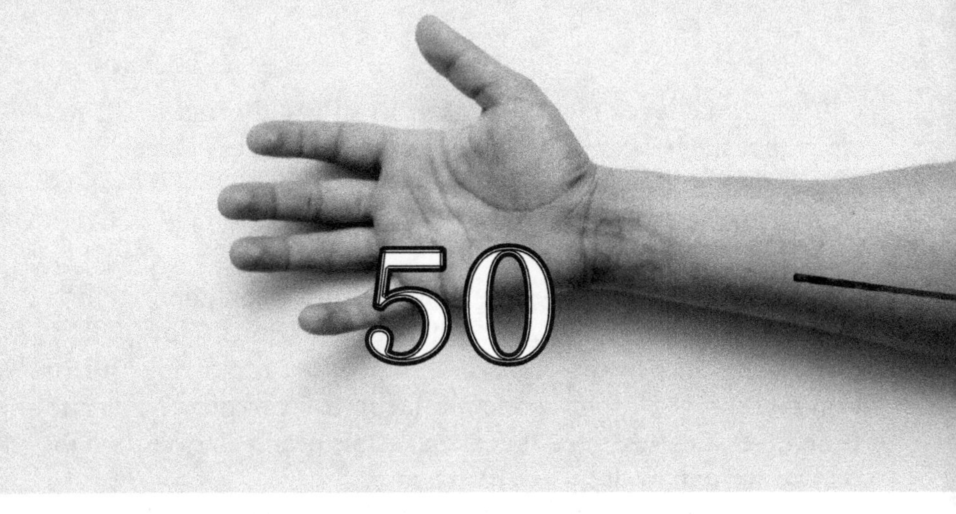

Leon appears behind Itra.

"Shit!" Ermal shouts.

Itra whirls around. He rolls to his toes. He twists and strains his neck.

"Hey now, I'm not that scary!" Leon teases.

Ermal shakes his head. "Remember, I'm armed." He pats his hip holster. "And a quick draw."

Itra falls back on his heels, reading Leon's face. "Where's Danae?"

"I was hoping you would know."

Itra frowns and furrows his brows. "Can't you use your ring to find her?"

Leon holds up his thumb. "I tried." He turns his thumb down.

Itra stares at Leon's hand.

"Kaly, Zana, and Vincent are inside."

"Do they know what happened in the suite?" Itra asks.

"Kaly describes it as a tornado like force," Leon says. "Enyo confirmed the suite's furniture was tossed around, and some pieces are broken."

"Anton and Elis?" Itra asks.

"Anton is back in his apartment," Leon says, biting the inside of his cheek. "But not with Elis."

"Where is my nephew?"

"With Perseus, according to Enyo and Hermes."

Itra balls his hands into tight fists. "Why would he take Elis?"

"Hermes believes that the reason I can't find Danae with my ring is that she is with or being protected by Princess Danae."

Itra's bottom lip quivers.

"And if she is protecting Danae and the babies, she is likely protecting Elis."

Ermal steps forward to rest a hand on Itra's shoulder. He lifts his chin towards the archway. "Where did the ember glow go?"

Leon gestures to the stone arch. "We had a clearing full of decaying fairies. A full distraction tactic from whatever got into the archives and the suite." Leon shakes his head. "I never thought you two were in trouble. I'm really sorry."

Ermal's eyes dart around. "Had a clearing full of what?"

Itra ignores Ermal's question. "I saw a blinding light from the endless stairs." Itra points to the ground. "What was that?"

Leon holds up his arm with the tattoo of the staff. "Mass destruction."

Itra blows out a breath.

Ermal raises his hand. "Fairies are real?"

Leon laughs. "You've met Teuta. And you still don't believe?"

"But!" Ermal stammers. "But she was real or is real. I mean, she's a real human turned fairy by Ember."

"Speaking of Teuta," Leon says. "When is the last time you saw her?"

Itra shakes his head. "Not since I was in the dining hall with the family."

"Can we circle back to fairies are real?" Ermal asks, pacing behind Itra.

Itra sighs. "What happened after you, um, used your light?" He gestures to Leon's arm.

"We made it to the dining hall before Ember sealed the doors, leaving Junior and Mui in the conservatory," Leon says.

"Did Chronos escape?" Itra asks, color drains from his face. "Are they under his control?"

Leon shakes his head. "Chronos is still in the hourglass, but he had an alliance with Prende."

"As in the goddess Prende?" Ermal asks.

"Yes." Leon reaches into his back pocket and pulls out a gold cuff.

Itra stumbles back.

"What is that?" Ermal asks, stepping towards Leon.

Itra yanks on Ermal's arm. "Leon?"

"Junior and Mui encountered Prende in the clearing." He places the cuff back in his pocket. "Ember sent Enyo and Hermes to assist."

"Enyo is here?" Ermal asks, straightening his shirt.

Leon winks at him. "You still crushing on her?"

Itra turns to face Ermal. "Is that so?"

"I ask one question about her," Ermal says. His cheeks redden. "And Leon won't let it go!"

Itra halfheartedly punches his shoulder. "She's a tough lady, good luck."

"Ermal likes them real old!" Leon teases.

"Ha, ha." Ermal frowns.

Leon laughs. "Long story short, Hermes threw the dagger he took from Junior earlier. It was a clean shot and sunk into Prende's chest. She dropped the cuff when she—died." Leon frowns. "Mui—Dita is working on him now."

Ermal stops pacing. "The giant Mui is inside?"

Leon nods.

"How bad?" Itra asks.

"Mui has lost a lot of blood." Leon shakes his head.

Itra mumbles a curse. "Bloody freaking nightmare." He kicks a small pile of rocks. They scatter out and land in a perfect circle. "What the actual…"

"A sign?" Leon inspects the rocks. "The two largest rocks are directly across from each other." He points them out. "Like their marks."

"What marks?" Ermal asks.

"The twins have a circle of twelve dots marked on an opposite shoulder blade. Emit's has a darker dot at the top and Ora a darker dot at the bottom."

"Do you know what it means?"

"We assume it means time but haven't really investigated it further." Itra runs a hand down his face. "Do you know how to find Danae and my babies?"

"Maybe," Leon says. "Kaly was summoned to the vault with Vincent a few minutes ago. Let's see if we can get you inside and find out what they learned."

"What do you need me to do?" Ermal asks.

"Can you check on Anton?" Itra asks.

"Of course," Ermal says. "What can I tell him?"

"Whatever you can remember between here and there." Itra states, tapping his head. "I'm not sure what Ember will let you recall."

"And I suppose I can call off the search party for you and the family?" Ermal asks.

"Maybe." Itra looks to Leon. "Should we look for Danae and the babies here, or are they out of our time?"

"Unlikely our time, but I would have an officer patrol the area just in case."

Ermal nods and hitches up his pack. He points to the archway and to Itra. "I'll wait to make sure you can go with Leon."

Leon mumbles the key to open a portal to the dining hall. "After you." He waves his arm to the portal for Itra.

"Thanks for running up to check on us again." Itra pats Ermal's shoulder.

"It's what friends do."

Itra sucks in a breath and nods to Leon. He exhales and walks forward. "Here goes nothing."

51

Teuta stands brushing off the dirt from the bottom of her dress. "Why did you bring me here?" She tilts her chin up to face the man shadowing the door to her cell.

"My wife's suggestion," the man says, stepping into the small, dark room.

His jawline visible but his face still dark.

Teuta squints. "Are you responsible for the attack today?"

"What attack?" Teuta straightens and strains her eyes to make out the man's features.

"You deny any knowledge of an attack?" He leans over to her eye level.

Teuta blinks twice and tucks her chin to her chest. "Zeus?"

"Who else?" Zeus laughs, straightening to his full height.

Teuta stares back at him, her jaw loose.

"Speechless?" He smirks.

Teuta swallows. "Why does the princess think I had something to do with an attack?"

"Trespassers inside the Castle of Teskom including the portal bound archives."

"Ember granted the entire family access to the archives, per Itra and Danae's request."

Zeus barks out a laugh. "Ember would never do such a thing!"

"You're wrong!" Teuta stomps her foot. "It was her peace offering to them since I retrieved the babies' minutes after they were born."

"Retrieved?" Zeus shakes his head. "Sounds like kidnapping."

"I am the messenger," Teuta says, balling her fists at her hips.

"You were until you let Prende and her husband inside."

"The attack? It was Prende?" Teuta taps her right foot. "How did she get inside?"

"She didn't, but her husband attempted to take time and the compass."

Teuta shakes her head. "Ember would never allow either of them access to the Castle of Teskom."

"Unless the messenger gave them access." Zeus nods and opens his arms to her. "You see why all fingers point at you."

Teuta chews on the corner of her mouth. "Are Prende and Chronos allies?"

"My wife believes they struck a deal before Chronos was banished."

"Chronos gained entry without an invitation. He could have easily given him the same access. I had zero knowledge of this alliance."

"You mean the vessel previously known as your brother, Pax?" Zeus raises a single brow and folds his arms across his massive chest. "Do you recall revoking an invitation for him?"

Teuta opens her mouth to speak but pauses. "I didn't… but Leon did."

"And was Leon the messenger when the vessel trespassed?" Zeus asks, raising the other brow.

Teuta frowns. "No. I was." Her shoulders drop and her chin falls.

"And when we're done discussing your role in today's events, we can discuss my daughter's death under your supervision."

Teuta looks up and glares at him. "Athena broke every oath to protect and serve the Castle of Teskom. Ember let her die painlessly. Trust me, I would have never been so kind."

Zeus snarls, but Teuta doesn't blink, keeping his stare.

52

"Kaly?" Leon turns in a slow circle.

The evening sky darkens the glass dome of the dining hall. He calls his staff and taps once. The warm ember glow highlights the drawn brows of Itra's face.

"Where is everyone?" Itra whispers.

Leon walks towards the war room on the far side of the hall, and the door swings open. He pauses mid-stride.

Ana steps out, wiping her cheeks.

"Mui?" Itra asks, stepping around Leon.

"Gone." Ana sniffles and nods over her shoulder. "Give Dita and Junior a moment."

"Of course." Itra steps back. "Where is everyone else?"

"Kaly went up to the suites to lay Zana down, and Hermes and Noel are up in the towers, keeping watch. The rest of the ladies are still in the vault with Vincent."

"Kaly's alone?" Leon steps forward.

Itra snags his arm and pulls.

Leon glares at him.

Itra taps his head.

"Kaly, are you safe?" Leon asks.

"Yes, but Mui didn't make it," Kaly says.

"Ana let Itra, and I know."

"Oh good! Tell Itra we have a confirmed location for Danae, the babies, and Elis."

"Where?" Leon turns to face Itra.

"Illyria with Princess Danae."

Itra raises a brow. "Do you want to fill me in?"

Leon smiles. "Kaly just confirmed that Elis, Danae and the babies are in Illyria."

Junior fills the doorframe.

"Junior, I'm so sorry." Itra walks towards him but stops, gauging his scowl and tear-streaked face.

Junior holds up a finger and points at Ana. "You knew this was going to happen!"

Ana sighs and pulls her hair up in a high ponytail. "It was a possible outcome, not a defined fact."

Itra sucks in a breath.

Ana's face and tone so similar to Iana.

"You could have said something." Junior advances towards her. "Anything!"

Itra steps in between them, holding his hands up.

Junior balls his fists.

"Trust me when I say I feel your frustration and grief." Itra points to Ana. "She couldn't stop it any more than Dita could save my sister."

Junior takes a step back and bumps into Dita.

"Did I hear you say they have a location for Danae and the children?" Dita asks, tilting her chin towards Leon.

"Yes." Leon releases his staff and marches past her. He steps just inside the war room and pauses. He takes a step back, taking in the giant figure draped with a white cloth laying on the table. He bows his head.

Enyo, Vincent and Xena appear next to Leon.

Vincent removes his glasses and bows his head.

Itra steps in and stands beside Vincent. He loops an arm around him.

Vincent looks up through glassy eyes. "Itra!" He tightly embraces him.

"Are you ok?" Itra asks, pulling back to check Vincent's forehead.

"Fine, fine. We know Danae and the children are with the princess."

Itra nods. "Kaly filled Leon in."

226

Xena looks Itra over. "Are you hurt?"

"No, just eager to get to them." Itra starts for the wardrobe.

"Wait!" Enyo says. "We need to confirm a few things with my sisters before we go in hot."

Itra frowns. "Are they working with us or for her?"

"Us." Enyo motions towards the dining hall door.

Itra hesitates.

Vincent smiles and pats his shoulder. "It's worth the wait to have a plan."

Leon shakes his head. "I don't like waiting either."

Xena chuckles and mumbles. "Understatement."

Itra follows Vincent and Xena. He shoulder checks Leon. "Grab a few cloaks just in case."

Leon smirks and races over, grabbing a few from the wardrobe. He tucks them behind his back as he joins the others standing around the table.

Ana tosses up her light stone.

A warm glow banishes the shadows of the room.

Dita gasps and points to the floor.

The mural under their feet swirls.

Vincent stumbles back and bumps into Junior. "Sorry."

Junior grunts.

Itra glares in Junior's direction.

The swirling action subsides.

"Oh, God!" Ana says. She covers her mouth and runs to the open door leading to the washroom.

Dita curses and runs after Ana.

"What in the hell does this represent?" Leon asks.

Leon traces the outline of a circle, divided in four equal quadrants draining into a dark hole in the center.

"The prophecy from the book," Xena says.

A book appears and drops to the table with a loud thud.

Leon whirls, calling his staff and double taps. The scythe glows over the book.

"Easy," Xena says, tugging on his elbow.

The book opens and flips to the same page Pemphredo read aloud.

Leon leans over the page. He turns to Vincent. "Translation. Please."

"Some context before I ask Vincent to read it." Xena gestures towards Vincent.

Leon nods.

"Deino and Pemphredo appeared in the vault at the request of Princess Danae to inspect the hourglass. There were three marks etched in the glass on the side we missed before all the action."

Dita and Ana walk back into the dining hall towards the table. Ana's face damp and pale.

"Would you like a moment?" Xena asks Ana. "Or do you want me to continue?"

Ana shakes her head and whispers. "Continue."

"The three symbols translate to begin again or tip the end and the phrase is bind my line with thine time."

The book lifts and turns towards Xena. She takes the book and looks over the page. "This is new." She turns the book towards Enyo.

Leon and Itra lean forward to look over Enyo's shoulder.

An illustration of a young boy and a young girl holding hands with their free hands raised towards another teen boy.

"The kids," Itra whispers.

Xena points to the caption. "Bind his line, to save time."

Enyo drops Ana's light and changes the warm yellow glow to blue. She hovers the blue light over the page. An image of a long bearded old man holding hands with a young girl appears behind the teen boy.

"What in the hell!" Leon attempts to grab the book, but it flies out of his reach.

Enyo tosses Ana's light back up. She reaches up and takes the book.

Leon mumbles a curse.

Ana clears her throat. All eyes shift in her direction. "The mural on the floor is the four dimensions merging into a new world."

Vincent nods towards the book. "A day will come when this world is one. A divine bride will lead the guide inside to begin again. He must tip the end. Four worlds will bend and fold to derive a world untold."

228

Itra's knees wobble. He pulls out a chair and sits. "The worlds end with Elis…"

"The divine bride is who?" Junior asks, leaning against the table.

The pages turn and stop, revealing the family tree of Ember. Enyo turns the book towards Junior. "Zana."

"Hold up!" Leon says. "She's a day old, maybe two, and you're telling me that her future husband is Elis?"

"Just explaining the information provided," Enyo says. "My sister Pemphredo has had one vision that may undo this prophecy." She glances at Xena.

Xena nods.

"A ruby stone embedded in pointed gold can balance the scale with the weight of the divine."

"I don't understand," Dita says.

"The message I received from Anubis when I touched the gold scale in the vault. Stack the stone against your own. A compass to guide is near inside. To begin again or tip the end. You must decide."

Dita shakes her head. "We have a trapped god in a tipped hourglass with an urtar stone. My father is dead. Four of Ember's assigned bloodlines need to be recovered," she chokes down a laugh, "and now we must find a ruby stone?"

"I believe the ruby stone is a family heirloom," Xena says. "Pemphredo mentioned she has seen me with this. I was gifted a ruby stone set in pointed gold as a wedding gift from my great aunt."

"We place Zana and the ruby stone on the scale and this end of the world drama is adverted," Leon asks, shaking his head. "Is that what you are saying?"

Xena and Enyo exchange a glance before facing Ana.

Ana nods and closes her eyes. Her face draws down into a frown before her eyes open wide.

"It's possible, but there is one thing in the way," Ana says. "The urtar stone is part of the ritual to balance the scale. The divine must carry the stone."

Vincent rakes a hand through his white hair, leaving it standing on end. "And the stone is with Chronos in the hourglass."

Itra pounds a fist against the table. "And my family! Where is the plan to retrieve them from Illyria?"

"My sisters suggested this castle is compromised as long as the hourglass remains here." Enyo moves across from Itra to meet his glare. "They're asking the princess to shield them in your own home."

Itra shakes his head. "And the plan is wait, um, no!"

Xena takes a seat across from Itra. "Pem and I will retrieve the ruby stone and return in a flash. Kaly and Vincent can research an alternative holding cell for Chronos and how to extract the urtar stone." Xena looks around. "Noel and Hermes?"

"Up in the tower keeping watch," Ana says.

"And Hermes can check on Elis." Xena reaches across the table, offering her hand.

Itra's eyes mist. "What choice do I have?"

Xena nods. "Pem and I will be gone for an hour or less." She vanishes from the chair.

Pem stands from a thought provoked sofa when Xena appears in the vault.

"What's the plan?" Avi asks, walking back towards Xena and Pem.

"Pem and I will return with the ruby stone. Vincent and Kaly will research an alternative for that." Xena points to the hourglass. "Ana believes the urtar stone is essential for the scale to work."

"We're letting Chronos out!" Avi shouts. "No!"

"We aren't doing anything yet." Xena frowns. "Just keep watch. We'll be back shortly."

Avi wrings her hands and nods.

Xena fingers her thumb ring and mumbles. A doorframe appears, outlining a small kitchen. Pem walks through first and Xena follows.

230

Avi blows out a long breath and slowly spins around, taking in the expansive space all to herself. "If I were to take the hourglass to the top of a volcano and throw it in, what would happen?"

"Time would end," a low pitch voice echoes from the other end of the vault.

Avi jumps. "Who's there?"

A tall man walks out between a stack of wooden crates.

"Enyo! Leon! Anyone!" Avi taps her amulet and moves to block the stranger's view of the hourglass. "And who the hell are you?"

"Perseus," he says and bends at the waist in a slight bow.

Leon appears beside Avi. He calls and double taps his scythe.

Enyo appears on the other side of Avi with her blades out and ready.

"What in the hell Perseus!" Enyo yells.

Perseus saunters towards them and the corners of his mouth curve up. "It's nice to see you too."

"Why are you here?" Leon advances, blocking his path to Enyo and Avi.

"You left the doors wide open," Perseus says, cocking his head to the side. "And I have a few trinkets I would like to retrieve."

Leon glares and closes the gap, raising his scythe. "Where is my sister, the babies, and Elis?"

"Safe with my mother."

Leon inches closer. "The only protection they need is us, their family."

"You really think they would have survived Perendi," Perseus says, leaning down level with Leon's nose. "If my mother didn't sweep in, they would have been taken again!"

"They were taken by your mother!"

Enyo quickly moves and levels her sword between them. "Take a second and back up." Neither man moves. "Both of you!"

Perseus obeys and takes a small step back.

Leon stands his ground.

"Why are you really here?" Enyo levels her glare at Perseus.

"To resume my role as messenger." He smiles. "And to meet our descendants." He winks at Enyo. "Not bad, right?" He admires Leon and Avi.

"You're the new messenger?" Leon asks. "What happen to Teuta?"

Perseus laughs. "Zeus is holding her for questioning."

"Why?" Avi asks.

"Like I said." Perseus folds his hands behind his back. "The doors are wide open. I entered with no resistance or notice. Teuta let all defensive shields down before the attack of Prende and Perendi."

"You really expect us to believe that Teuta would compromise the safety of time," Enyo says. "And the castle."

"Mui and Junior were under Prende's control." Avi states and shifts her weight to cock a hip out. "They could have unknowingly compromised the defenses when Prende was in range."

Leon leans forward. "Show us your forearms." He discretely checks his back pocket. The cuff still secure.

Perseus rolls his eyes. "Really?"

"Just do it!" Enyo says, flaring her nose.

He sighs and rolls his tight sleeves up to his elbow. "You realize I'm immune to the cuff, right?" He lifts and rotates his forearms.

Leon shakes his head.

"Actually," Perseus says. "You and your sister are immune, too. Oh, and of course, the twins." He points to Avi and Enyo. "But you two not so much."

"How is that possible?" Avi asks. She looks at Enyo, but Enyo shrugs.

"Call it a blessing or curse," Perseus says, "but once you're cuffed, any of my children, born after the mark vanishes, are immune from the effects."

"Who did that to you?" Avi asks.

"My grandfather." Perseus looks down at the floor. "His control actually killed him."

"Oh." Avi relaxes her posture.

Enyo stares him down. "Did Ember send you a personal invitation?"

"Not exactly." Perseus releases his hands and shrugs. "But I am the most qualified."

"Leon can handle the messenger duties," Enyo says.

"It's true," Leon says. "I have before and can again."

Perseus shakes his head. "No need, I'm here now." He takes a step forward.

"Not so fast." Enyo pulls her dagger level with him.

"I need confirmation of my sister and her family's safety." Leon swings his scythe.

A sliver of darkness hovers between them.

"Show me Danae."

The sliver remains dark.

Leon turns to Perseus and lifts an eyebrow.

"Show me my mother." Perseus states and nods towards the sliver.

53

Danae turns from the crib, searching the large room. "Who's here?"

"Sis, are you ok?" Leon says, staring at the live image of Danae in an old limestone suite.

"Leon?"

"Yes," Leon says. "Are you ok? Are the babies?"

"We're ok, but she won't let me see Elis." She looks around the room. "Is Itra there?"

"We found Itra," Leon says and glances at Enyo. Enyo frowns. "And the others are fine well, mostly. Mui is dead."

Danae covers her mouth. "How?"

"We can explain everything after we get you the hell out of there."

"The princess has blocked my use of this." Danae holds up her left thumb. "And she believes Elis was marked by the keeper's cuff when he was first taken by Chronos."

Leon mumbles a curse and looks over his shoulder.

Perseus is gone.

Enyo's skin prickles. She turns towards Avi, but the space is still dark.

"No!" Avi screams.

Enyo rushes to her.

Perseus plows past Avi and snatches the hourglass. He vanishes in two steps inches from Enyo's blade.

"Did someone just scream?" Danae leans over the crib.

"Perseus took the hourglass!" Leon taps his thumb ring. "We're coming for you. Be ready!"

A door opens to Danae's suite and a woman walks in with a tray of food.

Leon mumbles the sequence to open a portal and steps inside the room, scythe first.

"Ah!" the woman screams and drops the tray.

Enyo stands just inside the open portal, raising and pointing her sword at the woman.

The woman raises her hands and backs against the wall.

Danae picks up the twins. Leon rushes towards her and takes Ora.

"Take the twins." Danae attempts to hand off Emit. "I can't leave Elis here!"

"We'll find Elis," Leon says, handing Ora to Avi standing just inside the portal. "Go now!"

Danae turns to the open suite door. "Four, no five guards are approaching."

Leon nods and pushes Danae through.

The portal darkens and vanishes, leaving him and Enyo with the woman. He raises his scythe and Enyo pulls out her dagger, twirls her sword, and widens her stance.

"Please don't hurt me!" the woman begs. "I can take you to the young boy."

The first guard barges into the room.

Leon swings his scythe just above the woman's head and strikes the guard. His body crumples to the floor, his head falls at the woman's feet.

The woman faints and slides down the wall to the floor.

Enyo rolls her shoulders back as four guards rush in.

Leon swings high, disabling one and maneuvers away from a blade thrust towards him by another. He side steps the guard's second swing and drops low, extending his staff and tripping the guard. He steps on the tripped guard's chest, lowers the blade of his scythe to the man's neck.

The man freezes.

Enyo thrusts her sword through the abdomen of one guard approaching with a dagger raised. She blocks his strike with her own dagger. She uses his weight to crash into the guard behind him and they fall in a pile on the floor. The tip of her dagger impales the second guard with a long hiss. He fights for a breath, but Enyo presses the blade in deeper.

The guard's eyes bulge. He bucks away but then gargles and spits out blood.

She withdraws her blades and stands.

The guard cries out under Leon's boot. "Stop!"

"Where is the boy?" Leon asks, applying more weight.

The man speaks. "One floor up!"

The guard swings a free arm towards Leon, but Enyo blocks the blow with her sword.

Leon pushes the scythe to the floor severing the man's head.

"Bloody freaking mess." Leon looks Enyo over. "You don't have a speck of blood anywhere on you, how?" He looks down. His once light khaki cargo pants have splotches of red fading to brown.

"Off with their heads isn't my style." Enyo tiptoes over the arms and legs and checks the narrow stone corridor. "It's clear."

Leon leaps over the pile and follows Enyo.

She pauses after a few steps. "Do you hear him?"

A faint echo of a laugh.

Leon nods.

Enyo picks up her pace.

Leon silently follows.

She pauses again and peeks her head around the corner.

The staircase is dark but empty.

She creeps around the corner and stops on the first step. A large figure fills the landing ahead. She straightens and casually walks up.

Leon ducks back around the corner, out of sight.

"Have you seen my sisters?" Enyo asks, nearing the landing.

"Who do you think you are fooling?" the man asks.

Elis laughs again.

Leon white knuckles his staff and sucks in a breath.

Enyo moves up another step. "The princess asked for our help. Do you really think it is wise for you to stand in the way?"

The man throws his head back with a laugh.

Enyo doesn't hesitate. She bolts up the final two steps and levels her sword to his neck. She's close enough to see the whites of his eyes grow wider.

"Laughing now?" Enyo smiles and tilts her head.

Leon takes the steps two at a time and passes the two of them with a grin.

The man attempts to open his mouth, but Enyo uses the tip of her sword to shut it.

"Do it again!" Elis giggles.

"What this?" a woman asks. A buzzing sound grows louder near the door and quiets.

Leon risks a look around the door frame.

A small young lady is buzzing around the room.

Elis giggles.

Leon rounds the doorframe and holds a finger to his lips.

Elis notices him immediately, nods and stands.

The young lady doesn't turn around until Leon is touching Elis. "Sorry playtime is over."

"Aw!" the young lady screams.

Enyo mumbles the sequence and opens the portal just inside the room.

Leon steps through with Elis and Enyo follows.

54

Itra gathers Danae into his arms. He kisses her head. "Are you ok?"

Danae mumbles into his chest. "Yes, but Elis."

"Here!" Elis says, running towards Itra and Danae.

Leon and Enyo trail behind him.

Itra releases Danae and kneels with his arms open.

Elis jumps in Itra's arms.

"Leon!" Danae yells.

"Not my blood, sis," Leon says, hugging her neck and messing up her hair.

Kaly walks into the dining hall with Zana and nearly drops the baby.

Leon assesses his clothes. "Maybe I should change."

"You think!" Enyo back hands his arm.

Leon changes into clean clothes with a thought and jogs over to Kaly.

"What the hell happened?" Kaly whispers, hugging him close.

"We busted the family out of Zeus, hell or jail." Leon winks at Kaly's frown. "Enyo and I are fine and not a hair was harmed on the kids or Danae. Thanks for asking."

Kaly slaps his arm and shakes her head. "You're impossible."

"I second that," Danae and Itra say in unison.

"Seriously?" Leon frowns.

"So, what happened to the 'plan' first motto?" Vincent asks, taking Emit from Danae.

Emit coos.

"Uncle Leon went in scythe blazing." Leon takes Ora from Itra. "And I would do it again."

Xena and Pem appear behind Itra in the dining hall.

Xena shouts. "It's gone!"

Itra steps to the side, revealing Danae, and gestures towards the babies and Elis.

"But we made it," Danae says.

Xena's eyes dart around the dining hall. "The hourglass?"

"Perseus took it," Avi says, walking to Xena's side. "Did you find the ruby stone?"

She shakes her head. "No, it's gone."

"How did Perseus get to the hourglass?" Pem asks.

"He gave us a window to Danae," Leon says. "And while we were focused on her, he plowed through Avi to get it."

"Now what?" Pem asks.

Junior, Dita, Noel, and Ana walk in from the war room.

"We prepare," Ana says.

"Ana!" Elis runs towards her.

She bends and lifts him up.

He sniffs her neck. "You still smell like mama."

Ana pats down his curls and snuggles his neck.

"For what?" Pem asks.

"The end is near if we don't recover the urtar stone." Ana states.

"Near?" Leon asks, fighting a yawn. "Like how near?"

Ana shakes her head. "The visions don't come with a calendar."

"But are we talking hours, days, or years?" Itra asks.

Ana glances back at Junior.

He nods.

"The twins are five, maybe six years-old."

A collective sigh echoes around the room.

Danae takes in all the faces. "Where is Hermes?"

"A woman appeared and then vanished near the past archway," Noel says, scratching his beard. "He's checking on it."

Elis giggles. "A girl was waiting for Hermy. He was late!"

"He chose a girl over his obligation to protect and serve?" Junior frowns. "Disgusting."

Dita elbows him in the side. "I seem to remember the teenage Junior a lot better than you do!" She looks around the room. "Teuta?"

Junior stiffens.

"Still with Zeus," Enyo says. "Avi, can you please call in my sisters?"

Avi nods and holds the amulet. She furrows her brows. She shakes her head and closes her eyes.

Ana gasps. "They can't answer the call."

"Why?" Enyo marches towards Ana.

Ana holds up her palm. "They're locked up like Teuta."

Junior snorts. "And the one person who could likely bust them out unnoticed is chasing a girl."

"The princess mentioned nothing about Teuta," Danae says. "Are you sure she is there?"

Enyo nods. "Perseus claims Teuta's responsible for disabling the defenses when Prende and Perendi attacked."

Junior shakes his head. "Something has been off since we arrived."

"Reset?" Kaly asks.

"Why not?" Itra says.

"What do you mean?" Ana asks, releasing a squirming Elis.

A book hovers in front of Kaly. She passes Zana to Danae. "Six months ago, we found a few flaws with the security here. The passage resets the castle." The book opens and the pages flutter. It settles on a page with a single line of text. "Repair the old, fix, and fold to renew the castle to new and bold."

All the open doors slam shut. The floor shakes and rattles.

Elis runs to Itra and buries his head in his waist.

Itra bends and whispers. "It's ok."

A howl of wind rips through the hall.

Leon, Danae, and Vincent bend to shield the babies.

"To protect the ember in time," Enyo mumbles and steps beside Kaly. "Illyria of mine."

Xena, Pem and Avi step closer to Kaly. A whirl of air gathers around their ankles and blows straight up, lifting the loose hair of Avi, Pem, Kaly, and Xena.

Enyo continues as her braids release, and her hair lifts, connecting with the others. "Unravel the weave and hear us breathe. Bind our line to protect time, our legacy thine. Reset the walls, hear our call. Bring a shield for time, bind us all. Yield the fall." A final push of air twirls and intertwines their thick brown locks as one. "Bring us light to guide the night. To protect the ember in time, Illyria of mine."

Ora and Emit release a single cry.

The dining hall falls silent, and their hair unwinds, falling down all at once.

Noel gapes at Enyo's dark curls, standing on end fanning out around her oval face. He hides his smile behind a fist.

"Enyo, what did you just do?" Dita asks.

"Fulfilled my oath to Ember." Enyo pulls a section of her hair back in a quick braid. "Protect time."

"How does that little spell work?" Junior asks, shaking his head.

"We aren't witches casting spells." Xena scowls at Junior. "It's part of Ember's instructions."

The book, with the three haggard women on the cover, appears and opens in front of Junior.

Junior attempts to touch the book, and it flies just out of reach. He frowns. He leans over the page. "Bind us all?"

"The protectors of time," Enyo says.

Hermes slides into the dining hall and twirls in a circle. He looks from Leon to Junior and back to Noel. "What did I miss?"

"You ever duck out on your oath to protect and serve again." Junior points a finger in his face. "I'll make sure that door never opens again for you!"

Hermes frowns. "I was checking on a possible intruder and I have news."

Leon folds his arms across his chest. "Go on."

"Deino and Pemphredo planned their lock up to break Teuta out."

Junior snorts.

Noel glances at him.

Junior shrugs. "Not what I expected."

"Where are they?" Leon asks.

"Stopping to pick up something Pemphredo lost."

Leon raises a brow.

"You spoke with them?" Enyo asks.

"It was Pemphredo I was tracking through the archway." Hermes shrugs. "I didn't ask any questions. Have you met Deino? She is three times more terrifying than you." He points at Enyo.

Noel laughs. "That's hard to imagine."

"Damn right," Deino says, appearing next to Teuta and Pemphredo across from Leon.

Pemphredo hands Xena the ruby stone set in pointed gold.

"How did you find it?" Xena asks, turning it over. "I thought I lost it when it wasn't with my other pieces at home."

"The heirloom is mine," Pemphredo explains. "If it is lost in your time, doesn't mean it's lost in mine."

"Weird." Avi shakes her head. "Does anyone know where Perseus took the hourglass?"

"He is heading towards the bridge to nowhere," Pemphredo says.

"Do you think he is working with Perendi?" Enyo says, focusing on her sisters.

"No," Deino says. "We overheard Zeus and him arguing about the best place to hide the hourglass from the compass."

"What will Perseus do with it?" Danae asks.

"Drop it below the bridge." Deino states.

"Excuse me?" Leon puts a finger to his head and twirls it. "Are you nuts?"

"It's not a bad idea," Pemphredo says.

Danae and Leon gape at them.

"Far below the bridge to nowhere is the safest prison for the hourglass," Pemphredo says. "The ether spins between time and no time in an infinite loop."

"Whoa," Xena says, holding up a hand. "I flew under the bridge and down into the valley away from the usmu. If I made it out, how secure can that be?"

"Very secure," Pemphredo says, winking at Deino. "The princess swapped the hourglass when Perseus and Zeus were arguing."

242

"I'm sorry." Danae says. "Why would she do that?"

Deino smiles. "To lure the remaining fairies into the ether. There is no exit for the fairies if they go after the hourglass."

"And the urtar stone?" Pem asks.

"Secured in the hourglass inside the sundial if we need it," Deino says.

"Ana, what do you see?" Vincent asks.

Ana chews on the corner of her lip. "The same outcome. Five to six years and then boom."

"Do you want to vote on it?" Itra asks.

Some nod, others shrug.

"Raise your hand to get the hourglass back now," Leon says, raising his hand.

Junior and Enyo raise their hands.

"Stand down and wait," Danae says, raising her hand.

All but three raise their hands, excluding Teuta.

"It's settled." Danae states. "Teuta, is there a reason you didn't vote."

Teuta winks and raises her hand. "Tani!"

Itra shakes Danae. "Babe, we're home."

Danae moans. She snuggles in closer. "It's early. Are the twins up?"

"Danae, we are home, home."

Danae opens her eyes. The room is barely lit by the pre-dawn sun. She can make out her nightstand and dresser. "The twins!" She rolls to face Itra. She feels them close.

"Sleeping here." He rolls to his back and points to the bassinet on his side of the bed.

"Is everyone home?" Danae asks.

"Anton just called." He nods to the open door. "That's what woke me. Elis is back home asleep in his bed."

"Teuta?" Danae asks, rubbing her eyes.

Itra sighs. "Who else could send us home in a sleep induced like coma?"

Danae reaches up for her ember amulet, but her hand wanders around her neck. She mumbles a curse, recalling its fractured state back at the castle. "Are we going to forget again?"

"God, I hope so." Itra kisses her on the head. "I don't want to relive that nightmare again."

"We just resume our normal lives for the next five to six years?"

"Maybe?" Itra kisses her lips.

She sighs and folds into him. "If we can handle the last four days. We can parent twins, right?" She feels the vibration of Itra's chest under her cheek. "Are you laughing at me or with me?"

"With you," Itra says.

EMBER IN TIME SERIES

GUIDE TIME INSIDE

BOOK FOUR

KIM MALAJ

1

"Guide time inside."

"What was that?" Elis says, unlocking his locker.

"What was what?" Milio asks, sliding on his backpack.

"You said something about time inside," Elis says. He shoulders his backpack and grabs his skateboard before closing his locker.

"Nah," Milio says, grinning and nodding towards the door. "I was too busy gawking at the cheerleaders to speak." He falls into step beside Elis.

"Hmm," Elis says, stepping outside. He squints shutting out the glaring sun. "I could of swore you said something."

"Maybe it was Teuta?" Milio lightly punches Elis's shoulder.

Elis laughs. "Will you ever let that go?"

"You shouted Teuta in the middle of history class," Milio says. "Plus, that's only the third time I've dropped a reminder."

"Three is enough," Elis says, dragging a finger across his throat. "Bury that next to the insults about 'curly girly' hair."

"Zero puns left, no deal," Milio says, nodding towards the skate park. "Are you heading to the Dome?"

"Not tonight," Elis says, checking his phone. "The twins are heading to the house."

Milio frowns. "Aren't they like five?"

"Seven," Elis says, pocketing his phone. He drops his skateboard and places a foot firmly in the center.

"Ha, have fun babysitting," Milio says, dropping his skateboard and pushing off.

Elis shakes his head and watches Milio ride away towards the park before he pushes off. He glides in the opposite direction. He rolls down the sidewalk and cruises by a few lingering students at the corner.

A lady shouts, "Jace, no stop!"

Elis hops the curb onto the street to dodge the lady chasing her runaway toddler waddling at full speed towards a large dog. The dog licks the little man's face. The toddler bursts into a fit of giggles.

Elis chuckles. He looks over his shoulder to check for oncoming traffic, but flies forward off his board. He stumbles a few steps before he falls towards the curb.

Elis stands and inspects his jeans and shirt. A new grass stain and small tear in the jeans.

"Dang it," Elis mumbles, wrenching his board out of the sewage grate. He checks the wheels. "So much for brand new." One wheel is missing a chunk and the bracket is loose.

Elis plops on the grass and slides off his backpack. He loosens a strap and slides the board through. He adjusts and tightens the board to the backpack before he slides it back on. He hops up and brushes off the grass clinging to his jeans.

Elis checks for traffic before jogging across the street. He sticks to the sidewalks weaving around the afternoon shoppers and students milling about. He nods to a shopkeeper sweeping the stoop of a shop on his corner.

The shopkeeper smiles and waves with this broom.

Elis keys in the code to the building and strolls up to the third floor skipping every third step. He pauses outside his door and reaches in the side pocket of his backpack for his key.

"It's open," his dad, Anton, calls from inside.

Elis pushes the door open and kicks off his shoes. "You're home really early." He glances at the clock. "It's barely four."

Anton stands from the sofa and gestures towards the dining table. "Because we need to talk before your cousins arrive."

"What's that important?" Elis asks, holding up his backpack. "Can I at least put this in my room?"

"Sure," Anton says, reaching up to smooth and straighten his tie.

Elis walks to his room and sets his bag and board down in the corner. His laptop is open on his desk.

"Has he been in here snooping?" he mutters before walking back to the dining room. He sits down and Anton sits a bottle of water on the table.

"How was your day?" Anton asks.

"Besides busting a wheel on the way home… boring." Elis unscrews the lid and guzzles a third of the water.

"Is that why I received an email from your teacher today?" Anton says, sliding out the chair closest to Elis.

"What teacher?" Elis asks, folding his arms across his chest.

"Mr. Craven," Anton says.

Elis frowns. "Why?"

"According to him, today was the third time this week you have fallen asleep in his class."

Elis shakes his head.

"And that you called out a name last week that disrupted the entire class during an exam." Anton takes a seat and leans forward. "Care to share your side?"

Elis shrugs.

Anton mocks his shrug. "That isn't exactly descriptive. Try again."

"History is right after lunch, and it's warm." Elis fake yawns and leans forward. "It's like a—nap worthy environment. Plus, it's history."

Anton fights a grin. He keeps his expression even and stern. "Never let Kaly hear you say that."

Elis laughs. He recalls Kaly explaining the Illyrian Era during their last visit to the states.

"Elis," Anton says.

"Dad, it's not like I am failing," Elis says, squashing the laughter.

"That's not the point," Anton says. "Shouting during an exam is not exactly helpful for the other students who may be struggling."

Elis nods. "That only happened once."

"Elis," Anton says.

"And it was that same green-eyed girl I see in my dreams."

"Dreams?" Anton says, raising an eyebrow.

"I've told you about them." Elis stands. "I'll show you the latest one."

"Show me?" Anton asks.

Elis nods. He jogs to his room and rummages through his backpack before grabbing his sketchbook. He returns to the dining table and turns a few pages before he slides the sketchbook towards Anton. "This is the girl."

Anton stares at the big green eyes set in a heart-shaped face framed by wisps of dark raven hair. He traces the outline of the girl. "It looks real… like a photo."

"It's only a sketch, dad."

"Who is she?"

"Teuta, I think."

Anton shakes his head and pats down the hairs rising on the back of his neck. "And this is from a dream?"

"Dreams." Elis leans forward, pointing out the details of a stone corridor behind the girl. "It's more than that—I feel like I've walked through here."

"Like in person?" Anton asks, meeting his son's eyes.

Elis nods. "You believe me?"

Anton glances down at the drawing. "I do. Maybe it was when you were visiting Greece during spring break?"

Elis shrugs.

"Kaly mentioned her Aunt Xena took you and the twins to a dozen castles during the visit, right?"

Elis nods. "Maybe."

"And the name you shouted in class?"

"Teuta."

"Ok, so why do you think you shouted her name?" Anton asks, pointing to the girl on the page.

Elis sighs.

"It's not like you to fall asleep in class and you haven't talked in your sleep since you were six."

Elis eyes widen. "I used to talk in my sleep?"

"Full conversations," Anton says. "Your mom even searched your room for a phone once because she swore up and down there was someone talking back."

Elis frowns. "I had a phone when I was six?"

Anton laughs. "Absolutely not! You're changing the subject."

Elis shrugs.

"What made you call out and disrupt the class?" Anton asks, leaning towards Elis.

"She was falling," Elis whispers.

"Who is she?"

"Teuta," Elis says, clinching his fist. "I had her, dad, but she let go."

"Had her where?" Anton says.

"We were climbing down into a cave," Elis says, flipping a page back to a sketch of a dark cave. "And she slipped. I reached down and grabbed her hand. I was lifting her up, but she let go."

"And that's what woke you up shouting?" Anton asks softly.

Elis nods staring at the sketch. "It felt so real."

Anton nods and reaches over gripping Elis's shoulder. "You mentioned dreams. Does she fall in every dream?"

"No," Elis says, looking up at Anton. "That only happened once, but we were racing down a narrow path and then climbing down into a cave."

"We," Anton says, "as in you and this girl, Teuta?"

Elis shakes his head. "Zana, Ora and Emit were there too."

Anton's mouth falls open.

Elis slouches. He sticks his hands in his hair and lowers his forehead to the edge of the table. "It's nuts, I know."

Acknowledgments

This book and the inspiration for this series came from Art, my husband, and his desire to explore Albania, his home country. I've enjoyed being along—sometimes far behind—for the ride. He provided a stress-free environment to create and write. Thank you for the support and encouragement, and for making sure I always come down the mountain.

My thanks also to my faithful friend and lifesaver for this project, my editor, Jenny Leonard. Her wisdom transforms my vision for the book into a polished manuscript. You're a beautiful new mom, an amazing friend, and the best editor an author could ever dream of—THANK YOU!

And to my readers. Your support for this series is why I keep writing. Thank you!

About the Author

 Kim Malaj lives on a vineyard and homestead in northern Albania with her husband, Arti, author of Northern Albanian Folk Tales, Myths and Legends. Although she is a Show Me State (Missouri) lady at heart, she loves her life at Homestead Albania.

When she's not writing, she tends to the garden, orchard, vineyard, and livestock. She's also brewed up batches of raki and wine, and other sweet and savory treats made from the fruits and veggies produced in the garden. She is an avid photographer, an active blogger about the homestead, and a hobbyist drone pilot, learning the art of aerial photography and filming.

Visit the blog: www.HomesteadAlbania.com
For publishing news: www.KimMalaj.com